THE UNITED WORLD

THE UNITED WORLD 1

CRAIG PRIESTLEY

THE UNITED WORLD (THE UNITED WORLD 1)
Copyright © 2021 Craig Priestley

All rights reserved. No part of this book may be used or reproduced in any manner whatsoever without written permission except in the case of brief quotations embodied in critical articles or reviews.

This is a work of fiction. Names, characters, businesses, organisations, places, events and incidents either are the product of the author's imagination or are used fictitiously. Any resemblance to actual persons, living or dead, events, or locales is entirely coincidental.

Cover design by Sarah Carter.

First edition, 2021

10 9 8 7 6 5 4 3 2 1

ISBN: 9798580445274

SIGN UP FOR THE NEWSLETTER

Receive special offers, giveaways, bonus content, updates from the author, and be the first to hear about new releases: bit.ly/hearfromcraig

PROLOGUE

January 1st, 2020

The world waited in anticipation.

In years to pass, every lucid person alive would remember one of the most iconic moments in modern history.

In the crowd, news reporters disregarded personal space for the sake of vantage points.

Each and every news channel was tuned to the same event - regular programming only a mere commodity. Alongside the reporters, like predators cohabiting, social media influencers infiltrated, streaming to their increasingly large numbers of fans online from a variety of mobile devices. This occasion would result in millions of views, along with a massive opportunity for viral content.

Reporters had a job to do, while individuals chased everlasting fame with personalised footage: a giant circus led only by the hundreds of security officers who had a minimal chance of containing the tens of thousands that had gathered. Yet, there was little chance of an incident happening, for today was a day of celebration. Today was a day for peace.

Hushes rippled across the European summit; across the screens set up outside, and across the world that watched on a slight delay.

The ravaging destruction of forest fires, the growing concern over the spread of new and existing viruses, and the increasing demand of concrete actions to slow climate change had forced the world's governments to start working together.

Four people entered. They took centre stage in the circular arena that had become infamous over the last few years through a rising number of important gatherings and discussions, not only in Europe, but also across the world. A personal assistant twisted a stationed microphone on the table in front of her, causing a short wave of distortion to open proceedings. A woman waved away the assistant, who vanished as quickly as possible.

Prior to the meeting, she had announced the disbanding of the United Nations. It had served its purpose, but it was time for a new regime; it was time to issue in a new world order.

Mrs Phoebe von Beak was the person to introduce that today. The president appeared to be in her late forties, yet holding such an esteemed position as President of the European Union, required specific requirements. One of the most important was to be seen as an experienced and level-headed individual by her peers, resulting only from experience. Therefore, she accentuated her greying hair, allowing it to drop down smartly over her navy trouser suit and ensured that she spoke without a hint of vulnerability.

"Ladies, gentlemen, and people of the world. As you are all well aware, we are here today for one reason, and one reason only – the end of conflict, the end of national disputes. The end of war."

Mrs von Beak paused to allow the last statement to hit home with the people watching inside, and those outside cheering. Audible sounds echoed from outside the building, interrupting her; vuvuzelas and cheers in unison interrupted proceedings temporarily.

The president waited for a moment before continuing.

"Indeed, we have great reason to celebrate today."

More cheers greeted her.

She raised her hand, to which the crowd reacted and gradually quietened.

"Thank you, all." Mrs von Beak turned to the three people who stood with her. "And, thank you to these three gentlemen who stand beside me. Without their hard labour, dedication and vision to a common goal, none of this would be possible. The labour to work towards progress, the dedication to forgive and forget, and the vision for working in unison."

Crowds roared in celebration.

"We've already received signatures from hundreds of officials across the world, many of whom are in this very audience, but by my side at this moment are the final three we require. We have The President of the United States of America, the Chairperson of the African Union, and the Secretary-General of the Arab League. I think it's fair to say that the men and women in this building represent us all."

Mrs von Beak gestured towards the President of the United States, who needed no invitation to speak to an audience of this magnitude.

"Not only is today a great day for America and its people, but today is also a great day for the world. Today, America welcomes everyone with open arms. All borders have been disbanded, all military men will turn their focus inwards to uphold the law, and we cannot wait to join with our brothers and sisters in this proposal. God bless the United States of America, and God bless the world."

Cheers from outside joined the well-mannered round of applause.

The Chairperson of the African Union began in his native tongue, translated to English on the monitor behind him.

"Every country, city and village - all of the men, women and children - all of them, thank you for agreeing to the terms and making our dream a reality."

The African official finished his statement in English. "This Treaty will allow us access to better healthcare, larger quantities of medicine, and better education. Together, we are stronger. Thank you."

More cheers echoed around the arena.

The Secretary-General of the Arab League addressed the public in Arabic, again translated in real-time with only a slight delay.

"I speak on behalf of Islam, Christianity, and Judaism. I speak on behalf of all religions in our region. I speak on behalf of Iraq, Saudi Arabia, Israel, Egypt, Lebanon, Syria, and all of The Middle East's wonderful and prosperous countries. Today I ask that acts of violence across all nations to be halted. I ask that there is no more war over oil, and plead for there to be no more acts of terror due to religious beliefs: the need for conflict is over. It will take time, but the Middle East needs to come together, defiant, to make this change a reality."

The native Arabic audience members cheered first, followed shortly by the remaining public.

Mrs von Beak invited the panel members for a firm handshake, followed by a single nod of approval in their direction. She collected a document from the table in front of them and raised it in the air.

"Years upon years of negotiations have led to the creation of this very document, driven by Mr Candrade and his team. In it contains the details outlining the proposal of a worldwide government. We have four signatures left to make it official." Mrs von Beak offered the document and a pen along the line of government officials. The President of the United States of America signed, posing for photographs whilst doing so – followed shortly by the other two members of the panel. The Secretary-General of the Arab League placed the document back on the table.

Phoebe von Beak picked up the pen and paper once more and allowed the moment to wash over her.

"It is my honour to be the final member to sign this document, which will bring an end to closed borders, an end to racism, and an end to war. We are united, and it's only together that we can change the world for the better. There are new fossil fuel regulations that every business worldwide must adhere to, along with new recycling requirements. These changes will be challenging, but each will be a positive one – and the government is here to offer support. A welcome pack of the new Rules and Regulations will be shared with all business owners. Together, a united world will flourish."

As she took the pen and signed her name on the dotted line, a spattering of applause began, followed shortly by a standing ovation inside the summit. Outside the building, thousands joined in with the celebration, as did those watching around the world - for they had not just witnessed the dawning of a new decade, but the introduction of a new era.

The audience had witnessed what was already being described as the most significant moment in the history of humankind.

1

December 31ˢᵗ, 2020

In a dilapidated, single-bed apartment near Camden Town High Street, John and Nora Loche sat on their tattered and stained two-seater couch. In their eyeline, a scuffed television illuminated the room. Despite its broad back and relatively small screen size, it still worked well enough. Right now, they were watching the news. The report discussed the benefits that had taken place due to the formation of The United Word government at the beginning of the year.

John had never been sure about bringing a child into the London that he knew. His experiences were of the struggle to pay rent, the high levels of street crime, and the hate and disdain he witnessed in the eyes of strangers. However, the promise of a better and more open life, was one that both the government and his wife had sold him on.

Nora sat next to him, gently rubbing her large baby bump with both of her hands. A well-positioned cushion supported her lower back, as the cheap wooden coffee table supported her swollen feet.

"Cup of tea, my love?" Nora smiled in John's direction, a smile that could penetrate even the foulest of his moods.

"Of course." John leaned over and kissed Nora's belly, followed by her cheek. He walked over through the opening into the adjacent kitchen.

"I don't think it'll be long now," Nora said, taking a break from whispering pleasantries towards her stomach.

John collected the two plain white cups from the cupboard in the kitchen. He filled the kettle and flicked on the switch.

He wasn't ready.

"How long's not long?" John asked.

"Well, I don't think it'll be today," she felt her stomach for confirmation. "But, maybe tomorrow?"

"That soon, huh?" John laughed heartily, matching the volume of the rising boil of the kettle.

John was in his mid-thirties, while Nora was in her late twenties. He had never expected to settle down or even meet someone who would put up with him or his antics. He drank, he swore, and he knew that he wasn't the easiest to live with, yet somehow Nora accepted it all.

He opened the door of the fridge and sighed at its woeful contents: two cartons of leftover Chinese takeaway, two pints of milk and a large bottle of scotch. He collected the milk and the scotch and placed them on the side.

"Milk?" he enquired, unsure whether she could stomach it today.

"Yes, please," Nora responded.

John let the boiling water infuse with the pyramid-shaped tea bag in Nora's cup, before filling his halfway with scotch. Keeping it cold was something his father had done, and the habit had passed down to him. If anything, it saved the need for ice cubes.

John walked back through to his wife and settled next to her on the couch. Nora collected her cup of tea before taking John's arm and placing it around her shoulders.

The local news currently discussed the topic of climate change and the irreversible effects that humankind had already caused.

Following on from the sentiment of the news, Nora turned her thoughts to that of a serious discussion.

"We're going to be okay, right?" she asked.

John winced at the question. It was something he'd been putting off answering himself, never mind having to discuss it with his wife. He knew he would do everything possible to provide for their child. He would work long hours, put food on the table, and try not to lose his shit. He just hoped that would be enough.

John took Nora's hand in his. Their fingers entwined.

"I will always be there to look after you and the kid. I will do everything to give you the best life I can."

Nora rocked forward, awkwardly, due to the size of her baby bump, and placed the cup of tea on the small coffee table next to her. She looked at John and took his face in her hands.

"That is all I could ever ask for, my love."

They shared a gentle, loving kiss - not one of lust, but one of companionship - an embrace of togetherness.

John picked up his mug of scotch, took a large sip, and turned towards the television.

Since he was little, he had never enjoyed watching the news. It was just negative reports after negative reports – shootings, stabbings, homelessness, whatever it was, it was shown too much. There was enough stress on the table; who needed to worry about anything else?

John collected the television remote, placed one hand on Nora's bump, and began to flick through the channels.

"Right, so what are we watching then?"

* * *

As the receptionist placed the boiling hot cup of black American Joe on the table, the immaculately dressed Samuel Candrade took a testing sip. He let out an audible moan as the hot liquid shared responsibility in partially burning, and at the same time, satiating his tastebuds.

"That'll be all, Amanda."

The receptionist waited for a few seconds before she retreated from Samuel - and his jet-black hair that belied his actual age.

"Where were we?"

Samuel was sitting in an impressive-looking office, running a meeting with three foreigners who had joined him. Two of the guests were older gentlemen from India and Pakistan respectively, the third a younger woman from England. They seemed to take no notice that they weren't offered a beverage, as Samuel wrapped his fingers around the hot mug and gently blew on his.

"I was wondering about the report," repeated the Indian guest.

"Yes, yes, it's going as planned." Samuel retorted.

"The levels of violence are not retreating as we hoped they would."

"It is a long-term initiative. It won't be fixed overnight."

"I know, however-"

"The wheels are in motion."

All of the guests nodded at that statement.

"Have there been any problems to date?" the young woman enquired, speaking with a delicate Queen's English accent.

"All is running smoothly. As you know, it will take time for the operation to be a success."

The third guest spoke up, speaking in broken English.

"Things are the same. We want results. My people need change."

Samuel sighed internally and placed his cup of coffee down to the side, allowing him to gesture at will as he spoke. He'd had enough with convincing people that everything was running smoothly – which it was. However, he knew that he had to babysit essential and influential political guests from various countries; holding their hands to ensure them that their boo-boos would heal.

It made Samuel feel a little more than slightly agitated, but he hid it well.

"I assure you that the wheels are indeed in motion. It has been less than a year since the dawning of The United World. We have already seen an improvement in the decreasing use of fossil fuels, more than a one thousand percent increase in recycled goods, and scientists are informing us that at this rate we're on track to stabilise global temperatures at plus two degrees Celsius."

The English guest who, despite being in her early to mid-twenties, and commanded a certain air of authority, sat still as the two male guests shuffled in their seats.

"Yes, yes, climate change is all well and good - but there are still those who fight it," the Indian guest retorted.

Samuel held up a hand to allow him to interrupt.

"Yes, climate change was a large part of the worldwide initiative, as was the opening of borders, and the sharing of education and medical care for all. I think you'll find that so far all of these are on track to excel even our most optimistic forecasts, would you not agree?"

Three nods met Samuel's question.

"Of course, resistance is nothing more than human nature. Those who struggle to accept change adopt a fight or flight response."

"This will continue," the Pakistan guest added, his demeanour becoming more flustered by the second.

"For the foreseeable future, to some degree, it will continue," Samuel confirmed.

The Pakistani guest rose dramatically from his seat.

"This is not good enough. My men are dying in attacks."

"We have internal wars to abolish that are also proving difficult," the Indian guest added.

"And you? Miss…" Samuel pretended not to know the woman with whom he had many meetings prior to today.

"Cambersham, Emily Cambersham."

Samuel gestured for the VIP guest from Pakistan to return to his seat, which he did.

"Miss Cambersham, do you have any updates?"

"There is a clear split across the country; some celebrate the open border initiative, while others form groups to hunt down foreigners who have moved nearby, resulting in acts of violence. As we expected, it has created conflict in an already divided nation – as I'm sure is the case in the countries of these fine gentlemen."

The two male guests nodded and crossed their arms in solidarity.

"The prime minister is concerned. However, I have assured him that it is merely a teething issue, and over time the conflict will decrease."

"Good. Thank you."

"My pleasure."

"We have the world in the palm of our hands, gentlemen – and Miss Cambersham – it will take time, but soon it will begin to mould to our touch. The people will become pliable, and the world will welcome a neutral, unified government."

"And what of the modifications?" asked the Indian male.

"The tests have been a complete success, and we have begun to roll them out worldwide."

"When will we see complete results?" The Pakistan official asked.

"Ah. Now that is a fine question."

Samuel Candrade and Emily Cambersham shared a knowing glance, as the other guests shuffled at the annoyance of a long-term solution.

* * *

Nurses rushed around a chaotic hospital room, filled with the determined screams of different soon-to-be mothers, given privacy only by thin sheets of loose material in between.

A nurse entered the makeshift room that gave Nora and John some privacy.

"How are you feeling, Nora?" the nurse asked; either well trained at tuning out the screams of others only metres away or doing a good job at appearing to do so.

Nora gritted her teeth.

"Focus on your breathing, love," John reminded her before turning to the nurse. "Can we get a damn doctor in here? We need a doctor for Christ's sake."

"The doctor will be with you shortly."

John paced around the side of Nora's bed, ensuring that his large frame didn't knock into anything. He had seen Nora in discomfort a few times before – every time she cut onions, the one time when the knife slipped on an avocado and she cut herself - and the trapped finger in the cupboard incident. John had seen her cry, but this was another level.

The nurse snapped on a pair of clean latex gloves, raised the covers at Nora's feet, and began her inspection.

"Good, you're almost ready, I don't think it will be much longer."

Nora had suffered so much strain that her face almost seemed out of proportion. Her skin was grey and clammy, and her hair stuck to her neck.

"What do you mean you 'don't think'? Can't you see she's in pain? She needs more drugs and a bloody doctor." John found himself losing control of the volume of his voice.

The nurse, taken aback by John's tone checked on one more vital sign and then tapped Nora on her arm, squeezing it gently. She eyed John before she left.

"Useless," John said to himself, returning his attention to Nora.

He swept her sweat-soaked, brunette hair back from her neck, around her ear, and away from her face. He then picked up a white washcloth and dabbed at his partner's forehead and face.

"You're doing great, love."

Nora smiled back at him: a tired smile of resilience.

"We need drugs!" John yelled out to an empty corridor.

Another slightly dishevelled male partner peered around the separating curtains. John noticed a disapproving look and a potentially sleep-deprived tutting sound.

"Mind your own business," John suggested, gaining control of the tone of his voice best he could.

The man rolled his eyes before mouthing something to his partner as he moved out of sight.

"Nosy bastard," John mouthed to Nora.

Nora took John by the elbow as he approached the bed.

She looked into his eyes like she always did. It didn't feel like she just looked at the glassy exterior, but peered into his soul.

John had never felt as naked and vulnerable as he had when Nora looked at him like that. It caused his stomach to flip, and his heart to pulse.

He could tell Nora was in trouble. He felt it as he returned her gaze, he saw the resilience fade and the acceptance of pain and suffering stare back at him.

"Doctor. Get me a fucking doctor!" John broke the connection with his partner and marched towards the empty doorway.

"Doctor, doctor!" He shouted down the hallway. "We need you. Get the fucking hell in here right now!"

The husband with whom they shared the magical moment appeared again, this time approaching John. He was tall, around six foot three, but he was skinny. John was slightly shorter, but not by much. His broad shoulders and muscles he had gained from years on a building site would put him in good stead against most opponents.

"Will you shut up?" the guy inquired.

"What the fuck's your problem?" John turned his misplaced attention around once more.

"My wife's in labour."

"So?"

"Will you just be quiet?" the man closed the gap between them.

"Or what?" John retorted, closing the gap between them further until they came close enough to feel each other's breath on their faces.

"John, stop!" Nora weakly called out, to no avail.

"Why don't you go back to your woman," the man impersonated his tone.

John reached a single hand out and, palm first, pushed him in the chest, resulting in separation – and a sprawling six foot three soon-to-be-father falling across the room. On his way down, he caught a bedpan, which clattered to the floor.

A nurse rushed in and noticed the end of the quarrel. She took John gently by the arm. John turned around to face her, his blood pressure rising.

"Please, sir. I need you to wait outside."

John stood motionless, remembering the breathing techniques that Nora had taught him several years before.

"Please, don't make me call the police."

John looked over to Nora; he brushed free of the nurse's grip and walked over to the only thing that truly mattered to him.

"I'm sorry, love." He noticed that he was regaining some form of composure. "I'll just be outside, okay. If you need me, let me know, and I'll be right back."

Nora nodded and took his hand. John leant down and kissed the back of her palm.

"Okay, sir. I'll take you to the waiting room." the nurse instructed.

"I'll just be outside."

"I love you," Nora whispered through gritted teeth.

John kissed her hand one more time and then placed it gently back down on the bed. He turned to face the nurse and noticed the other man brushing himself down.

"No hard feelings, fella." John nodded in his direction as he exited the room.

Just as he left, he overheard the murmur of the man behind him - "bloody prick."

"What did you-?" John tried to turn but was stopped by the nurse who shepherded him away.

John took a deep breath in and released a long breath out, trying to control the fury of his beating heart. Breathe in. Breathe out. Step left. Step right.

He allowed the nurse to steer him along winding corridors to the waiting room.

"If you would please be seated in the waiting room, we will look after your wife." The nurse looked at him kindly, through tired eyes.

John felt his erratic heartbeat calming as he walked along the winding, white corridors of the mammoth hospital. He nodded in agreement.

The nurse walked him towards a seated area, which was partially filled with a wealth of weary inhabitants. Some families gathered, likely in wait for a child, while a few other single adults sat in wait – mostly men, but a few women as well.

The nurse placed him on the nearest empty row of seats.

"There's tea and coffee over there," the nurse pointed to a row of vending machines. "Along with other food and drink."

"Do you have any booze?" John asked, instantly regretting the question. The nurse ignored his enquiry.

"Mr, erm, Loche, is it?"

John nodded.

"Your wife will be fine." The nurse placed her hand tenderly on his shoulder. "She's in the best possible hands. I know it must be difficult, but trying to relax will be the best for everyone."

"Now, do you want a tea?"

John wanted a scotch. He shook his head.

"Okay, well if you need anything just follow the yellow line on the floor to Reception - it's only around the corner. There are nurses there who can update you on your wife and baby."

"Thanks," John turned his attention inwards, away from the nurse and the distractions around him.

"She's in the best hands. I'll be back to update you shortly," the nurse added before following the yellow line towards Reception.

John noticed a few onlookers who had taken an interest in him from around the room, his shaggy appearance not aiding their likely opinions. He felt his chest tighten but fought the urge to speak. All he wanted was to help and get Nora the best possible care. Instead, he sat back, closed his eyes, and rubbed his temples with his rough, yet comforting hands.

2

December 31st, 2039

Sat within a large studio in Manchester, a captivated audience waited for the live television broadcast to begin. It was one minute until nine in the evening, and the start of the broadcast.

The audience contained a mixture of people, of different ages and backgrounds, who sat in rows behind a string of cameras – allowing for the audience at home to view the show in virtual reality should they wish.

A well-groomed man in his forties, dressed in a grey suit, walked out on to the set. An announcement over the speaker system followed his introduction.

"Ladies and gentlemen, please welcome your host of the show; the one and only, David Stern."

A ripple of structured applause began, along with it a few cheers and woops from the older audience members.

David waved to the audience before sitting down behind a desk. The desk was positioned next to a couch, with a vertical screen situated next to it, allowing for video clips to be played – it was the classic talk show set-up that lived on throughout generations, modernised for a mobile phone-centric audience.

A young lady ran out on to the set, wiped David's brow and then applied a quick dab of makeup, before running off again seconds later.

The lights in the audience dimmed, and the red 'LIVE' letters lit up above the set. Theme music burst to life from the sound system.

"Ladies and gentlemen, boys and girls, I am David Stern. Welcome to The Stern Selection."

A sign that read 'APPLAUD' lit up, to which the audience obeyed.

"Now, wherever you're watching from, whether you're on your way to a New Year's party, whether you're travelling home for the holidays, or simply relaxing at home, we've got one heck of a show for you. Yes, ladies and gentlemen, we've saved the best guests until last. Tonight, on the show we've got the three most prolific influencers of our generation in the studio."

The screen next to David flicked on to a behind-the-scenes camera that showed the three teenage influencers sitting in a room backstage. The screen showed a close up of each as the host introduced them.

"That's right. We have Damien Zucheim, Sara Brealish, and the one and only Zach Power."

Zach did a peace sign to camera, before the crowd's attention returned to the host.

"And not only that, but we're going to talk to all of you wonderful people that are out and about. To the people on the street welcoming in the new year in what has become somewhat of a tradition. But for those of you watching at home, we'll be with you for the next three hours to see in the New Year, and the new decade, with style."

David adjusted his collar and looked into the camera to deliver a cutaway directly to the people watching at home.

"But first, why don't we have a look at some of the highlights from the past ten years? Roll VT."

David sat back in his chair, quickly joined by the sprinting makeup assistant.

The screen showed packaged highlights of the previous decade.

A slideshow of The United World began the montage. A well-dressed man in his forties spoke to a crowd. In the bottom, a title revealed the man as Samuel Candrade, President of The United World. Large text then flashed on the screen reading '2030'.

"It's been twenty years since the forming of The United World. Crime is down, homelessness has begun to shift, and there have been no acts of wars between countries. The tide is turning, but we still need your help. Let us make the next decade the best of humankind."

Roars from the crowd help to shift the highlights along - on to those of sporting achievements of various teams, including highlights from football, baseball, basketball and hockey. The most dramatic moments: the most spectacular goals and saves are shown as the numbers in the bottom begin to tick along with the year in which they took place.

A news report appeared next, discussing the rise of influencers back in 2035.

"Over the past decade influencers have all but taken over celebrity culture as we know it. No longer do we see billboards of movie stars or musicians. Behind me, in Times Square, you'll see Zach Power, a rising star in the influencer scene. His charismatic views on everyday life resonate with a younger audience, and it won't be long until he's at the very top."

Several videos of Zach Power cut over the news report and continue after. Videos show Zach on the big screen at Times Square, parts of his to-camera pieces where he smiles and wipes his hair from his face.

"Ladies and gentlemen, influencers are here to stay."

The report then shows a montage of influencers performing a variety of actions in homemade videos including cooking, sports, fitness, beauty and more – including Damien's fitness channel and Sara's vegan cookery show.

The years along the bottom continued to move towards 2039, as more images of moments from news reports, influencers, sporting, and cultural events wrapped up the three-minute-long video.

The applause button lit, and the audience at home was greeted once more with David and an appreciative studio audience.

"Wow, what an amazing decade. We'll take a look at some of those events in detail later, but first let's bring out our first guest, Mister Damien Zucheim."

The crowd welcomed Damien on to the stage with level applause.

Damien walked out on stage, dressed in a smart shirt and black trousers. He approached David and shook his hand before sitting on the couch.

"It's an honour to meet you, Damien. Almost everyone I've met, especially the kids, absolutely loves your channel."

"Thank you." Damien responded with a perfect smile.

"Seriously, my kids, my neighbour's kids, my friend's kids, they're all in great shape. Mine won't let us do anything in the morning until they've watched your videos and followed your exercise routine."

"If you believe in someone, believe in yourself," Damien replied - greeted by a round of applause from the majority of the audience.

"You're obviously in great shape. As a nineteen-year-old, shouldn't you be out drinking, getting yourself into a bit of trouble?" David jested.

"No," Damien replied. "That is only a distraction. What's important is self-growth and development."

David nodded, unsure where to take the discussion, before moving on to his next researched line of questioning.

"A little bird told me that you play six different instruments as well?"

"The piano, violin, cello, guitar, oboe and clarinet."

"Wow, I mean. When I was your age, I didn't even know how to make frozen chips."

A few of the older members of the crowd laughed, but Damien and the younger audience remained stoic.

"Anyway," David continued. "That is impressive."

"I do not do it to impress people. It is merely to aid my development."

"Fair enough and fair play to you. So, what's next for you then, Damien? Any aspirations of movie stardom?"

"No. I am perfectly content with creating content for my audience. Creating content that people can enjoy daily, matters much more to me than playing the role of somebody else in a movie. That seems alien to me."

"If it isn't broke, don't fix it! That's what they always say." David turned his attention towards the camera. "After the break, Damien here is going to talk me through his morning routine, and you may even see me do a press-up or two. We'll be back in a minute."

The lights faded, along with the audience's attention.

The makeup assistant ran out on set again. She dabbed at David's face as he talked. Other assistants ran out with padding for the floor.

"I'm so happy you're here. If you could try to lighten up a little, though. It's New Year's Eve. Everyone wants to just have a bit of fun."

The makeup lady finished with David and walked over to Damien, who waved her away, refusing her service.

"That is an out-dated notion."

"What? Having a bit of fun?"

Damien nodded.

"Alright then. Well, try to keep it light. Do you need a water or anything?"

Damien shook his head.

"Alright then, let's do this."

The crowd began to applaud as the lights rose, along with the countdown back to being live.

"Welcome back! So, Damien, you're going to show me how to get buff and look like you."

"It's quite simple, really," Damien began. "If you follow me, I'll show you how to get in shape."

David reached inside a drawer in his desk and retrieved a headband. He stretched it around his head. It read '#SuperBuff', to which some of the older members of the audience chuckled.

The two stood up and walked in front of the desk, where a matted area had been setup during the break.

"Alright then, go easy on me," David instructed as he followed Damien over to the mat.

Damien stood on the edge of the matted space and waited for David to join him. First, Damien bent down and touched his toes with ease. David struggled, but with a small bend in his knees, managed to reach his toes. The audience applauded.

"What else you got?" the talk show host teased.

Damien bent down to touch his toes once again, but after doing so, slid his hands in front of him. Moving his hands, he proceeded to a press-up position. Seeing the final part, the older talk show host simply dropped to his knees and braced himself for a push-up.

The fitness influencer drew one arm behind his back and performed five quick push-ups in a row. He walked backwards with his hands until his hands again touched his toes and then stood up straight in a single, graceful movement.

"Your turn," Damien suggested.

David put one arm behind his back, but after a split second his arm gave in, and he crumbled to the floor. Not wanting to be defeated, he returned to a press-up position and managed five push-ups, using both arms, and then walked his hands backwards towards his feet.

David let out a small cry before dropping to his knees and standing up in a typical fashion.

"My bloody back," David said before shaking Damien's hand. "Ladies and gentlemen, Damien Zucheim."

The audience applauded.

"Ladies and gentlemen, please be careful trying that at home, unless you're in better shape than me. Not difficult, I know."

David walked, gingerly sat down behind his desk, and removed his headband.

"Thanks for that. Any tips for older people like me, who might not be able to do all of the physical exercises like that one?"

"Yes," Damien began. "Don't worry about following routines, just be healthy."

"So, what you're saying is don't worry about it?"

"I'm here to help my younger fans. Maybe try stretching and walking more."

"Got it. Walk to the pub and stretch my arm as I pick up the beer - great advice."

Only the adults in the audience showed their appreciation for the joke.

"Well, for those younger people at home," David began to camera. "Here are a few highlights from Damien's vlogs over the past year."

The screen lit up with vertical videos of Damien demonstrating various exercises as the studio lights brightened. The makeup assistant sprinted over to David once more.

"Some paracetamol please, sweetheart," David asked.

The makeup girl topped up his makeup and sprinted off-stage once more. A few moments later, she jogged back gently, holding two pills and a paper cup filled with water.

She placed them on the desk, waited for David to take the pills and then ran off with the empty cup.

"Thank you," the host said.

The lights faded in as the video ended.

"Wow," David feigned enthusiasm in the guest's direction. "You are certainly in good shape, I'll give you that."

"Thank you," Damien replied.

"I think I'll stick to the single sit-up I do when I wake up in the morning, personally. Damien, thank you for inspiring a whole generation of people to stay in shape. Your influence has certainly been felt by many."

"My pleasure."

"Moving on, we're going to hear from Sara and Zach, but first it's time to hear from Miss Emily Cambersham of The United World."

A picture of Emily Cambersham appeared on the screen. Her youthful beauty had transformed into that of regal elegance over the years.

"It was over ten years ago that she was elected Head of Communications within T.U.W. I even had the pleasure of talking to her from this very desk a few years ago. Some of you regulars might remember that one. But what Miss Cambersham, Mr Candrade, and the entire team have done is nothing short of astronomical."

David turned his attention back to his guest.

"Youngsters like you, Damien, won't remember this, but I remember watching The United World being announced twenty years ago. They wanted to eradicate poverty, eliminate war, tackle climate change, and in general create a peaceful and thriving world without borders – and we're certainly getting there."

The screen updated with statistics.

"Homelessness has been reduced by over eighty-five percent worldwide. A living wage has helped the poor, and opened doors to others, creating a more balanced society. And there haven't been signs of war since the formation."

The screen updated again to the picture of Emily.

"I know a lot of you won't remember a time before we united, but today, boy do we have it good. And if the last ten years is anything to go by, then we're in for one hell of a good time in the twenty-forties."

The crowd cheered in response.

"I'm sure you're bored of hearing my voice by now, so here's Miss Emily Cambersham with her end of year message."

The lights dimmed, and the video of Emily played.

Emily sat behind a mahogany desk, with a vase of exquisite flowers carefully arranged by her side.

She talked to the camera with a thick, British accent.

"Ladies and gentlemen, I hope you are enjoying the culmination of another year's worth of hard work and dedication. We have had an exemplary year as part of The United World, meeting almost all set targets. However, there are areas of concern that must be confronted if we are to remain united. One of our key objectives was to become carbon neutral, and while action has been taken across the globe, there are still minorities out there who refuse to adapt. The same has occurred with crime: we've seen crime rates plummet worldwide, however acts of hate, greed, and selfishness continue to transpire. If we are to move forward, we must do so as one. After all, it is with one weak link that the chain will break."

Emily paused for a moment before continuing.

"Think of your families, your friends and your loved ones. We must stay on track and not let agendas slip backwards. Together we are united, and I wish you all a prosperous and gratifying new year."

The message from Emily Cambersham ended. David introduced his next guest, and the show continued its countdown to midnight.

* * *

"Ten, nine, eight, seven," the talk show presenter counted down the seconds to a new decade - joined by the audience and crew. "Six, five, four," the studio lights flashed on the count of each second. "Three, two, one."

Confetti rained from the roof of the studio, in-between the permanent fixtures and fittings. Coloured lights flashed around the studio, causing David to rise from his desk and jump around, energetically – his back pain seemingly alleviated for the time being.

"Happy New Year," David spoke to camera before rushing over to the three of his guests who sat on the sofa. He gestured for them to join him at the front of the stage, to which they followed.

The older members of the crowd belted out Auld Lang Syne as David linked arms with a couple of the influencers on his show. He faced the audience and spoke into the camera as the screen showed fireworks across London.

"Goodnight everyone!" David waved to the crowd as the lights dimmed. The screens showcased an impressive light display, led by drones, starting along the River Thames before reaching The London Eye. Thousands of flashing lights welcomed in a new year, a new decade, and unknown to all but a select few, a new authoritative regime.

3

January 1st, 2040

Empty bottles, leftover cans, and various remnants of street parties littered the streets of Central London. It was a new decade, and the public had welcomed it in style.

Masses of youths tidied the streets and collected rubbish from the ground, seemingly starting their new year's resolutions to help the community particularly early. Hundreds upon hundreds of teenagers occupied what would have otherwise been relatively quiet streets on the morning of January first. They walked in an ordered manner, assisting in the cleaning of their city.

There were no sanitation workers in the streets, no local authority staff in fluorescent tops, it was merely down to the youth – and they offered no complaints.

In Camden Town, a group of youths cleared the riverside market space that had existed for over fifty years. It was a Sunday, and that meant despite it being a bank holiday, people would be here today to sell food, drink and various wares. In order to do so, the litter from the night before must be cleared.

Reece walked along the canal, observing a group of girls and boys cleaning from afar. They showed no sign of hesitation or disgust for what they found in front of them; teens shovelled vomit into a bin bag like it was nothing but dirty clothes on their bedroom floor.

For Reece, today was not only New Year, but also his birthday. While others in his position might have wanted new clothes, a haircut, some warm food, perhaps even a shower; Reece found himself desiring none of them at this moment. The only thing that piqued his interest was the cleaning that happened across from him in the market stall.

A cold wind urged Reece to find shelter - his torn jeans and thick, but tattered top providing little protection from the winter air. He moved away from the open and positioned himself tightly against the wall. The six teenagers who he could see cleaned, unaware of his presence.

A grey-haired man entered from one of the arches that surrounded the market stall. He approached a few of the teenagers, but Reece was unable to hear the conversation. Reece moved closer, but something bugged him about groups of young people, unsure precisely as to why he chose to hide behind the stone bridge to remain out of sight and maintain a level of protection.

"Listen, kids. You don't need to clean. I've got people hired to come in," the middle-aged Londoner spoke to the group as one.

The young crowd continued, unperturbed.

"I know you're trying to help but, fucking hell I'm hungover. Listen, stop cleaning, I've already paid people to do it."

One youngster bent down and held a white bin bag open, into which another placed metal tins. The man approached the boy holding the bag.

"Look at me when I'm talking to you."

The older man pulled the boy up to his feet.

"Get the fuck out of here. I'm in no mood," he ordered.

The boy looked over the man's shoulder - silent, still.

The man waved his hand in front of the boy's face.

"Hello? Do you hear me? All of you fuck off. Fuck off, now."

The man turned around, met by the stares of the other five teenagers. They listened and stopped cleaning momentarily as the atmosphere shifted. Instead, they closed in on the man who had interrupted them on the first morning of a new decade.

"Don't get any ideas. I'll fuck you all up," he threatened the advancing teens, as he took a step backwards.

The sharp edge of a tin can sliced into the man's neck from behind. The man grabbed at his throat and stumbled around to see his attacker – the young boy, holding a white bin bag full of recyclables.

"There was no need to swear," the boy commented calmly before collecting the sharp, newly bloodied tin can, and placing it into the bag along with the others.

The surrounding boys and girls returned to cleaning as the middle-aged man grasped at his throat, unsuccessfully trying to cling on to life. He toppled to the floor with a thud.

Reece bolted from behind the stone protection, along the rocky canal path, into Camden High Street.

"Help, help." Reece ran towards some tourists who brushed him away. Reece continued his search. "Help! Somebody help."

Reece reached a man and wife, who were out for a morning stroll.

"Please, help, there's been a-"

"Help yourself, I don't have anything," the man responded before they continued their walk.

Reece tried the next person - a guy in his thirties, wearing a vintage Bring Me The Horizon t-shirt.

"Ring 999. There's been a murder."

The guy removed his glasses and studied Reece.

"Are you high?" he asked.

"No, listen. In the market, I saw it, can you call the cops?"

"Alright."

The man placed his glasses back on his face, pushed a button on the side of the wearable and spoke.

"Phone the police," the man waited. "Hey, yeah I'm in Camden Town, and a guy has just told me there's been a murder," he paused again. "I know, right?"

"Please, it was in the Camden market, I saw a group of teenagers do it."

"No way. Listen, he says a group of teenagers killed a guy in Camden market," he paused. "Okay, thanks."

The man pressed a button on the side of his glasses and removed them.

"Thanks," Reece nodded in his direction. "Will you come with me?"

"No way."

Reece was split in two: he wanted to flee, but a part of him also felt the need to keep an eye on the group. He hadn't stopped them from killing before, but he sure as hell could warn others. Fighting indecision, he ran back towards the market.

"Why don't you sign-on? Aren't you cold?" the man shouted back towards him, but Reece was too far away to answer.

Reece approached his previous vantage point stealthily. To his surprise, the youths were continuing as if nothing had happened. They had cleaned the area considerably in the few minutes that he was away, yet a dead man, and a large red bloodstain underneath him, added a certain level of untidiness to the floor.

Reece hid and waited. His heart fluttered, and his mind raced. What was he doing here? Shouldn't he just leave? Reece remained frozen to his hiding spot. Instead, he focused on his breathing, switching between rubbing his neck for comfort and blowing on his hands for warmth. On the odd occasion he allowed himself a glance, the teens were simply continuing their morning clean.

Police sirens wailed from a distance before they reached the intended destination. While Reece had been frozen in position, it had felt like a lot longer, but it only took a few minutes for them to arrive.

Reece watched two police officers step out of a car, which had pulled up on the pavement next to where he remained out of sight. He wanted to tell the police what he'd seen, but he'd been warned about talking to them. The law wouldn't understand his lack of identity, and questions would be raised.

Reece hid out of sight as the two officers proceeded across the stone path by the river towards the market square. Both of the officers were male. One appeared to be a rookie, following the more experienced of the two from behind as they entered the crime scene.

The young gang were finishing their clean around the lifeless body.

"Police! Put your hands up," the older police officer shouted.

Both officers removed stun guns from their holsters and approached.

"Stop what you're doing. Drop whatever you have in your hands."

The teenagers put down their rakes, bin bags, and other cleaning equipment to give the police officers their undivided attention.

"What happened here?" the police officer asked.

Both officers kept their non-lethal weapons aimed at the crowd as they approached the dead body on the floor in front of them.

"Interesting," the rookie officer considered. He knelt down to check for a pulse. He shook his head.

"What happened here?" the officer inquired, keeping his eyes on those around him. "What did you do to him?"

"He got what he deserved," one of the youths spoke. "We did what was right."

"What was right? You killed him?"

"No, I killed him," the boy next to the bag of recycling walked towards the cop.

"Down on the floor, now," the more senior of the two officers instructed as he replaced his stun gun with a pair of handcuffs.

"That won't be necessary," the boy responded.

Calmly, the other young offenders surrounded the murderer.

"Fine, I'll take you all in. Josh?"

The police officer looked over his shoulder to his young back-up. Josh was still kneeling by the body on the floor.

"Come on. Help me get these kids in cuffs."

Josh stood up.

"You little shits are all going away for this," the officer exclaimed. "Josh, what are you – come give me a hand."

Josh walked to his partner.

The youth in front of the officers outnumbered them. The older police officer returned the handcuffs to his pocket and retrieved the stun gun once more.

"I'm going to give you one more chance. All of you lie down on the ground, or I'm going to shoot the lot of you. You hear me?"

The police officer hit the floor, convulsing from an electrical current that ran through his body.

Josh stood over the body of his assigned partner in law enforcement, the person who had trained him and shown him the ways of the force. He also held the stun gun that was firing fifty thousand volts into the police officer's neck.

"Perhaps they did what was right?" Josh questioned the man twitching underneath him.

The police officer stopped his struggle and Josh eased off of the trigger.

"Did you see anyone nearby?" Josh asked the group, who shook their heads in return. "Alright, let's get these two cleaned up," he ordered to the young crowd in front of him. "We can use my car."

The group of youths, led by the young police officer, collected the bodies of the market owner and the officer's partner. They carried them one at a time to the police car and threw them across the back seats.

Reece made sure to hide as much as he could as they walked back from the car. What had he just witnessed?

The police officer and the young group returned to the scene of the crime, where they finished cleaning the mess from the night before.

Reece peered around the corner, saw an opening, and ran.

Thoughts pounded through his head, as did the blood through his legs. His limbs began to tire.

Could he ask someone to call the police again? And tell them what? They wouldn't believe him. Maybe he was seeing things? There was no chance of that, he thought.

Reece was out of sight of the market as he proceeded down the back roads of the quiet Camden Town. He allowed himself to rest against the brick wall of an alleyway for a moment, but the icy air kept him moving before long.

* * *

One side of a colossal office overlooked the English capital. In front of the windowed wall, Emily and Samuel watched over proceedings from a great height.

"How are the tests performing?" Emily asked as she allowed her pencil skirt to ride up her leg slightly.

A suited Samuel nodded to the side of her.

Emily looked down to the city below; from this distance, people seemed so far away.

"What happens next?" she continued.

Samuel turned from the world outside. He walked across the office to collect a crystal tumbler and an expensive-looking decanter that proudly presented a brown liquor.

Reaching the desk, he sat in a leather seat and poured himself a glass.

Samuel sniffed the drink that he had just poured.

"Don't you just love scotch?"

Emily turned away from the window and perched herself on the edge of the desk to continue her conversation.

"Sure," Emily answered.

Samuel slowly swirled the drink in his hand before taking a slow and gentle sip.

"Even the name, scotch. Do you know what it means?" he asked.

"Scotch?"

Samuel nodded, paying little attention to his counterpart.

"No," Emily admitted.

"In Gaelic, it means water of life. Isn't that rather apt?"

"It certainly is fitting," Emily agreed.

Samuel reached for a second tumbler on the desk and poured Emily a sizeable amount before passing it across to her.

Emily took the glass, sipped, and grimaced slightly.

Samuel let out a laugh.

"You still haven't got used to the taste?" He returned his focus to his internal thoughts. "Perhaps with more time, you will grow to love it. Go on, take a smaller sip."

Emily allowed a small amount of the liquid to pass her lips and flow down to her stomach. This time she did not allow herself a reaction.

"Just like this scotch, it's been a long road for us to get here - years of trials, years of dedication… years of sacrifice. But here we are."

Emily held the glass in her hand, content that she had appeased Samuel's love of scotch for the present time. She tried to ignore the gentle burning sensation in the back of her throat.

"Together we will create a better world."

Samuel stood up from his chair and closed the gap between the two of them. He placed a hand on her exposed thigh. She had always teased, she knew how to get what she wanted, and now was the right time to return the favour.

"How does it feel to be so close to what you've always wanted? To what you've always dreamed of, Miss Cambersham?"

Emily allowed her legs to open.

"Why don't you tell me?" she placed the scotch down on the table beside her.

Samuel grinned.

"Together, we shall make not only this country, but the world a better place. We shall create a world free of crime, free of murder, free of contempt."

Emily pulled Samuel in towards her.

"A truly united world," he added.

Samuel finished his drink in a single mouthful and allowed the tumbler to drop to the ground with a thud. He slowly unbuckled his belt and allowed his trousers to follow.

4

January 1st, 2021

John had been sitting impatiently in the waiting room for hours, and he was fuming. How dare they take him away from his wife and kid at such a critical moment?

People stole sideways glares at him. He ignored their tutting as he paced back and forth; unless they could tell him where Nora was, he could not care less.

A nurse ran through from Reception towards the theatre.

"Nurse, where's my wife?"

"She's in the operating theatre," the nurse said as she continued her journey.

"Can I go in?"

"Please stay there. She'll be fine." The nurse ran from earshot.

John turned around and punched the support of the plastic seat behind him.

"Fuck!"

Others that waited chose either to ignore his outburst or move away to protect themselves from further expletives.

John exhaled deeply and sat back down in his seat. He examined the large, rough knuckles of his right fist, which took no damage from the flimsy plastic chair.

Sitting was no good. He couldn't sit while Nora was giving everything in there to deliver their child. Maybe it was time for his fourth cup of coffee? No, that was just wasting money. Besides, he was on edge enough as it was.

John stood up and walked over to the corridor that led to the reception.

"Nurse? Nurse?" he shouted through the hallway. "Nurse?" he shouted louder - the hoarseness of his voice bouncing from the white, sterile walls.

A nurse walked quickly in his direction.

"Nurse!"

"Listen, Mr Loche, you can't keep shouting for us. We've got lots of patients to look after."

"How's my wife?"

"She's doing fine. She's fully dilated and with the doctors now."

"Can't I - please, can I go in?" John lowered his head, preparing himself for the answer that he knew was about to come.

"The best thing you can do for your wife, and the doctors, is to sit and wait."

"But it's fuck-" he caught himself. "It's so hard."

"I know, Mr Loche. I have to go, but is there anything else that you need?"

"I need to see my wife." He raised his head so that his eyes met hers.

The nurse looked away immediately.

"I'll see what I can do, but please sit down and try to relax, as best you can."

"How can I relax?" he asked to no response.

"I'll update you as soon as I hear anything," she said as she departed.

It had been hours. John had lost track of time, but he had been alone for at least six or seven hours. Perhaps more. He'd had no updates from nurses or doctors since he'd made a scene, and this waiting room was driving him mad.

Another guy in the waiting room began a conversation with him.

"It wasn't like this last time," he commented.

"No?" John asked.

"I was in there the whole time. Twelve hours, can you believe that? This time, they're making me wait out here."

So, it wasn't just him.

"It's ridiculous," another guy spoke up from across the room. He rose from his seat and walked towards the two of them, then sat next to the guy opposite.

"I'm Dave," he offered.

"Fred," the other responded.

"Can you believe they're making us sit in here? I've been here for hours," Dave continued.

"I'm going to get some fresh air," John cut himself from the conversation; if he had the strength to get through this, he had to focus solely on himself.

John collected his tattered, brown coat from the chair, threw it around his shoulders, and walked down a corridor that read exit.

* * *

Mechanical beeps and ear penetrating screams filled the operating theatre.

Nora lay on the slightly raised bed, gripping on to one side of the bed support with all of her might.

A doctor stood between her legs, reaching in to assist the baby out, as a nurse stood by her side.

"Push, Nora. Push."

Nora squeezed the rail as hard as she could. Along with the excruciating amount of pain she was in, her forehead felt like it was going to explode. She stopped pushing for a moment of relief.

"I can't do it," she gasped. "John? Where's John?"

"You need to push," the nurse smiled gently in her direction, wiping her face with a cloth. "You can do it."

"Push!" the doctor ordered. "We're almost there."

Nora's mind spun like a whirlpool of pain and confusion. The medication had created a numbness, penetrated by daggers that flew at her from all directions. They constantly reminded her of where she was.

Nora focused on her breathing. A deep breath in, and a big push as she breathed out. A deep breath in. A big push as she breathed out. Push. Push. Push!

Nora screamed, focusing all of her strength and anxiety on the delivery.

"That's it. Keep going," the nurse encouraged, but it didn't register with Nora.

Nora gave it everything: her last ounce of strength, and the final breath in her lungs – with every fibre of her being, she pushed.

A moment of panicked silence fell over the delivery room, broken only by the crying of a newborn baby.

The nurse left Nora's side to assist the doctor with the final parts of the birth. She cleaned the baby, clamped the umbilical cord and cleaned, as the doctor repaired Nora's wounds.

The pressure left Nora's body at once, and a wave of relief found her.

The nurse wrapped the baby in a warm blanket, ensuring to keep the newborn warm.

The doctor focused on Nora before cutting the umbilical cord and clamping once more. The nurse walked around to Nora.

"Here's your baby." The nurse approached Nora's side.

Nora rested her sweat-soaked head to one side and found herself smiling from ear to ear. Here was her baby - her and John's baby.

"Congratulations. It's a boy."

The nurse handed the carefully wrapped baby to his mother.

Nora took the baby quickly and carefully into her arms. She placed her face to her child's head and kissed his forehead gently.

He was like nothing she had ever known; he was the life that she had created. He was all of the sacrifices that she had made for the last nine months. He was her son.

The nurse placed a single finger on the newborn's neck.

"His pulse seems strong."

A tear of joy rolled down Nora's cheek, on to her child's crying face.

* * *

John removed the newly drenched hood from his head as he burst through the double doors back into the hospital.

He wiped his shoes on the welcome mat, shook the rain from his coat and proceeded through the hospital corridors.

John had managed to scrounge a couple of cigarettes from another soon-to-be father who couldn't stay seated. He hadn't smoked for a while, but it was mostly because he couldn't afford to, rather than a conscious decision to quit - that, and Nora hated it.

He paced for another hour outside, but it did no good. Plus, he didn't want to be away for too long.

John unzipped his coat and walked through the winding path, following the coloured lines back to Reception. That was - until he looked up.

A doctor and two nurses approached a crossroad ahead in a rushed fashion. They talked between themselves.

John overheard: "Loche ... special care... he's ready."

It caused John to stop still in his tracks. He kept his head looking at the floor so to avoid detection. He monitored the doctor and nurses from the corner of his eye, watching as they turned a corner to his left.

A sign loomed above his head, displaying the directions of many wards in this part of the hospital. The maternity ward was straight ahead, he knew that, but there were other sections.

The special care baby unit was to his left.

Fear grew in his stomach. Was his child alright? Was his boy okay? Was that where he was?

John waited for a second and then followed the signs.

He saw nurses exit to a room on one side and approached carefully.

The United World

John walked carefully as he approached the door, which had been left slightly ajar. Without thinking twice, he pushed the door gently and shifted out of the corridor, into the room with the newborns.

The room that welcomed him held tens of babies, some of whom were crying, all placed on what appeared to be small medical beds. Others remained relatively still.

Looking at the newborns, he hoped he would have some sort of connection with his son that would instantly allow him to know which was his. Either that wasn't the case, or his son wasn't here. Nevertheless, the doctor that exited into the closed door at the end of the room mentioned his son - he had a son. He would allow that to sink in later.

John walked through to the grey door that separated him from answers. He placed his ear to the door and listened to the few words he could comprehend.

"Loche… operate… son…Nora."

That was confirmation. John placed his hand on the cold, metal handle and pressed down. The door clicked open.

The room opened up to a doctor and two nurses standing over an operating table with a single newborn placed in the centre. The doctor, wearing surgical clothes and holding a scalpel, stood over the baby.

The doctor turned to face John. His mouth dropped visibly agape behind the surgical mask, and the four of them stood in silence for seconds; no one sure of the next move.

"What the?" John began as he walked into the room. "Is that my baby?"

"Mr Loche?" the doctor removed the mask from his face so that he could talk. The scalpel remained in his hand.

"Ai, it's Mr Loche. Are you going to tell me what you're doing to my kid?"

"I'm afraid you can't be in here. Nurse, please escort Mr Loche back to the waiting room."

The nurse nodded in his direction and walked over to John's side. She placed a hand on his broad shoulder; however, there was no way that he was moving.

After noticing John's desire to remain in the room, the doctor tried to explain himself.

"It's just a routine operation," the doctor began, but shortly after struggled to find his words.

The nurse by John's side moved away from him.

"Then why do the nurses here look like they've just shit themselves?" John pointed to the two nurses who had backed themselves towards the walls of the room. After he'd finished asking the question, one of the nurses made an excuse, opened the door and exited. The other scurried to the doctor's side.

"What's wrong with my son?" John said, placing his hands on the operating table. "Tell me!" he raised his voice.

The doctor and nurse used the table to maintain the distance between themselves and the massive, brute of a man who shouted at them.

"Mr Loche, listen."

"I'm all fucking ears."

"This is your son. We were just performing a routine operation that we perform on all newborns." The doctor turned to the nurse. "Why don't you go and get some help?"

The nurse tiptoed around the situation, past John, and out of the room. The two men, and a baby, were left to continue their discussion.

"What 'operation' then?" John asked, his demeanour not softening.

"Just a routine operation," the doctor's voice shook as he answered.

"Bullshit. What's that?" John pointed to the small metal tray that sat on the table next to his son, with a single miniature device in the middle.

The doctor picked the small tray up and placed it on the side behind him.

The doctor used one hand to gesture at John to calm down, while the other grasped the scalpel by his thigh.

"Mr Loche, if you would please calm down, we can go and discuss this in Reception."

John remained unmoving across the table.

"Your wife will want to see you."

John's shoulders fell, as did his desire to grasp the table tightly.

"Nora?"

"Yes, Nora. She's waiting for you and your son."

The doctor walked around the table, approaching John.

"She's been asking for you."

John lowered his eyeline to the floor. The doctor continued his approach.

"Let's go there now." The doctor placed a hand on John's shoulder.

The doctor moved closer to escort him out, but John noticed the reflection from an object in the doctor's hand by his thigh. He hadn't put down the scalpel.

"I want my baby." John turned his thoughts away from Nora.

"Please, Mr Loche," the doctor tried to reason with him.

John pushed the slim doctor away from his side and reached for his child.

The doctor held up the scalpel towards John, in a mixture of a threat and what appeared to be self-preservation.

"He needs to have the operation." The doctor's voice broke as he spoke. As John waited, the doctor lowered the scalpel down to his side once more.

"I'm taking him now," John confirmed.

"Nurse!" the doctor called, loudly through the open door. "Security!"

John walked around the table to collect his child. Should he turn physical, the doctor was no match for a man of John's size.

"I can't let you take him without his operation!" The doctor raised his voice, as he attempted to push John's large arms away from the table.

Adrenaline pumped through John's veins, and his fists tightened. John swung for the doctor but missed: he managed to keep his distance via the table in the middle of the room.

"What are you doing?" the doctor whimpered.

John lunged for the doctor. His fingers grazed the medical outfit, and his midriff fell on to the edge of the table. The momentary window allowed the doctor a chance to escape, which he grasped with both hands.

John began to run towards the door in pursuit, but he was stopped in his tracks by the wail of his newly born son.

Turning his attention from the doctor, and allowing his chest to rise and drop with a few deep breaths, he found his fists unclenching. He turned his attention to the delicate little person who lay naked on the metal table – covered only by a thin cotton sheet.

John placed his hands gently under his son, which he found difficult at first, but soon found a grasp strong enough to support his child's head.

"Sorry, I'm not very good at this," he said as he lifted the child to his chest.

John leant the crying baby against him. He clumsily shuffled the baby around until he had one arm comfortably hooked around so that he had a free hand spare. John collected the white cloth, wrapped it around his son and made gentle shushing sounds as he rocked him back and forth.

The adrenaline had dissipated, but his desire for answers' remained.

John walked over to the metal tray that the doctor placed on the side. The tray itself was nondescript, but there was a small item in the middle. It was no bigger than a grain of rice. It looked like some sort of computer chip.

"Mr Loche!" shouts came from afar.

John turned, made sure his son was secure, and ran.

He exited the room, ran past the chorus of crying babies, and back into the corridor. More doctors in blue and green scrubs approached. These ones, physically bigger. This was no time for a confrontation.

Running through corridors, taking sharp turns, and chancing glances at the signs, the new father made his way to the maternity unit. The voices faded behind him.

John's muddy footprints on the ground diminished after a while, along with any detection of his whereabouts. He had taken them in a random direction, but he knew the direction he needed to go. Unfortunately, clearly, the doctors did as well.

John slowed to a halt as he reached a doorway. He saw a sign to the side. He was close.

Bursting through the doors caused the baby in his arms to wail. This was no time for him to learn how to be a good father. He slowed his run to a jog and tried to rock the baby from side to side as he did so.

The child peered through barely opened eyes.

"Shush now. We're going to find your mama. Okay? It'll be okay."

John jogged towards an open doorway and peered inside. He was greeted with a few confused women, but none of whom was his wife. He tried the room next door.

John strode in, attempting to shush the child he gripped in his arms. The baby's screams welcomed attention from the mothers around him, all of whom were becoming attuned to the sound of the cries of their own children.

In the room, there were eight beds - mothers resting, either with their newborn, or else waiting impatiently. At the end of the room sat Nora.

John walked up to her calmly, wanting to draw as little extra attention as possible to himself. He approached the side of her bed and took her hand.

"Darling."

"John!" Nora responded, as enthusiastically as she could for a woman who had recently given birth.

John let go of her hand. He gestured for her to lie back, and placed a finger up to his mouth.

"You've got our son?" Nora smiled, a little deliriously from the drugs in her system.

"Listen. I know this is not something you're going to want to hear. But we've gotta get out of here." John rocked the baby back and forth.

"John... here." Nora opened her arms.

John gently placed their son in his mother's arms. She pushed herself so that she sat more upright and gently jiggled their son. Then she began to sing.

"Rock-a-bye, baby, in the treetop. When the wind blows, the cradle will rock, when the bough breaks, the cradle will fall, and down will come baby, cradle and all."

Her voice was fragile, and her tone sweet. John knew that she was destined to raise a child, and at that moment, as he listened to the sweetness of her song, his fears of being a terrible father started to fall away.

"Come on, dear. We have to go."

"Why?"

"It's serious. We have to go, and we have to go now."

"John. I can't."

Nora held their child to her bosom. He stopped crying.

"I'm sorry, love."

John removed the wires from his wife's finger and arm, so she was free to move. He collected her clothes from the bedside chair and placed her sandals down by the side of her bed.

"John, what the hell?"

"We have to go now!" John raised his voice but caught himself before he exploded. "We have to go. Trust me. It's for our son. We're not safe."

"But we need to stay here. He needs to stay here."

"He needs to leave, and so do we. Now."

John had made his case. He placed his hands on Nora's legs and gently pulled them towards the edge of the bed.

The two stared at each other.

John noticed the glaze in his partner's eyes, but not for a moment did she look away.

"Okay, okay. Hold on."

John helped Nora's feet find their way into her open-toe sandals, and then found her coat to place around her shoulders.

Nora placed all of her weight on her feet and, with the help of John's tree-like arm, managed to stand – albeit shakily. She let out a moan of discomfort but clung to her child with both hands.

"I'm sorry, love." John rubbed Nora's back. "But please trust me, I'd never do this if it wasn't important."

Nora placed one foot in front of the other and attempted a step successfully.

"Hold up." John returned to the bed and rolled up the top sheet. He placed it neatly over their child, to offer some warmth and protection from the rain. He collected the rest of Nora's belongings, and they walked towards the door – one unsteady footstep at a time.

So far, so good.

He knew that they couldn't run. So why hadn't they come for him? Surely, they knew where he'd be. Maybe they were just waiting outside the room to jump him?

They stepped out into the corridor but found themselves greeted by emptiness.

"I was thinking…" Nora began.

"Yeah?" John continued to look around him.

"Our son."

John nodded.

"What do you think about 'Reece'?"

John turned his attention to his wife.

"Reece?" It rolled off his tongue perfectly. "Ai. That'll do."

The United World

John allowed himself a smile as he supported his wife and his son on their walk through the winding corridors. It wasn't long until they were at the front desk. There would be no discharge form, no formal birth certificate of Reece's birth, but Reece existed – and he was the most important thing John could ever comprehend.

He would protect his son with his life.

5

January 1st, 2040

The beginning of the twenty-forties had not been quite what Reece was expecting. Witnessing a brutal murder was not at the top of his new year's resolutions. Luckily, he had managed to find acceptance in what he thought to be an isolated incident and was moving on from it relatively well. However, something plagued him - it wasn't the murder of an innocent man that burned into his memory; it was the vision of the young police officer turning on his colleague. He replayed the scene over and over, and it still didn't make sense.

Reece walked the streets for a few hours, unsure of what to do next until his aching limbs forced him to succumb. He slumped down in an alleyway and removed a packet of crisps from a knitted tote bag. On his journeys earlier, Reece had found some leftover snacks on the streets, and to his delight, a few cans of beer. He'd enjoy those later – it was his birthday, after all.

Reece took his time with the packet of salt and vinegar flavoured crisps. With each considered bite, he focused on the flavours as they prickled at his taste buds. He enjoyed the sharpness of the vinegar, but cheese and onion was still his favourite.

Sitting, sheltered, Reece rummaged through his possessions. In his bag, he had five more bags of crisps from the six-pack he had found earlier, an unopened chocolate bar, half a packet of digestive biscuits, a tattered, but dry, blanket, and three cans of lager. That would do for today.

Emptying the last crumbs into his mouth from above, Reece finished the packet of crisps, folded and placed it back in his bag. The sun would be setting soon. It was time for him to head home.

He wanted nothing more than to get wrapped up in some warm covers, and of course, to see his best friend. With a new focus in his mind and some crumbs in his stomach, he rose to his feet. His knees and ankles made a case for remaining sitting, but it wouldn't be long until he could rest again.

Reece exited from the alleyway. He instantly felt the cold air consume his body, probing through his skinny exterior to his bones and cartilage. He placed his hands in his pockets, dug his chin into his top, and walked.

The backstreets were quiet – most of the people were likely to be on the high street, or at the market, blissfully unaware of what had happened earlier. Reece had no desire to walk alongside others at this moment; he had seen enough, and he didn't know whether he could handle any more drama today.

The wind forced him to keep his head down, but every now and then he traced figures on the horizon; running, dancing shadows. He kept his distance as he walked into the icy wind.

Winding through backstreets, Reece found the path opened out to a large, mostly deserted, car park. Across from him was a large, dilapidated building that presented a no-longer-existent supermarket chain's logo on top of the closed entrance. The logo that may have once shone brightly, now stood dull and forgotten.

Reece broke out to a jog towards a boarded window, halfway along one side of the building. As he came within a few steps, he slowed his approach. Reaching out, he grasped one of the pieces of wood, and with a downwards pull, it moved enough to create an opening. Reece grasped the wooden barrier above it and repeated the movement, creating enough space for him to fit through.

Reece climbed through the opening, making sure not to drop any of his food or drink, and then returned the wood so that the gap was minimised. Stepping into the shadows, he knew where to place his feet. He knew that he needed to move to the right to get around the broken floorboards, after which he carefully manoeuvred his way around to the aisle. As he walked, he plunged further into darkness.

Proceeding deeper into the dark, cluttered, and vast space, with little visibility Reece heard the sound of footsteps.

The sound that came from directly in front of him quickened; a crescendo of steps accompanied by heavy breathing. Getting closer, and closer, the sound of the footsteps sprung towards Reece from the darkness.

Hit with the full force of the perpetrator, Reece fell backwards on to the floor. The wind left his lungs in an instant, and he found himself momentarily stunned.

The heavy breathing that he could hear around him became animalistic, as large teeth moved towards Reece's face. A wet tongue licked him.

"Hey, boy!" Reece rolled around on the floor, play-fighting with the dog.

The dog's tongue found his face again in the near pitch-black.

"Alright, alright."

Reece moved the dog away from his face, and collected his bag, which had crashed down to the floor – his beers might be shaken, but they were still intact. He removed a packet of crisps.

The dog sniffed and licked at Reece's hands as he opened the crisps – even before they were opened, the dog nibbled away.

The smell of cheese struck his nostrils as the wrapper split open. He placed it down on the floor, allowing the dog to wolf down the crisps as he collected himself.

Given a moment's rest, Reece found his feet and slung the bag over his shoulder. He patted the dog as his eyes began to acclimatise to the lack of light. The dog nuzzled his leg.

"Good boy."

Reece walked with the dog by his side.

The path opened up.

A warm light greeted them.

Defunct factory machines surrounded the large, concrete space. Machines that no longer had a use – that no longer had life – had been pushed against the sides of this open area.

In the middle of the open space, beneath a high ceiling with ventilation above, roared a fire. Tens of silhouettes enjoyed its warmth.

Reece walked up to the fire, sat down on the floor and leant back on his hands.

"Alright?" a female voice welcomed him.

"One hell of a day," Reece replied.

Reece sat up and patted the dog who had already made himself at home, lying down across his feet. He took two cans of lager from his bag and offered one to the person next to him.

"No, thanks. You have 'em."

Reece nodded, placed the spare can back into his bag, and then pulled the ring. Foam spurted out, causing the dog to shoot up.

The woman to his side laughed.

"Young' ns today. I dunno."

Reece brushed off the foam that had sprayed across his face and chest. The dog sniffed at him, but then settled back down by the fire.

Reece took a sip of the warm, and now slightly less carbonated, lager. Despite the taste itself being one he could take or leave, the drink was comforting. After these three beers, he should be able to get some sleep tonight.

"What happened then?" the lady asked.

"Mary, you wouldn't believe me."

"Can't be weirder than what I saw."

"What's that?"

"Just outside, down the road." She gestured the direction. "I saw these lads, messing 'round, you know how they are."

Reece sipped his lager and enjoyed the strength of the heat on his face. He slipped off his coat and placed it by the dog.

"They were joking, pushing each other 'round. And then one of 'em, he looked a bit young, he pushed the other into the road, right in front of a car."

Reece turned and faced Mary.

"And the other one, he decked him. Straight up, in the face. I didn't want to see no more, so I got out of there. Didn't want to be 'round when the cops turned up."

"Don't want to be near any cops," Reece agreed.

"And then George over there, he said he stopped a girl from stabbing this lady."

Reece nodded.

Mary grabbed Reece by his trouser leg.

"I mean a little girl. A kid."

Reece turned his attention back towards his beer, and a moment of inward reflection.

Others from around the fire nodded and waved in Reece's direction, to which he responded in kind.

"Alright, maybe you will believe me then," Reece considered.

He told Mary about what he saw. As he continued, others gathered around the fire to hear a story that some of them found shocking, and others simply accepted without a doubt.

After the witness report, a silence fell over the fifteen to twenty people whose lives depended on the warmth in front of them, and the scraps of food they had collected.

The United World

* * *

David Stern sat at the kitchen island of his large, luxurious home. Today was one of his few full days off this year, and having stayed up late last night for the show, he was relieved to be able to stay inside, and far away from the spotlight.

Others may consider his enormous, six-bedroom mansion overkill for one person; perhaps for some, it might feel vast and lonely. For David though, he relished the solitude. It was the complete opposite of his work, and in this large home, he felt entirely at ease.

Sitting alone in his open-plan kitchen diner, David tucked into his dinner, one slow and considered forkful at a time.

"Alexa, mood lights."

The lighting in the kitchen dimmed.

"Play my classical music playlist."

One of David's favourites by Chopin faded in at a comfortably audible level - wild, and beautiful piano scales filling the space around the television host.

David lifted his head to the ceiling and began to gesture notes with his knife and fork in the air. He took another mouthful of the chicken alfredo that his cook had carefully prepared for him earlier.

He allowed the sporadic notes to move him, as he swivelled around in his seat. He raised his fork and knife once more until the sound softened to a pianissimo section.

One of the things David adored more than having a private chef, more than his incredible home, more than wealth, was the music that surrounded and stimulated him at this moment.

David rose to his feet. He danced over to the fridge as the next song began, swirling with an imaginary partner. He removed a jug of filtered water, which contained chopped cucumber and mint, before pouring it into a glass.

He danced around the kitchen, arms high, swirling around the hardwood floor. His feet rose and fell with each step - the water splashing gently in his embrace.

The music stopped suddenly, causing David to pause in mid-stride.

The interruption of an incoming call replaced the sound.

"Hello?" David said out loud.

The call connected.

A female voice, with a distinct British accent, entered into his home.

"Is that Mr Stern?"

"Speaking."

David sat on the stool, took a sip of his flavoured water, and returned his attention to the half-eaten plate of food before him.

"Mr Stern. I saw your show last night. I have to say, I was moved by your words."

David tried to place a name to her voice.

"Nothing short of 'astronomical'," she continued.

"Miss Cambersham?" David managed to question, despite still chewing on a large piece of chicken.

"Speaking," she confirmed.

Although there was no way Emily could see him, David placed his knife and fork down, swallowed his food, and sat up straight. He turned his attention towards the direction of the in-built speaker.

"Wow, what a pleasure."

"The pleasure is all mine."

"What can I do for you?" David enquired.

"Mr Stern, I have been watching your shows for quite some time. I have to say that I am impressed."

David noticed some stray sauce on his chin, which he quickly wiped off with his sleeve. Receiving a compliment from someone with such authority caused his anxiety to make an appearance.

"I hope that you don't mind me contacting you directly, but I have a favour to ask."

"Of course. What can I do for you?"

"Today sparks the dawn of not only a new decade but a new era. I won't go into the details at this moment; however, I would like you to discuss what this means on your next show."

David took a moment to consider his conversation with one of the most powerful women on the planet. He fought his initial desire to decline and instead found a more thought-out response.

"I would love to. I will need to check with the producers, as they are the ones that plan the running order."

"Of course."

"What do you want to discuss? Is it regarding the new regulations?" David asked.

"Your next show is tomorrow, is it not?" Emily avoided the question.

"Yes, tomorrow at nine."

"Tell your producers that I am happy to be interviewed, live, on your show tomorrow. If you have them call my office, we can arrange the details."

David sat, unsure of what to say. After a moment of silence, Emily continued.

"I assume that won't be a problem?"

"No, No, of course not. I'll phone them right now. What shall I say the topics are?"

"Only the very future of humankind."

David needed to know so much more.

"Do you have any specifics? Is there anything I can prepare? Oh, and how long will you need?"

"It will only take a few minutes, Mr Stern, and don't worry, you needn't prepare a thing."

"Alright, I think that can be arranged."

"Very well. I shall see you at the studio tomorrow."

"Great! Well, thank you, Miss Cambersham."

The call disconnected, leaving David with his solitude, and half-eaten chicken alfredo once more.

The classical music returned, but this time, David remained in his seat and considered what tomorrow would bring.

If nothing else, it would be one hell of a show.

6

January 2nd, 2040

"TV off," Gary instructed.

In the front room of an open-plan, two-storey flat, a reality show had just happened to follow on from the previous programme. Not one for watching that kind of junk, Gary was initially hesitant, but after noticing the several attractive scantily clad women, he decided that perhaps it had some merit. That had kept his attention for several minutes, after which the constant chatter reminded him of its prevailing downfalls.

His flatmate, Marc, walked into the front room holding a box of half-eaten chicken wings.

"Nothing good on?" Marc asked, taking a moment away from his dinner.

"Nah. How are the wings?"

"Not bad. Not as good as that other place."
"How many you get this time?"
"Twelve, and an extra six."
Gary burst out laughing.
"Eighteen wings?"
Marc smirked.
"Almost your record." Gary continued.
"I'd offer you one, but eighteen is a solid, round number."
"True. I'll get a takeaway."

The two had been friends ever since they met on a sociology course at university. They lived together then, and despite both of them having lived with girlfriends in their time, ended up back together almost a decade later.

Being in their thirties, their lives differed somewhat to those university years - to start with they could actually afford to eat. Before universal credits came into play, Marc worked in marketing, and Gary worked in finance. They were tough jobs, with a high level of stress – but rewarding pay. They saved a reasonable amount, bought this property together, and reaped the rewards. Now, because of the government credit system in place, they quickly realised they had no need to work. They could live comfortably enough without a job and found themselves reverting to university living once more.

"Fancy a game?" Gary responded.
"Alright."

Marc sat down next to Gary on the large couch, which pointed towards a large flat-screen television. The edges of the screen blended into the wall seamlessly, creating a window of entertainment in the front room space.

"Play wrestling 2040," Gary instructed.

The television turned on silently, instantly loading the requested game.

"Set it up, won't be a minute."

Marc wolfed down the final three of his chicken wings as Gary set up a match. He chose a pre-made wrestler that combined a resemblance of himself with the huge biceps and washboard abs of a real-life wrestler.

Marc took a white napkin from his pocket and wiped the sticky barbeque sauce from his fingers. Gary passed him a wireless controller.

"I need to set one up," Marc commented, laughing at the absurdity of how strange Gary looked with a toned physique, covered in tattoos.

The match was not a short one. It involved chain wrestling, reversals, finishers, and after a while, weapons as well. The two of them attempted to out-do each other with innovative moves, including utilising elements of the environment for fun.

Gary cheered as his character finally managed to get the three-count following a brainbuster from the top of a ladder.

"You got lucky," Marc observed.

Gary stood up and flexed in front of his fallen counterpart. Marc focused only on the chance for redemption.

"Fancy another?" he asked.

"Sure, let me order some food."

"Alright." Marc walked through to the kitchen, taking his depleted box of wings with him.

"Order takeaway." The sound of the wrestling game dimmed.

"What cuisine would you like?" A female robotic voice responded.

"Chinese."

"Locating your nearest Chinese restaurant… Hing Oriental is that-?"

"Yes."

"Confirmed. What would you like to order?"

"Sweet and sour chicken, egg fried rice, barbeque ribs."

"Confirmed. When would you like delivery?"

"ASAP."

"Sweet and sour chicken, egg fried rice, barbeque ribs. Confirm order?"

"Yes."

"Thank you, your order will be with you shortly."

The sound from the wrestling game resumed.

Marc walked back in with a large glass of squash.

"That's so painful."

"What is?" Marc asked.

"Ordering. Surely there's an easier way"

"Could do it online?"

"Nah."

Marc sat back down, and the two of them resumed their game.

"Are we watching Stern tonight?" Marc asked.

"Can do."

"I read online that Emily Cambersham is gonna be on it."

"Like, actually on it?"

"Yeah."

"Fuck."

"I know."

"Something's going down," Gary suggested as he performed a jumping DDT to start the match.

"Gotta be."

"Heard some of the rumours?" Gary asked.

"Which ones?" March responded, reversing a suplex into a small package pin for a two-count.

"Come on, man!" Gary reacted to the pin attempt. The game had barely been going for thirty seconds. "The ones about the new government rules?"

"Yeah. Crazy if you ask me."

"Right?"

"Forcing that many people to suddenly change their behaviour?"

"It's embedded – just like my foot." Gary performed a spinning heel kick.

"People can change, though."

"Alright - let's say... someone told you that you couldn't eat chicken wings ever again."

Marc took a moment to consider his response, but before he could respond, Gary interjected.

"Exactly."

"I could do it."

Gary laughed.

"Is pizza still allowed?" Marc asked.

"Nope. No junk food at all."

"Shit. I wouldn't want to live in that world."

"You and me both."

After a few back-and-forth manoeuvres, Marc attempted another small package pin, and despite Gary mashing the control pad to kick out, this time he got the three-count.

"What the fuck?" Gary exclaimed.

"Yes!" Marc cheered. "Got you."

"Cheap win."

"Still counts."

"No way."

"Yes way. One all."

"Your order will be here in two minutes," the female voice interjected.

"Alright. One more match after food." Gary demanded.

"You're on."

"No cheap wins allowed."

"A pin is a pin." Marc suggested.

Gary stood up and walked through to the kitchen to prepare for his food delivery.

"I don't make the rules." Marc shouted through from the attached front room.

Gary collected a glass bottle of coke from the fridge, opened it, and poured it into a glass. He retrieved a plate, along with a knife and fork.

The doorbell rang.

"Get that will you, mate?" Gary asked, loud enough for Marc to hear.

The sound of the door opening and closing, along with a distinct whiff of Chinese food, reached Gary, causing his stomach to rumble.

Marc walked into the kitchen and passed the food over to his flatmate.

Gary served his food tower perilously high and attempted to walk back towards the couch – only a couple of prawn crackers that came free with the order, lost along the way.

"Set it up. Won't be five minutes," Gary instructed.

Marc returned his attention to the game and loaded up a hell in a cell match for their final encounter.

"Nice!" Gary responded as he bit into one of the barbeque ribs.

"You're going down bro."

Gary laughed it off and concentrated on his dinner.

"Did you hear back from the cops about your phone?" Marc asked – continuing the conversation.

"Yeah, fucking ridiculous. Nothing they can do."

"Really?"

"Yeah. Crazy isn't it?"

"And I thought uni was bad." Marc retorted.

"Not as bad as this."

"Yeah. Can't believe they had knives as well."

"Not going to lie, it wasn't the best experience of my life."

"At least you're alright," Marc added, as he chose his character for the next bout.

"True. I'll never go down that way again, either."

"I'll set yours up. 'Toonz' again?"

"Yep."

Marc took his friend's controller and selected his home-made character. He clicked play.

The entrances of the characters began, and while the two of them would typically skip them, Marc let them play out totally so that Gary could finish his food.

"How's the grub?"

"Decent. Ribs are good. Sauce is a bit crap, though."

"Should have got chicken with me."

"I would have, but you must have taken all the chicken wings they had in stock! Alright, two seconds."

Gary ran out to the kitchen with his half-full plate of food in-hand. He placed it on the side and quickly washed his hands.

"Let's do this!" Gary playfully punched his friend as he sat back down.

The two long-term friends settled in for what would be a long and intense match, where the victor would be decided through a deserved finishing move, in what would be their final ever encounter.

* * *

Emily Cambersham joined David on set, trailed for a moment by a sound operator trying to turn on her wireless battery pack.

For a moment, David wasn't sure whether she was actually going to turn up, and whether the phone call had been some sort of prank, but here she was. He had, of course, as one of the largest television hosts, interviewed her before. However, that was when she was an up-and-comer and needed all of the PR and media coverage she could handle. This time was different. She had claimed her throne on top of The United World and had no need to come back on his show. Perhaps what she needed this time, David thought, was a platform – and she had all the power in the world to get whatever platform she wanted.

"Just introduce me, and I'll take it from there," Emily insisted.

"Sure. Thanks again for coming on the show."

Emily waved his compliment away.

"What do you want to talk about? Normally I would talk to you before the show and help lead to a few questions."

"That's quite alright. I understand this is very last minute. I suggest that you simply join in when you feel is appropriate."

"Old school? I like it."

David pulled the piece from his ear.

"Let's do this properly," he suggested.

Emily smiled and nodded in return.

The countdown to the live show echoed around the audience. A member of the production team waved furiously in David's direction for him to replace his earpiece, but he waved them away.

'Three, two, one," the audience chanted, followed by a loud cheer.

The lights flashed, and the intro music played.

David spoke loudly over the music to the audience and people watching at home.

"Hello and welcome to a new decade. The twenty-forties are here, and do we have one heck of a guest to kick off the show."

The crowd applauded.

"I hope you've all had a great start to the year. We'll be taking calls shortly to hear how you saw in the decade, but first, we're going to get straight on with our exceptional guest. She's worked her way to the top of government, her proposal on carbon emission nullification has helped to scale back climate change, and she continues to pave the way for women in leading roles. Please welcome, Miss Emily Cambersham.

The crowd applauded her introduction.

"Thank you, David, it's a pleasure to be here."

"Emily actually phoned me at home yesterday, asking to come on today. Isn't that right?"

"That's correct."

"I was halfway through dinner, sauce all over my face, with half a mouthful of chicken, and then you called."

The audience laughed.

"Sorry for intruding," Emily said with a warm smile.

"Oh no, that's quite alright. It was just a bit of a surprise, to say the least – a very welcome one, mind you."

David paused for a second. Generally, at this moment, a producer would direct him with the next question to ask. He enjoyed the moment of freedom for a little too long, causing Emily to talk first.

"David, can I ask you a question?"

David returned his focus to the show at hand.

"Of course."

"What are your thoughts on The United World government body?"

David shuffled in his seat. He thought carefully of his words before he answered.

"Truly, please, there is no need to worry." Emily interrupted his line of thought.

"Alright," David began. "Truly, I think the coming together of nations and the worldwide peace treaty is remarkable. Many statistics demonstrate the rapid decline of carbon emissions and the slowing in the melting of ice caps – of which you've had a major hand in."

"I can sense a but coming?" Emily enquired.

"No, no." David considered his next words carefully. "It was an absolute necessity."

"I agree," Emily added. "Yet, I feel there is a hesitancy in your words."

"Miss Cambersham, I'm usually the one on here asking the questions," David joked.

"Oh, I am sorry." Emily softened her approach. "I would just like to know, as I'm sure would all of these people watching, what your thoughts are – positive and negative."

"Well. They are overwhelmingly positive," David began, allowing his words to flow this time. "However, I do wonder if everything is working how it should."

"That is interesting. Are there any areas in particular?"

David glanced at the producers to the side of the stage who frantically gestured for him to move on.

"You know what? Yes, there are a few areas, and what better place to discuss them than right here, live on my show."

"I couldn't agree more," Emily grinned.

"I think you're doing a fantastic job, Miss Cambersham, but there are a few things that irk me. The main thing is the world we're bringing kids into. It's all so regimented; I go and talk to kids, and they just seem so, I don't know, stoic, I guess? There's all of these influencers, but where's that brilliant spark, where's the creativity?"

"I see. Is creativity important to you?"

"Yes, it is."

"Is it more important than a prolonged peace?"

"Why can't both exist side by side?"

"I do not know the answer, but what I can say, is that so far, we've found acts of individualism to cause more problems than that of a group who pull in the same direction."

Feeling slightly afraid of arguing with his renowned guest, David changed the area of focus.

"And yes, there hasn't been a war since the formation, which is an astounding achievement, but the streets are still not safe. I mean, knife crime has recently been on the rise according to latest statistics."

"Thank you, David. It's refreshing to hear a public figure such as yourself, someone whom I respect, to let me know their true thoughts live on air. There have indeed been issues with country-specific crime. We expected crime to fall alongside homelessness and poverty, yet it seems that it is hardwired in certain communities and individuals."

David nodded.

"Do you know why I joined The United World, David?"

"No."

Emily wiped a single hair that had fallen across her otherwise perfect exterior.

"When I was six years old, a friend of my father abused me," Emily confessed.

The audience gasped.

"My father would leave me alone with his friend whilst he went to the pub. He would come back intoxicated, and when I told him what happened, he would hit me for making up tales."

Emily lifted her hand to her face.

"Are you alright?" David asked.

Emily nodded and continued her story.

"This continued for years. For years of my life, I was sexually abused by a friend of my father. This man had no empathy for another human being, and my father could not care less. It wasn't until the school teachers began questioning my bruised arms and black eyes, that anything happened."

"I am so sorry. That must have been incredibly difficult."

"Yes, yes, it was. The man was arrested, as was my father, and I was taken away from my family home, and placed into foster care."

"How have we not heard about this terrible experience before?" David asked. He remembered the need to reprimand his researchers after the show.

"It's not something I've ever spoken about publicly. I was given a new name to protect me from my father."

"I had no idea."

"After that, only ten years later, this excuse of a man was released from prison. They believed that he was reformed due to good behaviour." Emily took a sip of water from a bottle that was by her feet. "It was only two days until they found him next to a child that he had sexually abused and murdered."

David could find no words, so instead sat in silence.

"Ten years in prison, to come out and act again within two days. How is that right?"

David shook his head and fought back the tears that were beginning to surface from his guest's moving words.

"After a difficult upbringing, and I'm not trying to evoke pity - I had caring foster parents, but those actions from my childhood stayed with me. It was on my eighteenth birthday that I decided I had to do something to change this broken world. I vowed to not let another little girl be mistreated in that way."

The crowd rose to its feet. Applause echoed around every inch of the studio.

David stood to his feet and clapped, wiping away the single tear that had escaped and rolled down his cheek. He welcomed Emily to join him standing, and when she did, he greeted her with a hug.

The two of them sat back down, but the applause remained.

"Wow," David began. "Wow. For you to come out of that with this drive and passion for helping others. Just, wow."

"Thank you."

The applause faded as Emily took another sip of her water.

"That is why I forged ahead with a career in world politics. With Mr Candrade's help, we managed to succeed with the initiative all of those years ago."

"Ah yes, Mr Samuel Candrade, correct?"

Emily nodded.

"What can you tell us about him?"

"Well, as you know, unlike me, he prefers to avoid the spotlight."

A few of the audience members chuckled.

"But he is a wonderful man," Emily continued. "It is only because of his vision, his connections with world leaders, his financial backing, and his belief in me, that we are here today."

"Well then, I thank you Mr Candrade, because you have allowed this fantastic woman to come into our lives and change the world for the better."

The audience stood once more and applauded.

"Thank you. You are too kind." Emily breathed deeply. "But as you mentioned, it is not yet perfect. People just like the man who abused me are still out there. For every initiative we launch, there is a person that pushes back, a person that fights against peace and happiness. Those people will stand in the way of our attempts at reform. There is no place for people like that in our world."

"I couldn't agree more," David exclaimed, partly due to the rapturous applause from the audience.

"Therefore, even though yesterday was the beginning of a new decade, it is today in which we introduce the Public Protection Bill. I speak to all of you out there who have suffered, who have fought against injustice." Emily rose from her seat. "Today, I stand, not a victim, but a leader, your leader – a leader in the fight against evil. From today, I promise you that if you stand in line with government regulations, you will never have to suffer again. But if you break the law, then we will catch you, and this time there will be zero tolerance. Today is the true beginning of The United World: a world that stands against crime, against hate, against evil; a world that protects children and those who cannot protect themselves. To all out there who question this, I offer you a choice: you can choose to live in our world, or you choose to face the consequences."

Emily raised her voice over the rapturous rippling of applause.

"We have been working behind the scenes over the past six months on this matter. Many of you have already registered, many of you have received notice from your doctors or medical practitioners, but for everybody who has not done so, you must go and register to be part of this new world. We want everyone to be accounted for, and for us to be able to uphold the law, we need your full cooperation. For that reason, we are introducing a deadline to the registration process. We are asking that everyone go to their doctors, hospital, pharmacy, chemist, or town hall within the next forty-eight hours to do this. This is a worldwide registration, and available in all locations. So, if you're on holiday, visiting family, or in the middle of an expedition, go to your nearest town and register. It only takes a few minutes. This is your final chance."

"I've heard about the bill before. I'm sure we've all received the emails – but can you tell us, what exactly is this registration?" David interjected.

"Let me make this clear. In three days' time, the world will become divided, in order that we can unite. Those that choose to register, and those that have already done so, will become part of The United World... a part of our world. To those, we offer peace and prosperity. To those that choose not to register, you will be left behind. I urge you - no, I implore you, go and get registered tomorrow, and if that is not possible, it is imperative to do so within the next forty-eight hours."

David nodded and gestured for Emily to finish her sentence.

"From today, the world is, and will only ever be, united."

Following in the footsteps of the audience, David stood and applauded the most captivating, naturally charismatic, and powerful guest that he had ever interviewed on his show. Whilst his applause was genuine, he couldn't help but be concerned about the tight deadline of registration - and what may happen to those who choose not to fall in line.

7

January 2ⁿᵈ, 2021

The door to the small, damp flat, flung open.

John entered first, holding the door for his wife. Nora entered, cradling their newborn child, making sure that he was protected from the cold and rain.

Nora walked into the flat precariously.

"Sit down, love," John suggested. It was the very least he could do after forcing her to leave the hospital. After all, what type of idiot would do that?

Nora lowered herself slowly; her arms buckling slightly as she attempted to do so. John assisted her in making sure it was a smooth landing. Even so, Nora winced as she sat.

"The drugs might be wearing off," she suggested.

"Maybe just lie down?" John said. "I'll go and get some painkillers."

John took a peaceful Reece carefully from his mother, clutched him gently in one hand, and walked over to the kitchen.

As best as he could with his free hand, John looked through the few drawers and cupboards that may have contained some form of medication.

"Try the bathroom," Nora instructed from the couch.

John walked through to the bathroom and opened the cabinet - branded painkillers welcomed his search. He collected them, placed them in his pocket, and returned to his wife with a glass of water.

Nora had shuffled into a position where she could stretch out on the small couch. She sat up slightly as John handed her the glass of water and retrieved the packet of painkillers from his pocket.

John observed his wife closely as she took two tablets.

He noticed a spare cushion by the television, leant down whilst cradling Reece, and collected it. He placed it behind Nora's head to offer some more support.

"Is he alright?" Nora asked.

John looked at Reece. He was tough, he could already tell. For one, his child hadn't cried since they had left the hospital. John made sure to keep checking on him as they walked through the rain - yet, every time he was worried, Reece would simply stare back at him with undisturbed, unseeing eyes.

Nora mentioned that Reece couldn't see him yet, that he could only make out light and objects, but the way his child looked at him - he had never felt anyone look at him so closely. Nor had he ever felt more exposed.

"He's perfect." John smiled at his son and then his wife. "How are you, my love?"

Nora winced as she adjusted herself.

"Do you need anything?" he asked.

"Can you fetch me a blanket? And hand me Reece, he might need to feed."

John placed Reece down gently into Nora's hands.

He walked through to the bedroom and collected the duvet from the bed. He took it through to the front room and carefully placed it over his wife, and under his baby.

"You're going to be okay," John reassured Nora as he tucked her in.

John sat by Nora's side as Reece latched on to her breast. It was so strange seeing him do that so naturally.

"How does it feel?" John asked.

"So strange." Nora confided. "and a bit painful."

"I think you get used to it," John hoped.

John sat on top of the duvet, stroking Nora's leg as she fed.

"I think he's had enough," Nora said.

"Pass him here." John collected his son, placed him on his shoulder and patted his back gently. He had heard this was what you were supposed to do.

"I want to hold him." Nora pleaded as her eyes fought to remain open.

"It's alright, darling. You get some rest. He's just fed, I'll be fine with him for a little bit."

Before she could even manage to form the beginnings of an argument, she began to snore softly.

"Looks like it's you and me, pal," John whispered to Reece. "Let's give Mum some peace and quiet, hey?"

Reece threw up across John's shoulder, causing him to laugh.

"I guess I should have put a towel or something down, huh?"

John walked through to the bedroom and placed Reece down in the middle of the double bed. He took his top off and threw it on the floor. He collected a fresh t-shirt from the wardrobe and pushed the door to so that it was only slightly ajar.

"Hold on a minute," John talked to Reece as he collected a blanket from the wardrobe. He found one that was not quite as large or thick as their duvet.

"This will have to do."

John picked Reece up, removed the slightly cold-to-the-touch blanket that remained wrapped tightly around him from their journey, and placed him back down on to the bed.

Ignoring the urge to curl up in bed and get some rest himself, John made sure that the dry blanket was wrapped tightly around Reece, and then doubled it over to provide more warmth.

"You came so quickly, I forgot to even finish this off."

John walked to the wardrobe and reached on top of it. He collected a small baby's crib, which had no legs.

"It'll have to do for today."

John placed the crib on to the floor. He knew that the protective padding would still provide comfort, and the bars would stop his son rolling anywhere he shouldn't. He lifted his son from the bed, still wrapped in the blanket, and placed him gently into the crib.

He sat back on the bed, against the cushions and the wall, and placed his head back to allow him a moment to think. Reece's wail cut through any possibility of that happening.

"Sssh." John leapt to his feet and picked Reece up, instinctively. "You'll wake your Mum," he added.

Reece stopped crying, almost instantly.

"That's a good lad. I guess you can sleep in the grown-up bed for today."

John placed Reece back on Nora's side of the bed, before resting on it himself.

After kicking off his boots, John lay next to his son. He draped his arm around him for protection, and before he could count to ten, the world around him faded.

* * *

"John, John. Wake up."

Nora's voice caused John to open his eyes.

The sun that entered through the open curtains seemingly moments ago had now long gone.

"There's someone at the door."

John intuitively turned to Reece, who was peacefully asleep against his arm. He hadn't meant to fall asleep but obviously needed the rest.

"Who's at the door?" John asked, slowly regaining consciousness.

Nora held her stomach as she inched over towards the door. She looked through the peephole and walked back in.

"It looks like two men in suits."

"Shit. What the fuck do they want?"

John rose from the bed, careful not to disturb his sleeping son, and powered over towards the door.

"John," Nora whispered, grabbing his arm as he passed. "What have you been up to? Have you got in trouble again?"

"No, I promise. I don't know."

John considered who the men could be and why they were here. Instead of walking over, ripping the door open and threatening the two men, he tiptoed around and looked through the peephole himself.

The two men were big – not big enough to scare John but being two against one, he wasn't sure that he could take them. That didn't mean he wouldn't try, but the odds weren't in his favour. He felt the door vibrate against his cheekbone as one of the suited men bashed the door multiple times with his fist.

"Are they here for money?" Nora asked.

"I don't know." John thought for a moment. "Maybe they're from the hospital?" he suggested.

Oh, how he wanted to get rid of these two. He pressed his ear to the door.

John only understood a few words, but he caught the critical ones:

"I guess they're not here?"

More muffled words echoed through the door.

John turned to observe the men through the small fisheye lens once again. Within moments he was met by a close inspection of a brown eye. Shit. John froze, confident that any movement would be detected by the person on the other side. Instead, he met the man's searching gaze.

The larger of the two suited men backed away from the door, stepped aside, turned and forcefully planted his large boot in the middle of the door.

The reverberation of the door pushed John from the peephole to a standing position.

"If you're in there, we'll be back!" the more aggressive of the two shouted.

John listened to the footsteps as they moved away from the barrier that at this moment kept the peace.

After John was sure that the men were no longer on the other side of the door, he walked over to the window that looked out on to the street.

Peering through a small gap in the curtains, John made out the two large men exiting the communal entrance to his flat. They approached a large, black car, which they entered, and with the screech of its tyres, they disappeared.

John kept watch for a few moments, checked the peephole and then walked through to Nora and Reece in the bedroom.

"What do you think they wanted?" Nora asked.

"They weren't here to take a meter reading, that's for sure," John replied.

Nora lifted her waking newborn on to her lap, removed her top and placed Reece to her bare breast.

"How are you doing?" John asked his wife; the mother of his child.

"I'm alright," Nora responded in a hushed tone so as not to disturb Reece.

"How's the pain?" John asked.

"It's okay," Nora lied.

John could tell when Nora lied. First, she wasn't a natural liar. Secondly, she had a tell-tale look where she would move her eyes away from his before returning moments later.

"What can I do?" John asked, joining them on the edge of the bed.

"Nothing."

John sighed. The woman he picked was just as stubborn as he, only far more robust.

John shuffled gently along the bed and placed his arm around Nora's shoulder, allowing her to lean into his chest. With his other hand, he stroked the back of his son's head as he latched on to his mother's nipple.

"It feels so weird," Nora explained.

After a few moments of reflection, John spoke.

"I don't think we're safe here," he whispered.

Nora turned to face her husband; she placed a gentle kiss against his lips.

"As long as the three of us are together, I'll feel safe."

John hugged his wife tightly, welcoming her body into his.

"We'll rest tonight, but I think tomorrow we should make a move."

"Alright."

John took his hand from his wife's shoulder and stood.

"Do you want a drink?" he asked on the way to the kitchen.

"Just some more water."

John poured Nora a glass of water and removed the scotch from the fridge. It might be his last chance to enjoy that small comfort for a while.

The dark and unclear liquid splashed around uncontrollably before it settled in the cheap glass tumbler.

John walked back through to his wife. He passed her the water and sat down beside her.

"Are you going to be alright tomorrow?" he asked.

"Where are we going to go?" Nora replied, facing away from John. He understood why her focus was gripped to the child she had only just brought into the world.

"Wherever's safe," John replied.

"Well, how much money do we have? Can we stay in a hotel?"

"About a grand, all in. It'd run out pretty quick."

"How long do we need to be gone for?"

Deep down, John feared an answer that he could not vocalise. Instead, he played the fool.

"I'm not sure. Maybe a few weeks?"

"Suppose we could handle my father for a few weeks?"

John didn't reply.

"It's better than wasting all of our money on hotels."

Was it? John wondered.

"Listen, let's get out of here, check in to a hotel tomorrow, and then figure it out, yeah?" John suggested, hoping he wouldn't have to meet the man that he'd not seen in several years.

"A compromise." Nora twisted her neck so that she could throw a cheeky grin at John.

Even when she was in pain, sleep-deprived, and most likely experiencing emotional distress that he couldn't even fathom, his wife could always make him smile.

"You know me. All about the compromise." John leant over and kissed his wife on the forehead. "Listen, you get some rest. I can pack in the morning. I'll ring 'round and find a place."

"Thanks love, and-" Nora hesitated. "When are you going back to work?"

"I'm not going back there."

"Why not?"

"I don't trust any of 'em."

"John."

"They wouldn't even give me any time off, so I told them to go fuck themselves."

"John!" Nora raised her voice slightly. "How are we going to make money?"

"We'll figure that out on the way. They'll take me back in a few weeks."

"But we need to support Reece, you can't be quitting like that." Nora cooled her response, sipped a glass of water, and returned to giving their son lots of affection. "I'm sorry, I know it's all on you, but you need to be responsible."

John knew she was right. He would make sure he earnt enough to support them. Perhaps next time, he wouldn't storm off if there was an argument.

"Are you coming to bed with us?"

John sighed, thankful the argument came to nothing.

"Nothing in this world could stop me."

Nora cradled Reece, holding him tightly to her chest.

"Absolutely nothing," John whispered under his breath as he exited the bedroom.

8

January 3rd, 2040

Reece woke suddenly, startling the dog that lay across his legs.

He wasn't sure what time it was, but from his experience of sleeping rough, as well as the still darkness, he would guess it was somewhere between three and five in the morning.

Reece stroked the matted fur of his loyal companion.

"Sorry, boy."

Reece's dog didn't take long to relax and lie back down across his legs.

"I should really give you a name one day, shouldn't I?"

The dog didn't belong to Reece; therefore, he didn't feel like it was his job to give him a name. Even though he wasn't Reece's dog, on Reece's first day, he had come up and licked his hand. He was a good boy, no doubt about that.

Living here for so long, he hadn't ever had an owner. Perhaps it was time to give him a name. Reece closed his eyes and started to think about all of the potential ones that came to mind.

Unfortunately, Reece didn't know many people, and he hadn't heard that many names. He liked the idea of calling him George - after his friend, but it would only lead to confusing situations. Maybe he could name him after his Dad? No. Why did he think about John? Let's not go there, not now.

Reece sighed.

The dog stood up, walked along Reece's body and collapsed again across his chest. Reece ran his cold fingers along the back of dog's head.

Reece's sleeping situation wasn't anything to write home about. His bed, the naming of which was generous, provided some support at the end of the day. He previously had two pillows but recently gave one to a newcomer – one was enough, anyway. The old blankets he used were by no means clean, but they didn't smell – they were also dry and did a great job of protecting him from the elements. Also, Rex liked them. No, Rex didn't feel right.

It was cold outside of the blanket. He hated this time of year. His face was the only thing exposed during the night, but his hands were beginning to freeze. He stopped stroking the tangled fur of the dog and placed his hands between his legs. Geoff laid still. Geoff? Where did that come from? He definitely was not a Geoff.

The people here had helped set him up in an isolated area. Everyone stayed relatively close to the central fire.

However, it did go out each night. One or two people tended to keep it going as long as they could, but either sleep or a shortage of firewood would eventually result in a lack of warmth.

The warehouse provided enough protection, and it seemed like the right place for them to stay. Nobody appeared to come around to this derelict part of Camden anymore. He could see why. If he wasn't one of them, the large amount of homelessness would sway him as well.

But here he was, sleeping rough, accompanied by Sam? He looked at the dog that nuzzled into him. He'd never find a name that suited him.

Sleeplessness made him feel restless; it made his heart flutter. However, whenever he felt frustration rise, he always had his faithful companion to talk to.

"What do you want to be called? Hey?" Reece asked, more to himself than to the dog.

No name fitted, nothing felt right. Even though he wasn't technically his dog, he reminded Reece of someplace safe, he filled him with happiness - he made him think of home.

Home? The dog reminded him of home.

Reece had never had a home before, not one that he could remember, anyhow. This abandoned, derelict building was by no means his home, but the dog was. He was home.

"Home?" Reece said quietly.

The dog lifted its head, ears pinned back in an attentive state.

"You're my home, boy."

Reece removed his hands from the warmth of his blanket and tussled the face of his home.

"Home." Reece considered how it sounded, leaving his tongue. "I like it. What do you think?"

Home licked at his hands as he tried to stroke his face.

"Alright." Reece controlled his laughter so as not to wake other people who were only separated from him by makeshift blanketed walls. "Settle down, Home."

Home placed the full weight of his head back on to the midriff of Reece. In turn, Reece put his hands back inside the blanket and closed his eyes once more.

Memories of his mother and father escaped him. He remembered his Dad's features: as he closed his eyes, he pictured a haggard, unshaven, strong face with dark features. He saw his father's brown eyes that he had inherited, but his own hair colour was lighter than what he remembered of his father.

He also saw his father drinking from a bottle of scotch.

How old was that memory? Reece asked himself internally.

Reece opened his eyes and was greeted by two empty cans of lager that sat beside his bed. Perhaps he'd inherited that as well.

There was one question that plagued his thoughts each and every night. The question that entered his dreams, which quickly transcended into nightmares: why had his father abandoned him?

Reece squeezed his eyes tightly shut again. He wouldn't think about his father. Even though he tried repeatedly, he could barely remember any of his mother's features; he thought she had brown eyes, but sometimes they changed colours, resulting in him building his own picture. Instead, when he thought of her, he could almost feel her warmth – a radiating, loving blur.

Why did his mind do this to him? All he wanted to do was sleep.

At least he had Home with him, who he started to think of as his dog. He was the one thing that kept him going when he had no food, no drink, and no warmth.

Despite how welcoming people had been here, he knew that he had no real friends or family in this world. Home was all of that to him. He was loyal, obedient, and they were in this together.

Reece tried to make himself picture his face, his brown and black tufts of hair, his long nose, his soft ears.

If Reece could get back to sleep tonight, there's only one thing he'd be dreaming about; and that was Home.

* * *

Samuel Candrade placed his glass of scotch back on to the table in the London high-rise.

Despite being alone in his office, not a single thread of his expensive, dark suit, felt out of place. He leant back into his leather chair and waited for the right moment to address the person he was speaking to via a tiny wireless ear-piece.

"Yes, yes. The test went as planned."

For a man in his late fifties, Samuel was exceptionally well-groomed; so much so that when a colleague had referred to him as a silver fox, Samuel's receptionist countered with the description of a black panther. The comment drove temptation; Samuel's appetite for promiscuity had lessened only slightly with age. However, his devotion to Emily and their cause remained strong. Therefore, despite the occasional passing glance, the odd flutter of an eyelid, or the occasional brushing of an arm, his receptionist would remain nothing more than a fantasy.

"Nationwide launch is due to be a complete success. We should start seeing immediate results."

Samuel shook the thought of his receptionist from his head. It proved difficult in his office: it was large, had a view over London, yet it lacked features of any kind. Although, there was, of course, always top-shelf scotch.

"I understand that the way Miss Cambersham addressed the public was, how should I put it, unorthodox, but it was necessary. By showing that level of vulnerability, that level of humanity, it has increased the public perception of our cause."

Samuel knew that on a good day, he could win an argument against any credible professional speaker, as well as any president he had known, living or dead. It was a talent that came naturally to him, and with many years to practice, one he had mastered. This conversation with a director in The United World Results Team was no different. For Samuel, every day was a good day.

"With the actions that are about to unfold, we need every ounce of positive publicity… not that it will matter in the long run, but it will make the transition smoother."

Samuel collected his glass of scotch from the table as he half-listened to the continued conversation.

"Yes, and although it won't be simple in less developed areas, we should still see complete global results in a relatively short amount of time."

He waited for the question he expected to come, swirling his drink in the process.

"It's difficult to say. In multiple scenarios we ran, the impact was instantaneous, after which we expect to receive some resistance: there may be isolated groups forming, especially in areas we were unable to infiltrate. They will take a little longer, but in the UK, we're looking at an immediate effect - with perhaps a more conservative timeline of seventy-two hours for tangible results, which means there is likely to be a prolonged period, stretching over several months, for completion. We expect all countries in the West to be of a similar timescale."

Samuel poured the scotch into his mouth and swished it around like a minty mouthwash. After a moment he swallowed his favourite, yet expensive tipple, freeing him to end the call.

"Let's touch base again in seventy-two hours when the world will be a safe place to live in once more."

Samuel hung up. He leant back, lifted his shiny black shoes, and placed them down on top of his desk. He looked through the large window and down on to the streets of London below.

"TV on. Play BBC news," Samuel ordered.

What was seemingly a blank wall became a large digital screen. Samuel was greeted by a news reporter standing outside of the large building in which he sat.

The reporter finished her sentence and then started afresh.

"I'm here outside The United World Government Headquarters in Westminster. If we look over there-" The camera turned around. "You can see the Houses of Parliament that were once so prevalent in managing the country's policies."

The camera spun back around to face the news reporter. As it did so, people in the background were seen protesting with banners and signs.

"While parliament still has a pivotal role to play, it is clear that those in the building behind me have the final say. It was only this morning that we were informed, as were all of the media teams, to instruct the public to go to their nearest doctor, hospital, pharmacy, town hall, or designated registration office as soon as possible. As discussed previously, it has been confirmed that this is for the installation of a microchip. One reason is that it will allow for greater surveillance and help to lead to the eradication of criminal activity."

The news reporter walked to her side and invited protestors into the shot.

"As you can see, not everyone is on-board with the wishes of The United World. Sir, can you tell me your thoughts?"

A man in his forties held a sign that read 'What do we want? Freedom, when do we want it? Always.'

A group of people behind him chanted their motto as he addressed the reporter.

"It's obvious, isn't it? Just look behind me."

"Can you tell us more about your quarrels with the instructions?"

"What gives the government the right to monitor us? To track our every move? There are such things as human rights. We all have a right to privacy, and with this Public Protection Bill that they passed, I say fuck the government. Fuck them. Sitting in their ivory tower, they don't care about us."

The news reporter promptly removed the microphone from the protestor.

"I apologise for the language you may have just heard. As you can understand, tensions are high here. Let's talk to somebody else."

The reporter walked through the group of protestors who seemed to grow in size. She approached an older lady who was dressed in baggy, tie-dyed clothing.

"Miss?"

The older lady grabbed the microphone and made her statement directly into the camera, straight to Samuel.

"You cannot shackle us. We are human beings. We have a right to our freedom. You can pass whatever bills you want, but it won't change a thing."

"So you're not going to follow the instructions?" the reporter asked?

"Not a chance."

"Sir?" The reporter moved towards another gentleman protesting. "What about you, will you allow the government to install a microchip?"

"No!" he shouted, joined by a chorus of others around him.

"Not even if it means world peace?"

The man considered the question for a moment before selecting his words.

"You cannot simply castrate violence and hope that we can all live in harmony. Life doesn't work like that. Those of us who go and get chipped, surely, we're not the ones who need to? So, what's the point? Give up our privacy, our freedom so the government can check on us? We say no!"

"The government has warned those who are not chipped will be reprimanded."

"Warn is just a soft word for threaten. Let me ask, are you chipped?"

"I'm more interested in what you have to say."

"Tell me. Are you?"

The reporter allowed herself to show a moment of vulnerability as her expression changed from one of sheer professionalism to one of concern.

"Yes, I am," she answered hesitantly.

"Right. That was your choice. Did it feel right, when you went and got a chip inserted, or did you do it out of fear?"

The news reporter seemingly had no answer that would be appropriate on air.

"Your silence speaks louder than any words could. This government rules by fear. They are trying to remove our right to freedom!" The man turned to shout to his fellow people. "They can't take us all down, can they?"

"No!" came the unified response.

The proud protestor turned to face the reporter again; he leant in towards the microphone and spoke so that it would be crystal clear for those watching at home.

"There aren't enough prisons in the world to hold us."

The man turned to his colleagues and encouraged them to start chanting once more.

"Well," the news reporter began as she turned to face the camera. "There you have it. We welcome a response from Mr Candrade or Miss Cambersham from The United World on how they will deal with the situation in due course."

"Off," Samuel ordered from his comfy chair. That was enough news for tonight.

Samuel removed his feet from the desk and stood up. He walked over to the window.

"Why won't you just do as we ask?" he questioned aloud.

Samuel found himself looking down upon the people. Perhaps he was the closest thing to a God in this harsh world. If another God did exist, he certainly had no reason to believe in Him. It was Samuel who would step into the role that he had spent decades crafting. Samuel would watch over his people. He would cut out the cancerous parts of humanity and create a new order: even if it meant some painful decisions along the way.

9

January 4th, 2040

Marc woke to raps at the door.

Last night wasn't like others. Alongside Gary, he had spent it glued to the television, watching live updates on news channels – as well as conspiracy videos that were rife on the web. However, the one thing that did remain the same was the lateness in going to sleep.

He looked at his watch. It was a little past nine in the morning. Who would be bothering him at this time?

The rapping persisted.

Marc flung his legs from his bed and found his pyjama bottoms to hide his indecency. He collected his glasses from the bedside table and headed towards the staircase.

The two-up, two-down that they lived in left little to the imagination in terms of size, but the location suited them well. It had two decent sized bedrooms and a lovely open-plan feel below.

"Hold on," Marc shouted as he slowly descended each stair.

Marc reached the door, placed the chain across, and opened the door a fraction – a habit he'd developed from living in London for so long. He was greeted by a man in a black suit.

"Yes, how can I help you?" Marc asked.

"I'm going door-to-door to ask if you've registered yet?"

"For what?"

"The United World."

"Ah."

Marc was too tired for this. He broke, if only slightly, in his usually well-mannered response.

"Well, if I'd registered, then surely you'd know about it."

The man greeted his response with a smile – like he relished the challenge.

"You are quite right."

"So," Marc calmed himself. He found the cold air that intruded his maisonette to be as welcome as the early morning visit. "What can I do for you?"

"This is a friendly word to the wise - Mr Joylove, I presume?"

"How- Yes?"

"Be part of the solution. Run along today and get registered. All of the media hysteria is nothing to worry about. Get registered and live in peace and quiet. It's that simple."

"And, what if I decide not to?"

Marc felt the stare of the visitor intensify and leant against the door, fearing that he may force entry at any moment – he was certainly big enough to.

"We live in a free country. The choice is yours. However, I strongly advise, for your safety, as well as the safety of others, to register."

The line felt rehearsed and repeated.

"Thanks for visiting," Marc said, hoping to put an end to the confrontation.

"No, Marc, thank you."

Hearing the stranger say his first name creeped him out more than hearing his surname. He felt violated somehow – even if they did live in a world where data was everywhere.

Marc started to close the door, but a final message found him in time.

"Oh, and do pass this message on to the other resident, won't you?"

The door closed.

Marc locked the door from the inside. He turned around to see Gary coming down the stairs in his dressing gown.

"Who was that?" Gary asked, walking towards the kitchen. Marc followed him.

"Some tosser. He said we needed to get registered today."

"Fuck off," Gary suggested. "The only thing I need today is a cup of tea and a ton of bacon."

Gary grabbed two tea bags, placed them in cups, and switched the kettle on.

"He was proper weird, mate," Marc added.

"Just the government trying to control everything. You heard about the chips?"

Marc nodded.

"Yeah, well, it's all over the place that they are using the chips to locate people. That's how they'll stop crime, they'll constantly know where you are."

"We haven't got anything to worry about, though."

The kettle rose to a gentle boil.

"Not the point, is it? I don't want anyone tracking my every move. Imagine never having a moment of privacy again."

Gary poured the boiling water, collected milk from the fridge and finished his morning ritual.

"True. Cheers." Marc accepted the brew.

"You thinking about going?" Gary asked.

The two friends walked into the living space and sat down on the couch.

"No chance."

"Me neither."

"But that guy was freaky. I dunno."

"He's probably going around and threatening people to get chipped. Remember the rally last night?"

"Yeah."

"There's so many people, mate. Loads aren't going to be registered. What are they going to do?"

"You're right."

"We haven't got anything to be worried about," Gary added, before blowing on his cup of tea and taking his first sip of the day.

"I hope not."

"Let's see what the news says. TV on. BBC News."

The television came to life and switched to the desired channel.

The two former students were greeted by continuous reports of people all over the country. Whether interviewed as individuals or as rallies, they were vocal in their resistance to the registration.

"See. Nothing to worry about," Gary added.

"Do you not think the government might do something?"

"There are loads protesting en-masse. If there's enough people, they can't do anything."

"Fair enough. Cheers for the tea."

"No worries."

"We got bacon in?"

"Yeah, I'll put it on in a mo."

"Nice one."

The conversation, along with Marc's rumbling stomach, halted as Emily Cambersham appeared on the screen.

Emily talked directly into the camera from what appeared to be her home. The news reporter introduced her as quickly as she could, so as not to miss any of her speech.

"We're going over to Miss Cambersham now, who is giving a live public service announcement."

Emily began her speech.

"Hello again. As we've asked previously, we need every single person in this country, and every country watching around the globe, to go to their GP, their doctor, their nearest hospital, or registration office today. Today is the final day for registrations. Already billions of people worldwide have either registered or been registered previously. The cut-off is midnight, after which we can no longer guarantee successful registration. If you are unable to leave your property, for whatever reason, then there is a number you can call. Also, there is a website for you to enter your information, which will allow a member of the local government to visit and help you to register. Let me stress this again, this is the final day for registrations. After today, we shall have full transparency on who is part of The United World... and those who are not."

Emily took a breath. The news tickers along the bottom of the screen updated to display the phone number and website that people could visit.

"As mentioned in the media, everyone who was born before January first twenty-twenty needs to be registered. People born after this date are already registered. We are urging those twenty and over to register and be part of this new and improved world. We are being very transparent that today is your final chance. Please, I beg of you, go and register today. Be part of our world."

Tears appeared in the corner of Emily's eyes but didn't find their way to her cheeks.

"This is the first of The United World's daily updates. I will be talking to you again tomorrow, and the days following, with information regarding the fight against crime. As you all will be aware, The United World was formed twenty years ago with an aim to find worldwide peace. The Public Protection Bill will finally see it become a reality. Registration only takes a few minutes and will bring you, and your loved ones, a lifetime of safety and security. Those who have not done so yet, please go and register. Only then, only tomorrow, will I truly be speaking to The United World."

Emily smiled what appeared to be a sincere smile into the camera before the news reporter began reporting on what had just been said.

Marc fidgeted on the couch, unsure where to place his hands.

"Are you sure you're not going to register?" Marc asked.

"Nah," Gary answered confidently. "We all have a right to privacy, a right to express ourselves. Remember?"

Marc thought back to his studies; it had been a while since freedom had been focused upon.

"Yeah, of course, the Human Rights Act."

"Exactly. And do you remember the key points?"

"Treating people equally?"

"In a nutshell. It also allows us to have the freedom to express ourselves, as well as protecting us all from what the government are forcing us to do right now."

"Then, how are they getting away with it?"

"God knows, mate."

The two best friends sat, considering the options. Marc was unsure with where to take the conversation next and instead realised that he had let his tea go cold.

"Fancy another one?" Marc asked.

"Nah, I'm alright. I'll get food on in a mo."

Marc walked through to the kitchen, careful not to display his full cup to his closest friend. He felt torn. Gary was right, he had the right to make his own choice, and he had the option to refuse. Yet, there was something in the way the man at the door had looked at him that deeply concerned him.

Time for another cuppa, anyway.

He knew in times of indecision, his main course of action was to do nothing. He would sit here with Gary, watch some TV and maybe head out for a walk later. No one could deny him that.

* * *

"Home?" Reece called out.

Reece walked towards the extinguished central fire. He looked around the makeshift campsite for the homeless, and despite feeling closer to his dog than ever, realised that Home was not always by his side.

"Home?" He called out again, instantly regretting the volume of his yell.

Several of the sleeping bags that surrounded the site were filled with people trying to find sleep. It didn't really matter what time it was; they were entitled to peace and quiet if not much else.

Reece changed his approach. He walked towards some of the people that sat up around the edge of the room.

"Have you seen Home-" He stopped himself. "Have you seen my dog?"

He asked a few people around but was greeted with constant shaking of heads. He headed to the centre of the space. Some of the eldest threw items to where the fire was the night before.

"Setting her up?" Reece asked.

"You know it. Pass us that, will ya?" replied an elderly gentleman with rotted teeth.

"Sure."

Reece collected the wooden items that sat by the older man's feet and threw them on to the charred ground.

"You haven't seen my dog have you?"

"Yeah, he went off that way." The man pointed, his bare index finger appearing through a tattered, cotton glove with one fabric finger missing.

"Thanks, mister."

The man grunted.

The United World

Reece knew many of the people here, but at the same time, people came and went as they pleased. He learnt quickly, not to form too many unnecessary friendships.

Reece ran off in the direction the man pointed, out of the central area. There were no doors in front of Reece, just corridors filled with rubble and deserted equipment that had been pushed to the side, previously.

"Home!"

There he was. He appeared to be scratching at the floor, next to a pile of rubble.

"Home, what is it, boy?"

Reece reached his dog, who moved away from the area he was digging at. Home barked.

Reece looked at the ground. What had Home found? He knelt down next to the rubble and brushed some of the dust away. Something was sticking out from under a rock.

"Is this what you were after?" Reece asked his companion.

Reece placed his hand on the edge of what appeared to be a flat piece of laminated paper, and pulled.

The photograph came free.

Reece collected the dusty photograph strip, and looked at it, sitting cross-legged on the ground. Home nuzzled his face.

The strip contained four small pictures. All of them were of Reece as a baby, with his father and mother, posing for four slightly different photographs. It appeared that they were in a booth of some sorts.

The first photograph was of his father and mother smiling, looking into the camera. The second was of them looking at Reece. The third and fourth saw their smiles replaced with looks of worry across their faces.

Reece picked up the dusty photograph and placed it in his pocket. He had thrown it away a long time ago and regretted it soon after, and now here it was. Home had found it and, just perhaps, it was for a reason.

10

January 4th, 2021

John and Nora sat inside a small booth, cradling their newborn child. Nora balanced tentatively on John's leg, ensuring that they were both in the photograph.

The two of them smiled: Nora naturally displayed her teeth, while John felt like his smile was considerably more forced.

A white flash filled the space, momentarily.

"John…" Nora began.

"Now, Nora, we talked about it."

"I know, but they'll help us."

"I don't want to go to your parents," John exclaimed.

A flash caught them off guard.

"But you said we would!"

"I said we'd think about it, and I've thought about it."

"John!" she paused. "We are going to my parents. And you can either come with us or...."

"Or what?"

In the small space, John could feel his wife's body begin to shake with emotion on top of his leg.

"I don't know."

A flash cemented the moment.

"Nora," John pleaded.

"Let's just pose for the picture."

John noticed a tear trickle down Nora's cheek.

A fourth flash ended the session.

Nora rose from John's lap immediately, cradling her child in her arms as she exited through a partially curtained entrance.

John grabbed her by her free arm and spun her around. He wiped the tear from her cheek.

"Where you go, I go. Remember?" John forced the warmest smile that he could.

Nora rested her head against John's chest. He ran his fingers through her hair and stood there as she sobbed.

"It'll be alright. We'll be alright."

The tears dried up.

Nora lifted her head and looked at the man who promised to protect them, through sickness and in health, for better or worse.

"I am going to my parents. So, that means you're coming with me."

John sighed.

"Fine."

He looked over at a slot on the edge of the photo booth; the pictures had just developed. He collected the strip of four photos and passed them to Nora without looking at them.

"If we're going to your parents, I'm going to need some time to get a few things."

Nora nodded and looked at the strip. She seemed in a daze as she lost herself in the first photographs of their family.

A drink was the main supply John needed right now. If he had to face the arsehole of a man, aka Nora's father, then that would help.

John walked around the shop, collected a few bags of crisps and snack bars for the road, a couple of bottles of water, and the most potent pain killers he could find. He then approached the counter. He looked at the options of spirits behind the counter.

"And a bottle of JD," John added as he placed the food items in front of the cashier. It wasn't his favourite, but it would do.

John removed a bundle of cash from his pocket, found a few ten-pound notes and paid the cashier.

"Alright love, let's go," John called out to his wife, who hadn't moved since he last saw her.

The two of them left the store side by side. He could tell his wife was in pain, but she kept moving. She held little Reece to her bosom as tightly as he'd seen anyone clutch anything before in his life. John instead clutched the plastic bag containing the liquid courage that would help with the journey ahead.

Last night's hotel bed was pretty comfy and relatively inexpensive. They had managed to get a crib added to the room at late notice, but Nora wouldn't put Reece down. After they lay down, John had nodded off quickly - he needed the rest, but he still noticed, more than on a few occasions, when Nora paced around the room to comfort Reece.

"Is he alright?" John asked as they walked to the side of the road in front of the superstore they had just left.

Nora bounced with him up and down, swaying him side to side gently in the process.

"I think so."

"I - you're doing great." John comforted Nora.

"Do you want to know something?" She asked.

John nodded.

"I've got no idea what I'm doing."

John let out a laugh.

"What?" Nora asked, allowing a small smile to appear on her face.

"Seriously?"

"No."

"I couldn't tell."

"Good. It's crazy, you know, having another little person to look after…"

John let her words sink in before she continued.

"The three of us is all that matters."

Nora leant towards John and placed a gentle kiss on his lips. It was the first time they'd kissed in days.

John's cheeks flushed. Even this many years into their relationship, a tiny spark could ignite in a moment.

"So how are we getting to my parent's place?" Nora asked.

John walked closer to the pavement and held his thumb out in the road.

Baby Reece began to cry.

"It'll be okay, little buddy," John added.

The United World

Nora continued to bounce up and down, swaying Reece to and fro.

"How are you feeling?"

"Fine."

John was sure she was putting on a brave front.

There was no way her stitches had healed entirely yet, and he could sense her discomfort with every step they took. He hated having to drag her from professional help, and from the rest that she desperately needed, but something told him they needed to leave. John always listened to his gut, and alcohol only strengthened his self-belief.

They'd find a lift and then she could take some more medication – that would make him feel a bit better.

John focused on trying to catch eyes with cars that flew past at speed. He took Nora by the hand. He pulled her and their crying baby a little closer to the edge of the road. Surely someone would stop to help.

Cars whizzed by.

Only a few minutes passed before a stranger answered their call.

The green estate car pulled up on to the curb. The driver appeared to be an older gentleman. He wound the window down on the passenger's side to speak to them.

"I don't suppose you could give us a lift?" Nora asked.

The man looked at Reece, and then at Nora and their child.

"Sure. Where you heading?"

"As far towards Cambridge as you can take us."

"What you heading to Cambridge for?"

John began to answer but thought against it. Nora's innocence would shine through.

"We're on the way to see mum and dad. We've been kicked out of our place in London." She told a half-truth. "We're desperate."

"I'm heading to Hitchin, but if you need a lift, I can run you over to your parents' house."

"Oh, if you could, that would be amazing."

The man nodded, his grey moustache gently bobbing up and down in time with his head movements.

"Thank you." John smiled in his direction. He knew this kind gesture was more for Nora and his child, but nevertheless, it filled him with hope - a dim and slow-burning hope, that there was still an ounce of kindness left in the world.

"Get in." the stranger offered.

John opened the back door for Nora, who ducked her head and sat herself down slowly on the back seat. John closed the door, walked around to the other side, and entered the vehicle himself. He placed the carrier bag down by his feet, and his hand on the leg of his wife.

"What are your names?" the man asked as he indicated and turned back on to the road.

"I'm John, and this is Nora."

"Nice to meet you, I'm Stan."

"Thank you, Stan," Nora added.

"And what's the little guy's name?"

Stan adjusted the rear-view mirror so he could check on the child.

"This is Reece," Nora answered.

Reece, their child: it was the first time that they'd told anyone else his name. He suddenly felt the urge for a strong drink.

"And how old's Reece?" he asked – now driving along a busy road out of London.

"Erm," John began to count the days in his mind.

"He was born on Friday, so I guess he's three days old." Nora finished John's thoughts for him.

"Wow, only three days, huh? And you're doing alright being up and about?"

"Yeah," Nora responded.

"We're taking it slowly," John added. "But that's why we need to get to her parents' house."

"Sure," Stan responded. "What type of low life would kick you out with a newborn? Sometimes I don't understand the world today."

John and Nora looked at each other.

"The world is messed up." John answered.

"Too damn right. Wouldn't have happened twenty or thirty years ago, I tell you that. People nowadays, all they care about is money. Money, money, money." Stan ranted. "Well, I'm sorry about your situation, but your parents can help you?"

"Yes." Nora added.

John noticed the energy fading from his wife, along with the crying of his child. It was amazing how in sync they seemed already.

"Do you mind if they take a little nap?" John asked.

"No, of course not. Why don't you close your eyes too? You must be shattered."

"Yeah?" John asked for confirmation.

"Close your eyes pal, I'll shout when we're coming up to Cambridge."

"Thank you."

John looked over at Nora and Reece, who already appeared to be half asleep. He closed his eyes and rested against the car's window. The vibrations stopped him from finding comfort, so he placed his arm against the window and leant on it. He would never be able to get comfy enough to doze off. At least he could rest.

John battled with the images in his mind. He saw a picture of a doctor holding a scalpel, he watched as the doctor cut into Reece's head, and placed a chip into his brain.

John struggled with the vivid images that flooded into his mind.

"John?" Stan whispered. "John?"

John opened his eyes, finding his eyelids to be heavier than he remembered.

"Yes?"

"We're almost in Cambridge."

"Already?"

Stan laughed gently.

"You've been snoring back there for about an hour."

He didn't even realise he had fallen asleep.

"Really?"

"Mmhm," Stan confirmed.

"Alright." John placed his hand on Nora's face and watched as her weary eyes met his. "What's the address, lovely?"

Nora closed her eyes again, but before she did, told John and Stan the address for her parents.

"Alright, it'll only take me one jiffy." Stan entered the postcode into his old-fashioned GPS system that took up a large amount of space on his dashboard.

After a few moments, the GPS system sprung to life.

"Ah, we're only a few minutes away," Stan said. "Thanks."

John placed his head back on the headrest and watched as Nora and Reece rested. He listened to them and focused on the sound of their breathing. He knew what Nora sounded like; the gentle breathing through her nose, indicating that she wasn't fully asleep yet. But Reece - he could hear his little lungs inhaling and exhaling. He listened to his baby, who was making the tiniest noise that was new but somehow felt familiar.

"It's amazing, isn't it?" Stan interrupted as they turned off down a side-road.

"What is?" John asked quietly.

"Being a dad. Best feeling in the world."

John considered the question. He was only just getting used to it.

"Mine have their own lives now, they're all grown up, out the house. My daughter has her own house, two kids, nice fella, not got much time for her old Dad, anymore. Enjoy this while you can. Before you know it, they'll be all grown up, and you won't hear from them for weeks at a time."

At least then he wouldn't be such a hopeless father, John thought.

"Alright, if you want to wake your wife up, we're just a minute or so away."

Nora opened her eyes.

"I'm awake." She turned to John. "You were snoring."

John rubbed the back of his neck.

"So I've been told. Is he asleep?"

"I think so."

"They sleep a lot more at that age," Stan interjected from the driver's seat.

"The nurse said it's normal for them to sleep a lot. It'll be better when he can lie down properly."

"And you," John added.

The car slowed and pulled in towards the curb.

"Alright, is this the place?"

John looked out of the window. He'd only ever seen this house in pictures Nora had shown him.

Instantly he felt the blood drain from his face.

"This is it." Nora said. "Thank you so much. You have no idea-"

"That's alright." Stan interrupted. "Not a problem at all."

"Thanks, mate." John gulped. He grabbed his carrier bag and exited the car. He walked around and helped his wife out on to the side of the street.

The car beeped as it drove off, leaving the two of them outside of the large detached house that stood before them.

"It'll be okay," Nora assured John. He was not so confident.

Nora led John by the hand up the small driveway, past a parked BMW. The family of three approached the front door.

Nora rapped the knocker on the door three times to announce their arrival.

John noticed the curtains shift to his side. Moments later, the lock turned, and the door swung open.

"Darling!"

Nora's mother stood before them; her arms open.

Nora walked forward, carefully protecting their child, and leant in for a hug.

"And who is this?" she asked.

"His name is Reece."

"Isn't he adorable? Come on, you must be cold, come inside."

"Is Dad here?" Nora asked.

"Yes," came her only response.

John was hoping they'd been lucky. Still, Nora and Reece needed a warm bed tonight – him, not so much.

Nora walked in through the welcoming doorway, looking over her shoulder as she did so, most likely to ensure John followed. He did as he was asked. Nora's mother closed the door behind them. She locked the cold air out, but also the three of them in.

"John. What's it been, two, three years?"

"Something like that. Nice to see you again, Patricia."

"And you."

A cough interrupted the near-niceties.

"John," boomed a low male voice.

"Andy."

"It's Andrew," Nora's father corrected.

John knew he preferred being called Andrew, but he couldn't help himself. He felt Nora dig at him in the ribs with her elbow.

"Hello, Daddy."

Nora moved in between her husband and her father, before closing in and placing her free arm lightly around his neck.

"Hello princess."

"This is Reece." Nora attempted to show off her child.

The man grunted in response.

"Now, now, you must be tired," Patricia began. "Why don't you kick off your shoes and go and take a seat in the living room? We'll bring you a nice warm cup of tea through."

"That'd be nice, Mum."

"Don't get too comfortable," Andrew warned John directly.

Nora slipped off her shoes, allowed John to follow suit, and lead John through to the living room – cradling Reece all the time. She'd already mastered multitasking, John thought.

"Idiot," John muttered under his breath. For Nora's sake, he made sure it was soft enough for her father not to hear.

"He's my family."

"He shouldn't be."

"I can't. John. I'm too tired. I just can't deal with it."

"Alright, alright." John stopped his wife from spiralling and instead helped her lower herself gently on to a soft cushion, before sitting beside her.

"Please be nice."

Moments later, Nora's parents walked through the door, her mother carrying a tray topped with porcelain cups, a jug of milk, and one large vintage teapot.

John shot up to his feet and took the tray from Patricia.

"Where shall I put it?"

"On there, please," she gestured towards the coffee table that lay between the sofa and three individual cosy chairs. "Thank you."

John placed the tray on to the table and sat back down.

"Right then, what are you doing here?" Andrew took them by surprise.

"Daddy," Nora appealed.

"Don't 'Daddy' me. I don't want him in my house."

"Mum?" Nora looked for support but found none.

"Andrew," John tried to get off on the correct foot. "We're extremely sorry to come and take you off guard. Truly, we wouldn't have come if it wasn't an emergency."

"Go on," Andrew offered.

John thought on his feet.

"We've been evicted. It's not that we've not been paying the rent. It's the landlord, real slimy, we couldn't do anything, selling up and left us on the streets."

"We don't have anywhere to go. And we've got this little one to look after." Nora took over.

"Why's that my problem?" Andrew asked, bluntly.

"Please. I'm in so much pain." Nora let her guard down.

As much as it hurt John to hear the truth, he saw it have an affect on her father.

Andrew rose to his feet and approached John aggressively.

"You're supposed to protect my daughter, and now you can't even put a roof over her head?"

John started to rise to his feet, but Nora wisely pulled him back to sit down. He was doing this for Nora. He needed to be strong.

"I'm doing the best I can."

"Well it's not good enough, is it?"

John gritted his teeth.

"That's why we're here. We need your help."

"You need my help, hey?" Andrew contemplated his words. "You need my help. Tell me, boy."

This idiot. He couldn't handle idiots. He was on his last straw.

"I need your help."

"Hmm." Andrew backed off from his dominant stance over John and sat down.

"And I need your help too, Daddy." Nora added, sounding younger than John had ever heard her. "Can we just stay for a few nights, until I've recovered?"

Andrew considered the statement for a moment. Eventually, he waved his hand in the air and responded.

"Fine."

"Thank you."

"Milk and sugar?" Patricia asked, rising to serve the refreshments.

"Just milk. Thanks," John answered.

Andrew turned his attention back to John.

"If you're staying under my roof, you're to do as I say. You'll get up first thing and do as I ask. Understood?"

"Yes." John sighed.

"Yes, what?"

John knew what he wanted to hear, and this wasn't the time for arguments.

"Yes, sir."

"Good. Oh, and no drinking."

John hadn't the strength to argue.

Andrew noticed the contents in the carrier bag.

"Speaking of which, pass me that bottle will you?"

John collected the bottle of JD and handed it to Andrew. He wouldn't be getting it back. His hand was quickly filled with a cup of freshly brewed tea from Patricia.

"There's to be no noise, whatsoever." Andrew rose from his chair and left the room with the bottle in his hand. "I'll be in my study. Patricia, lunch is to be served at one."

"Yes, dear," Patricia answered.

It had taken John everything to get through the encounter. History had been swept away for Nora's sake, but he could never forget. And above everything else, he would never forgive.

How long would they need to be here for? Perhaps John could look in the paper for some cash in hand building jobs around the area? Then he could find them a hotel.

"Is there a local paper around here?" John asked.

Patricia nodded and exited the room, leaving the husband and wife alone for a few seconds.

"Thank you." Nora said the instant her mother had left the room.

"I'm doing this for you, the two of you." John said.

"I love you."

"Just keep him away from me."

Baby Reece woke up and began to cry. Instinctively, Nora lifted her loosely fitted top and placed her breast next to his mouth. The baby latched.

People at his old job had told John his life would change, but he didn't think it would be by this much.

Look on the positive side, John thought. At least they were safe for now.

11

January 5th, 2040

Reece woke to the pressure of Home's paws pressing into his midsection. Quickly after waking, he heard low-levelled screams from all around.

"What the fuck?" Reece asked as much to himself as to his dog. He buckled quickly into a seated position.

Home ran off, growling at a low level.

Reece bounced to his feet, threw on his overcoat, and placed his boots on as quickly as he could, before running after his dog.

"Home!" Reece ran out of his small section into the large area where people had congregated. He dodged past people, and noticed couples comforting each other, hugging, around a depleted fire.

"Get the fire on," Reece shouted to the crowd.

He noticed a few people move, following his command.

An old lady grabbed him by the sleeve, halting his journey.

"This is the end. The end is here." She repeated.

Reece pulled his sleeve free.

"You'll be alright."

"The end… the end…" she continued to repeat to herself.

Reece shook the ramblings from his head and continued over in the direction of his companion.

"Home!"

Reece noticed Home growling at a small broken section of the wall which protected the inhabitants of this slum from the outside elements. He dodged past a few of the other inhabitants until he met up with his four-legged friend. He placed a hand on Home's fur to comfort him.

Noticing a small gap in the wall, Reece peered through. Movement. Was that what Home was growling at?

"Easy, boy." Reece tried to calm his dog.

Reece moved Home from the small vantage point that allowed him to view the world outside. He noticed the icy cold air lick his face as he moved closer.

Reece could see several people moving through the gap. Luckily most were far away, but Reece couldn't remember the last time he had seen as many people close enough to see, or close enough to hear.

Piercing screams were followed by moments of silence until screams rolled again from another direction. It reminded Reece of the wailing of an ambulance siren, just a lot more terrifying.

Focusing on what appeared nearest to him, Reece saw a single person holding a long metal object, standing over someone on the ground. He was just close enough to see red liquid drip from the piercing instrument, down to the body below.

Home nudged at Reece's legs, but Reece pushed him away.

"Stay…" he ordered, turning to his dog. "And be quiet."

Home barked in disapproval to Reece's command.

Reece placed a finger to the front of Home's snout; all he received was a wet, slobbery tongue for his trouble.

"Quiet," he tried again.

Reece focused his attention back through the gap in the wall.

Where he was looking before was only what appeared to be a body. A motionless, lifeless, lump lain across the landscape. But where had the killer gone?

Reece pushed his face forward into the gap as far as he could to widen his field of vision. There. He saw the person. They were closer now. They walked over to a lady who appeared to be pushing a pram. The killer walked with intent towards the mother. It could have been his mother. He approached her from behind, raised the long, metallic object above his head, which glistened in the morning sun, and closed in for the kill.

"No!" Reece yelled.

The man turned and looked in his direction.

The woman looked behind her, screamed and then ran forward, pushing the pram in a frantic jarring motion as she ran. The killer seemed unsure about whether to chase, but by then it was too late, the lady was far gone. Instead, he approached Reece's direction.

Shit! Reece thought, ducking away from the gap that gave away his location.

Home began to growl.

Reece ducked down to his dog's level and placed his fingers quickly around the snout of his canine. He knew a bark was only moments away. He felt the reverberation of Home's growl through his fingers.

"Quiet boy," Reece whispered.

Reece's heart drummed violently in his chest. He felt it hard to catch his breath, even more so as he focused on attempting to be quiet. Reece concentrated on his breathing best he could, to slow his heart rate. Breathe in, breathe out. He tried to focus.

A distant scream interrupted his calming attempt. Another thought ran through his mind - had the killer left them and found another victim?

He could chance a look through the gap. Perhaps that was the best move.

Reece stood slowly from a squatting position and looked through to the outside.

A large knife thrust towards Reece's eye between the gap in the wall. Reece managed to push himself backwards from the wall to avoid the prodding movements of the weapon. He had managed it with only fractions of a second to spare.

The killer removed the knife from the hole and looked through it. He stared at Reece.

Reece had expected the person to look deranged. He expected to notice a maniacal twinkle in his eye, but this man – no, this boy, looked like every other teenager Reece had seen on the streets of Camden. There was nothing maniacal about him, except for the weapon in his hand, and the intent in his heart.

He had expected a verbal threat to follow, but none did.

Instead, the boy stood at the gap for a moment, watching Reece, taking in the surroundings that he could see.

The gap emptied, revealing the cold sky in the distance. Perhaps the boy had retreated.

A thud vibrated through the brick wall in front of Reece, causing Home to bark. The boy was trying to force his way through the wall. A few more thuds came, but to no avail – the brick would surely hold against this teenager's light frame.

The thuds stopped, overlapped by the bark-turned-growl of Reece's companion, which slowed soon after. Home jumped up to the gap, but Reece beat him to it. Peering through once more, Reece saw that the boy had gone.

He looked around as best he could from his limited view. There were still people further in the distance, but nobody directly ahead. He strained his vision to the left, and then the right, but saw no-one.

They were safe.

Reece scratched Home's head in appreciation of the protection, before tussling his dog's face between both of his hands.

"Good boy."

Reece checked the hole one more time, before following his steps back towards the fire. Home followed by his side.

"What was going on over there?" George caught him off guard, stopping them at the entrance to the main area.

"Some guy going around trying to stab people," Reece responded factually.

"Really? Heck. But you're alright? Fire's starting, come and tell me over there."

They walked over to the fire, which had just sprung to life, and sat by its banks. They were joined by others who circled the heat source.

"Where's Mary?" Reece asked.

"Not sure. She was getting wood for the fire."

"Hope she's alright."

"She's a tough ol' bat that one."

Reece chuckled, but instead of filling him with warmth, it instead left a lingering feeling of worry and uncertainty.

"So, tell me what happened then, from the start." George rubbed his hands together in front of the fire, which was beginning to warm the area.

"I looked through the wall over there." Reece pointed. "I saw a guy, young, about my age, maybe a bit younger – I saw him holding a weapon over someone. Then I watched as he walked towards a lady pushing a - one of those things on wheels."

"A pram."

"Yeah. Anyway, he went over to her, pulled the weapon above his head, and then I shouted out."

"Did it work?"

"Did what work?"

"Shouting. Did the lady get away?"

"I think so."

George placed his dirty hand on Reece's shoulder and squeezed.

"Then well done. It's not every day someone can say they saved a life." George smiled before placing his hand back in front of the fire's warmth.

Reece sat uncertainly. All he had done was warn her.

"But then he saw me. He came over and looked straight at me."

"Damn."

"But the thing is, he just looked, I don't know… normal."

"Always do."

"Huh?"

"The craziest out there are often the ones that hide it the best."

"Really?"

"Well look at us. None of us are hiding it very well, are we? And most of us are harmless."

Reece thought about George's words. Something still dug at him.

"And then he went."

"Just like that?" George asked.

"Just like that," Reece confirmed.

"Blimey. Must have given you a fright."

"Sure - and this one here too."

Reece looked at Home who had just settled down next to them and placed his chin to the warm earth. If he could, Home would lay by the fire all day – apart from when he needed to take a leak.

"How's camp?" Reece asked.

"Same as normal. Few people seem to be out. Had to have a word with that old bag last night." George pointed in the direction of a woman who sat rocking back and forth behind them.

"Ah yeah, her."

Reece recognised her as the woman who had warned him of impending doom.

"Alright, you old bag?" George shouted in her direction.

She continued to stare into the air, rocking back and forth.

George made a circling gesture with his finger around his ear to indicate that she wasn't all there.

"Gotcha." Reece understood, but he wanted clarity. "I'm just going to check on her."

"Alright."

Reece stood up; causing Home to raise his head with a questioning glance in his direction. It appeared he was more interested in the fire and placed his head back down by George's foot.

Reece approached the old lady who was chanting on his approach.

"Are you okay?" he asked.

"The end. The end is coming."

She grabbed at his clothes with bony fingers.

Instead of fleeing, Reece bent down and looked at her. She had thinning grey hair, dirt-covered overalls, and where she once might have had a full set of teeth, the ones that remained were yellow and decayed.

Reece took her ice-cold hand in his and sat before her.

"What's coming?" Reece asked.

She looked at him, her eyes cloudy and white.

"The end. The end is coming."

"What end?" Reece asked - trying to warm up the hand he had taken in his.

The old lady leant in. Reece tried his best to not pull away from the body odour that greeted him.

"Death. We're all going to die. The end is coming. Death is coming."

"Is there anything we can do?"

"No, child. You can't outrun death. It is inevitable."

"But surely-"

A sharp silver blade appeared suddenly from the throat of the lady, as an object pierced her neck from behind. The lady grabbed at her throat, clutching at the sharp point as it was pulled backwards through where it had entered.

Reece jumped to his feet.

"Help! Help!" he shouted out instinctively, backing away from the body of the lady who fell forward and collapsed to the ground.

The teenage killer looked at him with a stoic expression. The boy from the wall had found a way in, after all.

Reece retreated towards the fire, facing the killer as he approached. The boy held the large knife in his hand aggressively, waiting to pounce.

Panic set in within the confines of the safe house for the homeless. All those who were sitting around the fire either fled or ran to Reece's side. They would not let a person in here threaten their kind. George joined Reece by his side, as did Home.

The boy did not slow his approach. Instead, he stepped methodically towards Reece, George, Home, and two others who had joined them. They stepped backwards, in-line with his reaction.

"Fuck this," one of the homeless guys said, as he pounced in the direction of the killer.

The killer, armed with the quickest of reflexes, simply slashed and side-footed the lunge. The homeless man was met with a swift and lethal slash to the throat.

"Sid!" George shouted.

The killer looked down at the body by his feet. He seemed to consider the death that had resulted from his hands – but there was an absence of emotion. He continued walking towards Reece.

The group back-peddled around the edge of the fire; Reece felt the warmth burn against the bare flesh of his face. But something caught his attention, something that shimmered with the reflection of the fire - he noticed something in George's hand.

"I've got this," George whispered to Reece.

Reece placed his hand on George's arm to stop whatever he had planned.

Before George had time to argue, the killer pounced forward, stabbing at the air in front of their chests.

Even though they outnumbered the teenager, there was no way for them to take him on while he wielded such a massive and deadly weapon. But Reece couldn't flee. He had to protect his family.

Reece was being backed into a corner - as were his dog and friends.

George stepped forward and thrust his hand towards the stranger's body. Reece saw it happen before he had a chance to object. Unfortunately, the teenager saw it as well.

The blow that George had intended was intercepted before there was any chance of damage being inflicted. The large knife cut through the skin of George's arm with ease, causing the shiny object in George's hand to fall to the floor, and him to retreat.

They were running out of space to back into. Reece glanced behind them, seeing only a corner behind them.

Blood trickled on to the floor from George's wound.

The man thrust the knife forward at George once more, this time attempting a fatal blow.

Home jumped forward and caught the teenager's arm between his snarling teeth, deflecting the blow away from its intended target. Home bit deep, locking his jaw and shaking his head from side to side on the arm of the killer.

The killer stepped backwards, giving Reece a chance to dart around him. He noticed a whining sound, but it wasn't coming from his dog.

"Get him off," ordered the teenager.

"Good boy!" shouted Reece.

The teenager collected the blade in his free hand and raised it above Home.

"No!" shouted Reece.

The killer pointed the blade at the scruffy Alsatian.

Reece noticed the shiny object on the ground. He moved.

The killer held the blade still, shaking only in his hands from the jarring movements caused by Home playing tug of war with his other arm. He was hesitating.

Reece dashed behind the killer, collected what turned out to be a pocketknife from the floor, and in one swift move planted it into the side of the killer's neck. Reece pulled the knife back, causing blood to spurt from a vein.

The boy dropped his weapon and reached for the wound. He sank to his knees, Home still grasping his arm.

The boy's face turned white quickly, so quickly that it frightened Reece: the killer resembled a ghost in mere seconds.

"Leave it!" Reece ordered; the feeling of desperation being replaced by one of guilt. Home let go of the boy's arm, which he held up to the wound to join his other hand.

It was no good. Despite trying to cover the wound with both of his hands, blood only collected and trickled through his fingers: life escaping, falling away into the cracks below.

"I…" the teenager began. "I love dogs."

Reece felt on edge. He was ready for a fight. He bounced on his tiptoes, unsure of what to do with his energy. He looked at George, who appeared to be feeling the same.

Home approached the intruder, who was visibly fading. He whined, and to Reece's surprise licked at his face.

"Home!" Reece ordered the dog to return, but this time, his command was ignored.

The teenager's hands dropped to his side, revealing the full extent of the point of entry from the pocketknife, which Reece still grasped tightly in his right hand. The boy crumbled backwards to the ground.

Home placed his chin on top of him and whined.

Reece stood, shaking, uncertain.

Arms enveloped him from behind, causing him to spin around and hold the knife up aggressively.

Mary's shocked face greeted him, as she backed away with her arms raised.

Reece dropped the pocketknife to the floor and fell to his knees.

"I'm sorry," he said.

Mary placed her arms around him once more, clutching his head to her stomach.

Tears found him, joining the river of blood below.

"It's okay," Mary comforted him.

Reece cried uncontrollably.

"Shush, shush. He's gone now."

George walked over to him and placed his healthy arm around his shoulder.

"You saved my life."

Reece pulled away from Mary's damp t-shirt that clung to his face.

George took Reece's face in the palm of his hand.

"You saved all of our lives."

Reece fought the tears back. He used the sleeve of his shirt to help him. The other homeless man that Reece didn't know placed his hand on his shoulder as well.

"Thank you," he said.

"I…I…" Reece tried to form his thoughts out loud but was unsuccessful.

"I know, champ," George said. "It's over now."

Reece pushed himself to his feet.

"Home?"

Home lay across the dead teenager.

Reece hung his head, and shame filled his stomach. He felt a sudden urge to be sick.

Mary gave George a big hug and looked at his arm.

"Let's get that cleaned up," she said.

Reece approached the teenager who lay motionless on the floor. He saw the large knife that, without doubt, was used to take so many innocent lives, before he sat down next to him.

Reece saw the teenager's face. There was no way he was older than sixteen. He didn't look like the violent type. So then, how could he have done this?

Home whined.

"I know, boy," Reece sniffed, and patted his dog.

"Come on, lad."

George offered his hand out to Reece, which he accepted. George pulled him to his feet with his good arm. Together they left the lifeless killer who had tried to put an end to their lives.

A killer.

An emotionless killer

An emotionless killer who, for some reason, had a strong affinity with dogs.

12

January 5th, 2040

Marc barged in through the front door.

"Fucking hell!" He shoved the door closed.

"You alright, mate?"

Gary helped him in, quickly locking and bolting the door behind him.

"It's crazy."

Marc paced through to the kitchen and placed the two carrier bags on the side. He noticed his hands starting to shake.

Gary wasn't far behind and placed a hand on his shoulder.

"It's fucked."

Marc found himself beginning to cry.

"What did you see?"

"We need to barrage the doors and windows. I don't know what else to do."

"Was it that bad? Gary asked.

Marc's silent response seemed to catch Gary off guard.

"What did you see?"

Marc began to unpack the milk, bread, and tinned goods he had gone to stock up on. He had carried as much as he could home, without impairing his movement too much.

"Mate?" Gary tried to catch his attention.

"Chaos. I saw absolute chaos." Marc answered. He then continued to unpack the items into the kitchen cupboards to try and calm his nerves.

"Are all the curtains closed?" Marc asked as he positioned the last tin of baked beans.

"I think so."

"Go and check," Marc ordered. "And make sure the windows are closed."

Gary went to do as he was told, but before he had the chance, Marc grabbed him by the arm.

"Don't let anyone see you."

"I won't."

Marc released Gary, who exited to check the windowed areas of their property.

After collecting a glass from the cupboard, Marc poured himself a water and sat down on the sofa.

Moments later, Gary returned.

"Alright, they're all closed. Now, will you tell me what the hell you saw?"

"People, everywhere, all over." Marc took a sip of his water and then placed it to one side. He planted his head in his hands. "People being killed. I saw people with knives, walking around. I even saw someone strangling a lady. Was like being in a real-life first-person shooter."

Marc looked down at his now still hands, contemplating how someone could do such a thing.

"Fucking hell, mate."

"I chickened out. I should have helped her."

"No, No. Mate, this isn't your fault. You did the right thing coming back here."

"Cheers," Marc said, letting a sigh leave his chest.

"So, what the fuck's happening?" Gary asked.

"It's gotta be the government, right?" Marc suggested

"Maybe."

"That guy who came over, he threatens us to register - and now this? Can't be a coincidence."

"I guess not." Gary mused.

"Do you think we'll be alright?" Marc asked.

"I," Gary paused. "I don't know, mate."

"TV on. Play BBC news." Marc ordered.

The screen turned on, to a montage of distressing images.

The news ticker along the bottom read:

"BREAKING: The United World begins. Full co-operation is required."

The montage continued, showing clips of people dying on the streets, fires all over London, and homeless people asking for help. The images continued then faded out.

The female newscaster who had been covering the last few news reports sat inside the studio, alongside a colleague. In the background, a few people could be seen working away at desks.

"Some disturbing images from around the country today, as individuals who oppose The United World have taken action."

"Bollocks!" Gary and Marc both said at the same time.

"That's right," the male news presenter continued. "These actions just demonstrate exactly why The United World is an absolute necessity."

"We apologise if you found those images disturbing, but it's important to show what is happening on the streets all around the country. It's important to show how people are taking violent actions against innocent individuals."

"It's been happening for too long," the male newscaster, who would generally stay impartial, voiced his verdict.

"Earlier today, we received the following message from Emily Cambersham on the sanctions taken by The United World to stop these acts of terrorism."

The studio faded to a video of Emily Cambersham sitting at The United World Government Headquarters. She sat in a chair and talked directly to camera.

As always, she did not only deliver a straight message, but teased and tantalised with how she pronounced with such elegance and grace.

"My people, my fellow British Citizens, and indeed, my fellow citizens all across the world. I welcome you to the dawning of a new day."

Emily collected a letter in front of her in preparation for reading a quote.

"I believe it was Thomas Fuller who was the first to notion, and I quote, 'It is always darkest just before the Day dawneth'. He was a wise theologian, and many more have followed on to use that quote across history. It is now that I too say that darkness is merely a prerequisite to light."

Emily placed the piece of paper back down on to the expensive wooden desk in which she sat.

"It saddens me greatly to hear of the acts of terror occurring both across the United Kingdom and indeed, the world. I implore the people taking these actions to stop, lay down your arms, and join us in creating a truly peaceful and collaborative united world."

"I don't believe it," Marc interrupted the speech on the television. "She's the worst of them all."

"Always knew there was something about her," Gary added.

"They're feeding people lies. This is so fucked up."

"How it's always been, mate. Government lying, trying to form us all into a nice little herd for them to manage."

"But this? This is messed up. The people I saw earlier, they couldn't have all been terrorists, surely? That old lady? No chance."

"It's horseshit mate. I wouldn't be surprised if they're the ones attacking everyone," Gary suggested. "I mean, think of that bloke who came around and threatened you."

"Really? The government would do that?"

"Who knows? I wouldn't put it past them."

"No chance. Outside was crazy. If it's like that everywhere, there will be thousands that die."

"Mate, if it's that bad outside, it'll be millions."

The two of them sat in silence and focused back on the television report.

"Thank you to all of those who followed the registration protocol. Thanks to your registration, we can ensure that you are safe and that no harm comes to you. So, if you registered, please don't fret at the actions happening outside. Now to those who did not register, I urge you to go to your

GP, local surgery, hospital, or pharmacy and register as a matter of emergency. I will say this only once. If you have registered to be part of The United World, you are safe. We will protect you. However, we cannot protect those who are not registered. The decision is yours, and I hope, for your sake, that you will make the right one."

The final statement, although sounding threatening, danced from her lips enticingly: she could read a murder report and make it sound like a warm and cosy bedtime story.

"Be safe. Be strong. We shall get through these times together and emerge as one great, united nation. We shall emerge as The United World. Thank you."

The news cut from Emily's speech back to the news reporters on Marc and Gary's screen.

"There you have it – and Miss Cambersham couldn't make it any clearer, could she?" the male news reporter began.

"It is as clear as day. If you are registered, the government will help to protect you. If you're not registered, then they simply cannot help."

"Can't help, or won't?" Gary asked.

"Again, we ask those watching at home who have not yet registered to go to your local doctor, pharmacy, or your nearest hospital to do so. There's even an online service where you can get an official to pay you a visit if you're not able or willing to leave your property."

"I bet it's that bloke from the other day," Marc added.

"Probably."

"The advice is clear. Complete your registration as soon as possible."

"TV off," Gary said.

The screen turned off, leaving the two near life-long friends in silence.

"Sorry. I've had enough," Gary added.

"Me too."

"It makes me so, ah!" Gary jumped up to his feet and clenched his fists.

"I know." Marc remained sitting.

"How the fuck do they think they can drive us into a corner. Forcing us to register."

"What do you want to do?" Marc asked.

"I don't know. I really don't have a fucking clue."

Gary unclenched his fists and stared at the closed curtains that separated them from the madness of the world outside.

"Shall we just register?" Marc asked.

"It feels wrong," Gary responded.

"If it's a choice between registering and being safe, or not registering and having to deal with that... I don't know."

"It's a basic human right to have freedom of choice."

"But the government aren't giving us a choice."

Gary turned around to face his friend.

"There's always a choice."

"What do you want to do?"

"The media is obviously on the government's side. The people out there deserve to know the truth." Gary thought for a moment. "Set up the lens in the study. I'll be up in a minute."

"Alright." Marc stood up and went to exit the room.

"Make sure to enable the VPN," Gary added. "Literally, as soon as you turn it on, get the VPN on."

"Will do."

Gary walked through to the kitchen as Marc headed upstairs.

Marc headed to the small area on the landing where they had set up a desk. They had two similar sized bedrooms, but the small study space was one they shared. It had a small desk, a single black faux-leather chair, and an old-fashioned but slim wireless desktop computer and curved monitor.

Marc opened one of the desk drawers and collected a round, wireless eyeball with an automatic fastening stand on the bottom. He placed it on top of the monitor, and it clasped in place.

Marc turned on the computer, which booted instantly, and ran the VPN programme. He then checked the drivers, which instantly checked that the eyeball lens was installed.

"We're going to need these," Gary said as he entered the study area holding a four-pack of beers.

Gary snapped one of the cans from the cardboard binding and handed it to Marc.

"Cheers mate." Marc rose from the chair and offered Gary the driving seat.

Gary sat down, freed a beer for himself, and placed the other two on the desk.

"If we hide and bury our heads in the sand, the government wins." Gary began as he cracked open his beer. "We need to share what we know. Grab a chair."

Marc exited into his bedroom, collected a small chair, and placed it back in front of the computer, next to Gary.

"We're going to live stream. All we're going to do is talk about what you saw outside, discuss what the government are saying, and give our thoughts. Sound alright?"

"Definitely." Marc rubbed his fingers through his hair in an attempt to make it look reasonable.

"I'll set up a brand new account. Hold on."

Gary clicked away, and in moments he had created a new account. On YouTube, he set the account name as The United Resistance, and the logo to be a hand-drawn red cross that he found on Google Images.

"Alright, that'll do. Are you ready?"

Marc took a big swig of his drink and nodded.

Gary started a new live broadcast, named it "The United World Exposed – What's really happening?" and began to live stream.

Marc moved about in his chair to try and position himself properly in the frame of the shot that Gary had set up.

The stream began.

"What do we do?" Marc asked.

"We just talk," Gary answered.

"Is there anyone watching?"

"Not yet, but maybe they'll find this later."

After a few awkward seconds of adjusting his seat, Gary began.

"Hello, YouTube. We're streaming to you today because what the news is telling you is a lie. What they're doing is forcefully ordering you to register, which is against the Human Rights Act of 1998 that still applies today. What the government is asking us to do is a clear and obvious breach of our human rights... and to be fair, is downright unlawful."

Marc noticed the number of people viewing increase from zero to one, then two, and continue to slowly rise.

"The government is feeding us lies. We don't know everything that is going on, but we have a first-hand witness.

He's seen things outside that you need to know. Go on, mate."

The numbers rose into double figures. Marc noticed a few comments appear in the live chat; most of them derogatory against the appearance of them both. The words did nothing to calm his nerves, but he told his side of the story anyhow.

"I've just seen some of the comments, asking who are these two fat blokes sitting at their computer, and fair enough."

Gary interrupted.

"We're not as fit as we used to be, but that's got nothing to do with this stream. We're here to bring you the truth."

Marc nodded in Gary's direction and continued.

"I went out earlier to grab some supplies, and what I saw was absolutely crazy. I still can't even get 'round it." Marc took a breath. "I was outside for about ten minutes, just popping round to the corner shop, and in that time, I must have seen tens, if not hundreds of people being attacked."

"And did they look like people opposing The United World?" Gary asked.

"Well, I scarpered, couldn't catch my breath."

Some of the comments again focused on the shape of the two men. However, the number of viewers had already risen into the hundreds.

"But most of the people attacking others were young. I mean like kids and teenagers. It's crazy."

"Really?" Gary asked. "But kids and teens nowadays are known for being extremely reserved and well behaved."

"Trust me. I couldn't see all of them, but I did see a teenage boy kill an older lady I recognised."

"A teenager? How sure are you that he was under twenty?"

Gary had turned interviewer to help Marc from rambling, which he had a tendency to do.

"Oh, one hundred percent," Marc responded.

"But that's strange, isn't it? The government told us that everyone under twenty was already registered. Isn't that interesting."

"And all the others looked young to me."

"So, if that's the case, then surely the people who are attacking others are actually part of The United World, and not opposing them?"

"I would guess so."

The two friends had stumbled on the answer to their conflict live on a stream, with an increasing viewership every second.

"And another thing," Marc began. "The people I saw being attacked; they didn't look like a threat to me."

"How do you mean?"

"Well, the old lady, I've seen her around, and she seemed nice enough. And the others, they didn't have any weapons that I could see."

"Can you tell us more about what you saw?"

"The young people were attacking some older people. That was it."

"Did they have weapons?"

"The young ones did yeah, most of them."

"Did you see what kind?"

"I didn't really see it. I was crapping myself, to be honest, and I legged it home. Didn't have time to film it - but I did see someone being stabbed."

"Thanks, M..." Gary forcefully stopped himself from revealing Marc's name... "Mate", he instead transitioned to as smoothly as he could.

"If anyone else has seen anything their end, please say so in the comments," Marc added.

The two of them watched the comments for a few seconds – the number of live viewers already approaching a thousand.

"Ah, here we go," Gary began, scrolling through the comments. "Tom in Cambridgeshire says that his wife was taken today."

"Man, Tom, I'm sorry," Marc added.

"He says that he was looking outside of the window upstairs, and he saw her get taken just before she got to the door. He thought they were police. He says a group of men in black took her away into a car and drove off. He then heard people knocking at his door, calling his name, so he hid in the bathroom and locked the door." Gary finished reading the first account.

"Bloody hell. Anyone else?"

"We've got someone from America reading. Hello Cory. Cory said he was stabbed by his own son. What the hell? Cory, is that real?"

"Cory, what happened?"

They waited for Cory to respond. They noticed the speed in which comments appeared to be rapidly increasing – as was the viewership.

"Thanks, Cory for responding so quickly, here we go..." Gary continued his leading role in the live stream. "Now I don't know if this is true or not, I just want to say that, but let's take it on face value for now.... Cory said that he was visiting his son's house. He was cooking breakfast and then, well I won't repeat the swear words he's written down…. Let's say he used some colourful language, shall we? Then his kid came in and stabbed him in the back. He was stabbed multiple times before he turned around and knocked the knife out of his hands. He called an ambulance, but no-one came. He says he ended up locking his son in the basement because he was trying to kick and punch him as well."

"Jesus Christ," Marc commented.

"I see Cory's commented again. He says that he swears it's true. Alright, Cory, we believe you."

"Damn, there's so many," Marc added.

The two of them looked through the comments and focused on a few more cases. Marc and Gary read them out loud to the tens of thousands that had stumbled upon their stream from all around the world.

"Listen, there are tens of thousands of us in this chat. Share this with your friends, your family, your colleagues. Let's get everyone in here and share their stories. We'll stay streaming now for a bit, and then we'll be back later today, I hope you'll join us then. There's already tons of people on here, I mean, the government can't take us all down, can they?"

Comments flooded the chat, so quickly that each one could barely be seen - 'no', 'never', 'liars', 'fuck the government' and others sped by.

"But first, let's read some more comments," Marc suggested.

"Yes. And thank you for joining us. Together we are going to get to the bottom of what exactly is happening out there, and what The United World is really up to."

The two London lads continued reading comments as their audience steadily rose into the hundreds of thousands.

The United Resistance had begun.

13

January 5th, 2040

D avid felt something deep within his core that concerned him.

The butterflies that surfaced before a live show hadn't stopped, but they had undoubtedly subsided over the years. However, today, they fluttered uncontrollably. He felt something more as well, certain anxiety - something he felt in the air.

A knock at the door interrupted his train of thought.

"Mr Stern. We're ready for you," a female voice instructed from the other side of the closed door.

"Thanks," David replied, loud enough for his assistant to hear.

David took a deep breath.

The things he saw on the way to the studio today concerned him. Luckily, as usual, he was couriered by a chauffeur, but even with tinted windows, he couldn't ignore some of the scenes that they drove past. Even his regular driver, a guy called Dom, who was usually the definition of professional, couldn't maintain his steel. He did, however, get David to the studio safely.

David took one last sip of his water, rose to his feet, and exited the room. He was greeted by his assistant; a lady in her twenties who wore a headset with a microphone piece. A make-up lady was also waiting and instantly attempted to dab at his face to touch up his makeup. The three of them walked through the corridors.

"Andrew has dropped out at the last minute, no one can get hold of him." His assistant told him the bad news.

"Just what we need! Anything else?" David asked as they approached the side of the stage.

"We've heard about a live recording, that you might want to look at. Perhaps it could be worked as a replacement?"

The assistant pulled out an electronic device and played part of the YouTube clip from The United Resistance channel.

"It's gone viral," his assistant added.

"Tell me the gist of it?" David asked.

"It's these two guys, they seem normal enough, your 'average Joe' types. They started a stream questioning the government's motives, questioning The United Governments registration and what it actually means for people."

"Isn't that a bit heavy for the show?" David considered the option. "It might be too much for the audience. Why don't we see if we can get someone from The United World to speak to us about it?"

David had always had an interest in journalism; it was what drove him to television in the first place.

"It'd mix the show up a little bit, keep everyone on their toes."

His assistant nodded.

"Remember the number I gave you for Miss Cambersham? Maybe try that one first."

The assistant ran off to make the call.

An announcement introduced David and the show to the crowd once more. David walked on stage, waving to those in attendance.

"Thank you, everyone, for coming," David said loudly; his microphone not yet set up to play his voice across the PA system.

David sat down at his desk – his home away from home.

The makeup girl dabbed at his face, leant back to observe her work, and then made a few small adjustments. She then ran off stage.

On this stage, he felt safe. David found himself surrounded by his television family, along with an audience of friends.

An assistant ran out, turned on a microphone pack that was placed in his pocket, and then exited quickly.

The countdown to the show began.

For the first time in as long as he could remember, the audience did not chant along.

His show, like other live events, was known for having a fun, almost carnival-like atmosphere. There was always a buzz in the air, a certain aura that anything could happen. Today, something had changed.

He looked over to the side of the stage where a producer signed three, two, and one to him.

"Hello everybody, I'm David Stern, and this is The Stern Selection."

The applause sign lit up, greeted only by a few claps from staff.

"Well, it looks like we've got a bit of a quiet audience today. That's alright, no, it isn't - because it's my job to cheer you all up, get you on your feet, and get this place bouncing."

He heard his producer talk through on his earpiece, delivering news about Emily Cambersham.

"Tonight, we've got – yes, I'm just being told now. We've got a live video call with the one and only Miss Emily Cambersham."

The audience applauded gently.

Finally, David thought.

"But that's not all, we've also got television personality Gino Divo from Cooking across Italy, and the music of Nothing Further on their comeback tour."

The crowd sat, silent.

"Alright. Well, it's shaping up to be a great show. Without further delay, why don't we move straight on to our first guest? It's one that we're no stranger to on this show. Miss Cambersham, can you hear me?"

The vertical screen next to David switched on to show Emily Cambersham sitting at her usual pristine desk.

"Hello David, how are you?"

"I am great, thanks for asking. Thank you so much for appearing on the show at such late notice."

"My pleasure," Emily replied softly.

"I mean, no other show could just ring up, and get the head of communications on the line, could they?"

Emily smiled and appeared modest.

"Miss Cambersham, we'll get straight to it. I'm sorry this is not a softer subject to approach." David paused, realising how much he was relishing interviewing a person of such power, without a revised line of questioning. "We have received a video, which you may be aware of. It's called The United World Exposed."

Emily's armour of natural beauty and trained composition remained intact.

"Now, no-one knows who these two guys are. It seems like they're from the UK, but from what I've read, no-one's been able to track them down yet. Can I ask you about some of the things they've been saying?"

"Of course."

David gestured to his assistant to come on stage – it was taboo, and it broke the fourth wall, but at this moment, he didn't care.

"My assistant is just writing down some of the comments, give me one second."

His assistant ran on stage with a tablet, almost tripped, and then ran off once more.

David tried his best not to laugh.

"Thank you. Ah yes," David turned his attention to the device. "They claim that acts of terrorism happening across the world, are not acts against The United World, but are likely – and I'm just reading here what my assistant has written – likely from younger generations, who have already been registered. Now, if that is the case, how could those acts be against The United World?"

"Well, David, the registration process is not a simple one. We have not been able to register each and every young person in this country, or indeed the world. There are a few that oppose the government and stand against what we aim to achieve."

"If you'd allow me to ask, you're saying that the attacks that many of us are witnessing are from people who are not registered?"

"That is correct."

"But then, why do initial reports suggest that it's mostly the elderly that have suffered in these attacks?"

Emily chose not to respond. David noticed a change in her demeanour – that was all the invitation he required.

"As statements have said, there is no requirement for under twenties to be registered, most likely because they already have been – that's a fairly small leap to make. Then it'd only be a handful of those that aren't registered, those perhaps without homes, maybe some who have slipped through the cracks. There wouldn't be many, especially in the United Kingdom."

Emily allowed David to continue.

"The amount of attacks reported, it doesn't correlate. Surely, if the majority of attacks are the young on the old, it would be from the registered?"

"Did you register, Mr Stern?"

David shifted uncomfortably in his seat, both from the change of subject, and the way in which she used his last name.

"Me? Erm…" David didn't want to alleviate parts of his audience who chose a different path.

"I understand, you don't want to offend any of your audience by revealing one way or another; very political of you. However, you can't sit on both sides of this situation."

David looked around and caught the eye of his producer who gestured for him to hurry the show on.

"With all due respect, my registration isn't important. I'd like to know whether you had anything to say regarding the self-proclaimed resistance?"

"Oh, but whether you registered or not is important - it's imperative. Whether you registered defines either you are part of The United World or are against us. The question is a simple one."

David had never seen the alluring nature of his guest transform into that of a shadowy figure that looked down upon him. Yet, he noticed the change as Emily continued.

"Let us find out," she added. "Thank you for allowing me to be on the show again. Perhaps, I'll see you again."

The video-link disconnected, and the video turned to black.

"Well," David began, turning in his seat. "We didn't get any definitive answers, but a big thank you to Miss Emily Cambersham for coming on the show at such late notice."

The crowd stared.

"Moving on. After the break, we'll hear from our other guests. We've got a great lineup for you-"

David heard his producer talking in his earpiece.

"It is time for a commercial break. I'll see you all in a few minutes."

David noticed the crowd rising to its feet, as one.

The large display showed David sitting at the desk wearing a silent look of concern.

"See you soon."

David stood up from his desk and walked to the side of the stage, ignoring the waves of his producer who ordered him to go back out.

The empty desk was left on air for all to see before moments later, the 'Live' display turned off.

"What the fuck are you doing, David?" his producer asked.

"Something's wrong," David said, only inches away from the audience-observed set.

"Sure, the interview was strange. But that's what you get for going on the fly."

"Come on. That's not what it was." David's producer was obviously annoyed at him for taking charge of that section of the show. "Something's wrong. I mean, have you ever seen an audience so... so dead?"

"No, but it's live television. Anything can happen."

"That's what I'm worried about." David said, before turning to his assistant "How long have I got?"

"Ninety seconds," his assistant advised.

David struggled with his choice. He peered around the curtain to observe the audience. They stood, in unison, in wait – for what, David had no clue.

"No way. I'm sorry. I'm out of here." David turned around to walk backstage before his producer grabbed him gently.

"David, come on. We're due back live, in what, a minute? What the hell? Get a grip. We've been through worse times."

"This is different."

His producer leaned in close so that no-one surrounding them could hear.

"Listen, David. We're at the top right now. All it takes is one fuck up, something like this, and then you're back presenting those shitty daytime shows. Alright?"

Taken aback by the tone of his producer, David was unsure how to respond. He hadn't got this far in show business without dealing with pricks before.

"I'm sorry. Just get back out there and give the audience what they want."

"I'll go back out, but I'm telling you. Something's up – I mean, look at them, they're just standing there."

The producer leant around the corner and saw for himself.

"They're just waiting for you to come back, most likely for a standing ovation. You're worried about nothing."

"Fifteen seconds, David." His assistant warned.

"Alright." David thought for a moment, before addressing the show's producer. "Line up a highlight show, and should anything happen, get it loaded. Alright?"

His producer smiled, patted him on the shoulder and nodded.

"Three seconds, David," his assistant shouted.

David ran back on stage, counting down in his head. He took no notice of the crowd as he ran and sat back down at his desk, introducing the show again mid-sit.

"Hello again! Welcome back to the-"

David looked up at the audience, despite the spotlights that lit the stage and targeted his line of vision, he had always been able to make out the audience. It had helped him in the past connect with his crowd, but right now it did him no favours.

The young audience marched towards him as one.

David bounced on his seat, rising again as soon as his bottom had been planted. He found his feet, using his desk as a barrier from those that approached.

David looked directly into the camera.

"Everyone at home look for answers. Something's not right. Something's wrong. Search for The Resistance on YouTube and decide for yourself."

The first row of the crowd climbed on to the stage, followed by the second.

David ran from stage, straight past his producer, assistant, and makeup lady who had her brush out in preparation.

"David, what the fuck? We're live!" his producer shouted from behind.

A scream followed, trailed by another.

David ran through the corridors backstage, at least the audience wasn't aware of the intricacies of the winding pathways. He dodged left and right, quickly running past some people he recognised and others he didn't.

More screams echoed throughout the cement walls behind him.

"Run, get out of here!" David shouted to a group of workers in front of him.

David ran past the production office, took another right and reached a set of emergency exit doors that he had often found himself sneaking out of after a late finish. This time, however, he burst through them in one swift motion, causing an alarm to sound.

The cold air welcomed him out on to the street, as did the streetlamps outside.

He almost knocked into an older passer-by, who was walking through the area. The person instantly recognised him and tried to ask for an autograph, but David slammed the doors behind him shut, which cut off the alarm, and kept moving.

"Jerk!" he heard the so-called fan shout in his direction.

He ran up the street but noticed something strange; there were a lot of people standing at that end – perhaps a protest in the capital?

He took a few steps up towards them but noticed them all staring in his direction.

David pivoted on the spot and began a slow, but deliberate jog, as to not attract much attention. Looking over his shoulder at the crowd that now began to follow, he ducked off around one of the many side roads around the Manchester studios.

The streets were dark. He couldn't remember the last time he'd walked the streets at this time, except for the occasional post-pub evening. But that was always with friends or near his home, not in the city like this. There was a chill in the air that frightened him.

A nearby scream pierced through the silence. David turned and looked in all directions, whilst he continued his retreat, but couldn't see anyone – probably for the best, he thought.

If he continued down this road, took a right up ahead to get back on to the main street, he should be able to catch a taxi from around there – he thought to himself. It was as good of a plan he could muster mid-jog.

David continued, with the occasional glance over his shoulder. There was a right-turning up ahead. Perhaps it was all in his head.

Another chilling scream put a halt to those thoughts.

Adrenaline pumped, causing his legs to move quicker, and quicker – he found himself sprinting towards the corner, which he took without hesitation.

David darted from the road out on to the high street. He slowed for a second to look at what surrounded him.

All around there were small skirmishes; small fights – creating a chorus of screams from all around. A few of those who had been victorious raised their heads, almost in unison and looked in David's direction.

An explosion burst from a nearby building, almost knocking David off of his feet, causing him to stop. Feeling the heat warm the side of his face, David turned to see a building becoming engulfed in flames.

There was a taxi rank up ahead. Run David, run.

David's legs almost gave in - that was how out of shape he had become in his sedentary mid-life routine, but the adrenaline kept him moving. Although, now, he was finding it hard to breathe.

He looked around, noticing people moving, chasing him.

Another step forward, and another, he was almost at the taxi rank.

A second explosion from behind kept the adrenaline pumping.

"Taxi!" David shouted, raising his hand in the air and waving it in the direction of the old-fashioned driver pool that still served the Manchester area.

"Taxi!" he tried again.

David slowed his steps to a walk, his chest rising and falling uncontrollably. He could feel a fire in his lungs, but not enough air, not enough oxygen.

He gasped sharp breaths. He tasted fire.

David leant against a post, noticing a driver coming towards him.

His vision began to blur, and his legs began to wilt.

Running up behind the driver was a small kid, but he was no ordinary child. He was a kid that was wielding what looked like a machete.

"Watch out," David failed to say, moments before the darkness found him.

14

November 1st, 2022

"Daddy?" Reece cried.

"He'll be here soon," Nora comforted her toddler.

Her son had grown up so quickly, Nora thought as she bounced him up and into her arms. She still cradled Reece like a baby, even though he was almost two.

Reece squirmed in her arms, so she placed him on her lap, facing away from her. She reached over for a toy, shook it to demonstrate the sound it made when shaken, and handed it to him.

Reece threw the toy across the living room.

"Daddy!" he cried.

"Shut that bloody kid up!" her father shouted from the other room. "I'm trying to read."

A door slammed, causing Reece's cry to become constant.

Nora bounced Reece on her knee - up and down - to try and comfort her son, but right now, it seemed to be providing none. Raising a child was hard. No one had warned her just how tiring it was. Sometimes a part of her wished she could just run away - no, that wasn't true. All she needed was just a good night's sleep, and some peace and quiet for a few moments.

Right now, that looked a distinct impossibility.

Where was John?

Nora's mother entered the living room, bringing her a cup of freshly made lemonade. She picked up the toy that Reece had thrown and placed it back next to Nora.

Patricia sat down next to her, took Reece under the armpits, and placed him on to her lap.

"Hello, little man," she greeted him with a broad smile.

Nora relaxed for a moment, leaning back into the cushion behind her.

"Why don't you have a little rest? You look exhausted." Patricia asked.

"No, no, I'm fine," she insisted.

Patricia sang gently to Reece; a song that she faintly remembered from her own childhood.

"Rock a bye baby, on the treetop, when the wind blows, the cradle will rock…"

It took Nora back to her childhood. It took her back to the evenings when her mother would sing to her as she cried - to all of those times she'd notice her mother coming in to console her with a black eye or a bleeding lip.

She hadn't really thought about her father for such a long time.

"Wee little fingers, eyes are shut tight. Now sound asleep until morning light."

Reece's cries halted, and his eyelids dropped.

"I used to sing that to you as well. I don't suppose you remember?"

Empathy rose within Nora. In her tired state all she could muster was a smile as she took her mother's hand in hers.

"Thank you," Nora said as she closed her eyes.

"What for?" Patricia asked.

"Taking us in… convincing Dad."

Her mother waited a moment before replying gently.

"Your father is, well, he's a complicated man. You know, John reminds me-"

"John would never hurt me." Nora interrupted, opening her eyes and sitting up alert.

Her mother stood up, passing the not-so-light toddler over to Nora and on to her lap.

"I better get started on dinner," Patricia said as she exited hastily.

Nora refocused her attention on her child. It seemed that most days were one long blur that toyed with consciousness.

John had made her agree to not having a mobile phone. He was so over-the-top with all of his crazy thoughts about the government. As if anyone would care about the two of them. The idea was for him to work some jobs, always cash in hand, and save up enough to get back on their feet.

Well, that plan started almost two years ago, and here they still were – wait, here she was; sitting, waiting - caring, crying.

She wanted to scream. Her emotions would rush up from inside her and spill out, destroying everything that they touched. But instead, she passed Reece his favourite toy. Moments later, she collected the toy from the floor and tried again.

* * *

John took a long walk back to the house. It should only take him around twenty minutes, but this route took almost an hour and a half – what with the quick stop off for a few drinks to take the edge off.

He'd found himself drinking even more regularly than usual. The work was hard, but that he was used to - building work was his bread and butter. But it was the life that he struggled with. How could he, as a man, live under the same roof as Andrew? Andrew, for Christ's sake.

He clenched his fist and ground his teeth.

No, he wouldn't get upset. He stopped in his tracks and focused on taking three, deep, long breaths.

The sun had set a while ago. Perhaps he should stay out here, find a place to sleep? Was that even really an option?

John started walking again.

It was a shame, but he could not care less about the people he walked past – a few of whom tried to catch his eye and say hello. He also had no desire to take in any of the surroundings of this place, which would never be home. He'd simply get back, accept his fate, and then tomorrow would be the same.

John couldn't even go into the off-licence and pick up a bottle. The last time he did that Andrew poured it down the sink in front of him. It was only cheap stuff, but it would have helped.

He'd earned another ton today. It was nothing compared to the amount of work he'd done, but what was left of it would go with all of the rest.

When he got this job last year, he set himself a goal: five grand. If they could save five grand, then that'd be enough to get them out of the house. Five grand came and went, and yet they stayed. Where would they go? That was the problem. So, he set himself a new goal, ten grand - that would surely be enough for them to live off.

Well, this hundred would put them up to around twelve. Perhaps it was time to get out.

When Andrew left the house, Patricia had looked on the computer for them at apartments in the area. They all needed a background check, and he couldn't risk it. What if they came for him again? What if they came for Reece?

Ominous clouds formed above. John noticed the temperature drop. He turned up his collar and shrunk into the rough fabric. He hoped it wouldn't rain, because it'd mean he'd have to hurry.

After he decided there was no possibility of renting a property through legal means, he'd asked around some colleagues at the building site. One almost came through, but then at the last minute, he had demanded five grand for a deposit, and nearly twice the rent.

It seemed like being on the run had its difficulties.

He felt stuck, in limbo. Every day he noticed his boy growing older, with no plan to offer him or his wife a home.

Rain started to fall.

John begrudgingly quickened his pace.

Twelve grand, it sounded like a lot, but with hotels, and looking after Reece, they'd burn through it in a few months.

But they couldn't stay here much longer – he definitely couldn't stay here much longer.

The house grew in size as he approached, until it towered over him.

The pub called to him; its sweet nectar enticing, but instead he raised his hand to the door and knocked.

He heard the keys rustle inside. Of course, he wasn't allowed a set himself. It was merely a demonstration of power. He heard Andrew shout from inside.

Behind the door fell quiet, as John stood, attempting to protect himself from the rain, which grew in force.

He rapped again. He knew they were home.

He heard Nora shout and rapped once more.

It was all a game.

"Andrew, can I come in?" he asked, eventually.

The door opened a fraction.

"Only if you say the magic word." Andrew's beady eyes observed him through the crack.

How he'd love to just go to town on him.

"Please," John managed.

Andrew opened the door, putting on a façade.

"Why are you just standing out there? It's pouring down. Do come in."

John walked in past Andrew, but quickly found his spirits lifted by Nora's arms wrapped around him, along with a kiss planted on the bare part of his bearded cheek.

"Where have you been?" Nora asked him, quiet enough to not make a scene.

Andrew walked away, muttering something under his breath as he went.

John waited for Andrew to leave before he removed the money from his pocket for a moment.

"This is what I've been doing."
Nora sniffed near John's face.
"You've been drinking."
"Just a quick one on the way home."
"Do you know what I've been putting up with here?"
Reece began to cry from the living room.
"See," Nora said before turning towards the living room. "Mummy's coming."

From one workplace to another, John thought - as if twelve-hour shifts weren't enough by themselves.

John took his shoes and jacket off and walked through to the living room.

Reece's cries stopped instantly. The two-year-old toddled over to his father as quick as he could and reached his arms out to him.

John lifted his son up in his arms.

"Hello son," John said. At the same time, he playfully threw his child up and down, in a controlled manner.

"Careful!" Nora almost shouted from the sofa.

John stopped and placed Reece back on the ground. He ruffled his hair and was greeted by a simple stare.

"Can you get the bath ready?" Nora asked. "I'll bring him up in a minute."

"Of course." John summoned the strength to keep going for a little while longer. He walked upstairs and before going to the bathroom, entered the spare bedroom that they'd called their own.

John walked in, took out his cash once more, and lifted the mattress.

He took hold of the pillowcase, which contained his savings. Something didn't seem right. He was sure that it was heavier yesterday.

John picked up the pillowcase, blood rushing to his face, he poured it out on the floor and scattered it.

"What the fuck?" he shouted.

John counted. There wasn't more than a few thousand here.

"What the fuck!?" he roared. "Nora?"

John turned to see Andrew standing in the doorway.

"You? What did you do?" John said, rising to his feet.

"I've taken money for your board," Andrew said.

"That's my money." John approached.

"I think you'll find it quite reasonable. Five hundred a month for, what, eighteen, nineteen months?"

"You said we could stay here." John was within inches of his father-in-law.

"So, I did. I guess I neglected to mention the rent." Andrew smiled.

"You don't even need the money."

"I might donate it, you know, to a good cause."

John felt the pressure in his temples rise. He grabbed Andrew by the shirt with both hands.

"Give me my money," John demanded.

"I think you'll find it's my money now."

"Give it back."

"I think not."

Nora approached the argument.

"John, what are you doing?" she asked.

"Stay out of this. Your dad has taken our money."

"Is that true?"

"Just for board and meals," he responded. "Quite reasonable, if you ask me."

"Why do you think we were staying here? Give it back." John found his grip on Andrew's top tightening further.

Andrew smiled in return.

"You devious excuse of a man."

Andrew's smile disappeared.

"Get out," He ordered.

John's let go of Andrew's shirt.

"Now. Get out of my house."

"Andrew, come on." John pleaded. The rage he felt turning to hopelessness.

"Daddy?" Nora asked from behind.

"This man is no longer welcome in my home," Andrew confirmed. "Either you leave right now, or I'll call the police."

"Give me back my money, our money."

Andrew took out a mobile phone and pressed nine three times. His finger hovered over the call button.

John retreated into the bedroom and counted the cash quickly - there was around three thousand left. He gathered half of it.

He pushed past Andrew, shoving him into the hallway as he approached his wife.

"I've left you half, okay?"

John began to walk past his wife but was stopped by Nora's arms around his shoulders.

"Daddy, come on."

"No, he's done. You've got five minutes to grab your things, else the police will be on their way."

Andrew exited downstairs.

"I'm so sorry," John averted his face from Nora's eyeline..

Nora pulled his chin up to look at her.

"Listen, I'm sorry I've been so snappy lately." Nora began to cry. "It's just been so tough."

John placed his hands around her waist.

"It's alright, love. I know it's hard. But we'll get through it, alright?"

"Together." She added. "We'll get through it together."

"I think you should stay here."

"What? Wherever you go, I go, remember."

"I know, but at the moment we can't afford to look after Reece. I've got enough to look after myself for now. I'll work every day and bring you your half. Alright?"

Nora looked unsure.

"Another few months and then we'll leave."

"I don't know if I can do this anymore," Nora whispered.

John pulled her into him.

"You're the strongest person I've ever met."

Nora fought the tears back and sunk into John's arms.

"Listen, I better get my stuff together. He's not bluffing."

"What shall I tell Reece?"

"Tell him I have to work away for a while."

Nora nodded. The couple entered the bedroom, where they both packed a bag of clothes for John.

"Promise me one thing," Nora said.

"What?" John asked.

"Don't leave us."

"I won't. I promise."

John and Nora collected the last of John's things.

"One minute!" Andrew shouted from downstairs.

"Alright, I better get going. I'll be back tomorrow."

"Promise?"

"I promise."

Nora kissed him on the lips. She held the embrace for a few seconds before John pulled away.

"I love you," she added.

"And you," he responded.

John headed downstairs, trailed by Nora.

"Thirty seconds. Cutting it fine." Andrew admonished them as they approached.

"I'm going, alright."

John put on his shoes, threw on his jacket, and pulled up the collar to cover his neck. He collected a sports bag full of clothes from Nora.

"Ten seconds. Nine, eight."

"Bye, Patricia," John shouted.

"Seven, six."

"Bye, love. See you soon." John kissed Nora on the forehead.

"Five, four, three."

"Bye champ, see you soon!" John called to an onlooking Reece.

"Two."

John interjected the count and held up his middle finger to Andrew.

"One," John said as he opened the door. "Bye, Andy," he added, swinging the door shut behind him, as he stepped out into the dark, cold night.

15

January 6th, 2040

In the large, minimalist office, the digital clock on the wall turned to 09.00.

"Welcome. Thank you all for coming." Samuel addressed a long table of colleagues. "We're here to look at the results to date of the final phase. "Load slide one," he ordered.

A chart appeared with a linear scale, depicting criminal acts over the past twenty years. The line had decreased to a low number where it had tailed off and seen a slight increase recently.

"As you can see, a united government, with freely available healthcare, universal credits, and better educations, has seen a decrease in criminal acts. However, as you can see more recently, there has been a slight reoccurrence."

A tanned, older gentleman, with a thick Spanish accent, decided to take the opportunity to ask a question.

"Why is this happening?"

"Thank you," Samuel continued, motioning to Emily sitting beside him. "Miss Cambersham will provide you with data on the next slide, which should answer your question."

"Load next slide," Emily began.

A slide that showed approval levels of The United World reflected the previous slide – with approval levels increasing, but with a decrease recently.

"As you can see," Emily pointed in the direction of the chart. "Approval levels have always been high, but recently, there has been a slight decline – which we believe correlates to the levels of crime, and homelessness, increasing slightly over recent months."

"Will it continue?" a female Indian guest asked.

"This is why we've moved to the final phase of the plan," Emily answered. "Load next slide."

The next graph contained an age range of criminal acts.

"As you can see, the number of crimes committed by those under twenty has fallen to almost zero, whilst the age ranges above that have reduced, but tend to fluctuate. Next slide."

The slide contained a graph-like diagram with three different coloured lines.

Samuel spoke through this slide.

"These are the three areas of human behaviour which we can curtail. To simplify matters, we have grouped them into three well-known categories: the ego, the superego, and the id. Now, with a reduction of one of these areas alone, you leave an individual unbalanced and prone to behavioural issues. The data in those under twenty has demonstrated that balancing, and where necessary slightly toning down all three areas, has resulted in model behaviour. Load next slide."

The next slide showed a diagram of the human brain and the area in which the microchip is fitted.

"As you are all aware, the technology has been upgraded to accommodate adults, which will allow our entire population to become model citizens, and finally result in peace. Unlike the first-generation that was fitted in children, the second-generation works through live monitoring of chemicals. When chemicals are imbalanced, the technology reacts, releasing a minute pulse to stimulate the reduction of certain parts of the brain. The technology is painless, seamless, and has a near one hundred percent performance success rate. Load next slide."

The next graph showed steeply rising lines of deaths, followed by it quickly reducing to zero.

"This chart depicts the number of expected casualties in the UK." Emily talked through the chart, continuing their well-rehearsed presentation. "The projection is expected to be similar in other countries, but the curve will be steeper in some areas, and less in others. As you can see, we are currently seeing a large spike, and this is expected to continue over the next few weeks…"

Emily paused, causing Samuel to jump in.

"The lives lost will not be in vain. These people, those who have chosen not to be part of a united world, will be remembered as the ultimate sacrifice. The lives lost today will result only in thriving lives tomorrow."

Emily took a sip of her water.

The spike in deaths loomed large over the captive audience.

"Load next slide," Samuel ordered.

A final slide loaded, with multiple projections in various chart-formats.

"However, as you can see, following this difficult, but necessary time, we shall prosper. Take note of the projected levels of homelessness, crime and poverty falling steeply, and reaching a base level of almost nil."

The audience rose to their feet, and one by one began to applaud Samuel and Emily, who remained sitting.

Samuel offered Emily his hand. She obliged. They stood united in front of the leaders of multiple countries - in front of the most powerful politicians in the world.

"Thank you." Samuel smiled. "It is with each and every one of your country's dedication and support that this project can become more than just a theory. Please."

Samuel gestured for everyone to sit back down, which they did. Samuel and Emily followed suit.

"What are the next steps?" a member asked.

"Miss Cambersham? Would you do the pleasures?" Samuel asked.

"Of course," Emily responded. "The next phase has already begun. It was instigated through the activation of the Bluetooth transmitters in those born after the uniting. Those individuals are responsible for seeking out those who are not part of The United World and convincing them to join."

"And if they refuse?"

"Refusal is not an option." Samuel interrupted. "The projection is that within the next month ninety-nine percent of the world's population will be united. It will take longer to identify a few others and shift that final percentage, but we shall get there, in time."

"Who is the one percent?" another guest asked.

"Those are people of whom we have no records," Emily answered. "Some people, often born into poorer communities, are not registered and live outside of our system."

Samuel continued. "As I'm sure you can all comprehend, even a miniscule percentage of the world living outside of the government delivers great risk."

"How will we drive it down?" a man in his late sixties asked.

"First, the focus will be on those that we can see. After which, those that live off the grid will be searched for, and-" Samuel considered the next word carefully, "enlisted into The United World."

"Very good."

"Are there any further questions?" Samuel offered an invitation, to which no one responded. "Perfect. Thank you all for your time. I hope that you enjoy your stay in the capital. Drivers are awaiting all of you downstairs. In the current climate, although you'll all be perfectly safe, we recommend heading directly to your hotels."

A few members of the room agreed, some nodded, and others simply rose to their feet and collected their things.

Samuel and Emily saw the men out of the large boardroom, nodding at each person one-by-one as they left the room.

The door closed behind the last guest, leaving Emily and Samuel alone.

"Fancy a drink?" Samuel asked.

Emily shook her head.

"Is there something the matter?" he asked, slowly moving closer towards her.

Emily stood unmoving, taking a moment to consider her response.

"No, nothing."

"Good," Samuel observed her for a moment, before relaxing. "Come, let's check in on the lab."

Emily nodded, and the two most influential individuals on the face of the earth headed out of the room. They strolled past Reception, and into the elevator.

* * *

Perched around the fire, Reece sat next to George and Mary. Many others huddled around the warmth nearby. Home looked at Mary attentively as she reached into her pocket.

"Your mother wanted you to have this."

Mary retrieved a tattered piece of paper and handed it to Reece.

"What is it?" he asked.

Home sniffed the paper and tried to nibble at it.

"Open it," she said, gently pushing Home's mouth away.

"What does it say?" Reece asked.

"Your mother gave it to me when she left you. She warned us about, well, this. We all thought she'd gone a bit bonkers, to be honest with you, but she made me promise that if anyone started coming for you, that I'd give you this letter."

"And you're just giving it to me now?" Reece's voice rose slightly towards the end of his question.

"It's alright, champ." George placed an arm on Reece's shoulder. "We didn't want to worry you."

They wouldn't do anything to harm him, Reece thought. He calmed himself and prepared to hear from his mother for the first time in over fifteen years.

'My beautiful Reece,

For your sake, I hope that you never have to read this letter.
I hope that I'm just imagining things, but I fear that your father is right.

First I want to tell you how much I love you…'

Reece skimmed across the words to the next sentence. Now wasn't the time to allow emotions to get the better of him.

'If you're reading this, then I am no longer by your side - no longer looking after you, protecting you, and for that I am sorry. I left you with Mary as I knew that if worst came to worst, she'd raise you like her own.'

Reece looked at Mary, who smiled gently back at him.

'So, I guess the worst did happen. In that case, I have some things that I need to tell you.

You mustn't trust the government. Do not trust the police, do not trust the doctors, dentists, and if you need to, seek medical assistance from friends and those that you can trust. This is of grave importance. Mary, if you're reading this, please make sure that this is carried out.

Everything that was happening from the second The United World began seemed a little too coincidental. I wanted to believe in the vision, as so many others around me do, but it all seemed a little too good, a bit too perfect.

Your father suspected that they were microchipping babies as they were born, for some sort of mind control. I know that seems crazy, maybe we are just crazy, but I've seen the scars. It terrifies me. We were on high alert, but trying to get on with life, and then your father was taken.

I was hoping that one day he'd just show up on the doorstep, telling me how sorry he was for leaving, but that hasn't happened. I wanted to go after him, I tried, but you were too small, you needed me.

Your father and I made a vow to always be by each other's side, and it's where I must go. Now that you're a bit bigger, I have to try and find him.

I don't know where he is, but I know where to start, The United World headquarters in Westminster.

I hope that you're doing well, that you're growing up to be a fine young man, and I pray that you never have to read this letter and I'm just being stupid.

*Love always,
Mum xxx'*

Reece dropped the letter down from his line of vision. Time passed as he stared into the fire.

"Are you alright?" Mary asked.

Reece nodded, failing to completely understand what he'd just read. The crackling and popping from the fire danced in the silence.

"When did she give you this?" Reece asked.

"When you were little," Mary replied.

"And you've not seen her since?"

Mary shook her head and placed a hand on Reece's knee.

"She's been gone all this time, and you've not gone to look for her?" he asked.

"Reece," Mary tried to comfort him.

"No." He shuffled away, causing Home to spring to his feet. "You've known all this time. The government took her, and you didn't do anything." Reece stood.

"It's not like that, we were trying to look after you."

"What? And raise me here?" Reece threw his arms up, to point at the warehouse-come-living space. "Well, thanks for that."

"Reece, come on." George stood and walked towards the boy.

Reece backed away.

"No, screw this." Reece threw the letter to the ground, where it fell open. "I'm outta here."

"Reece," Mary attempted to reach out to him.

"You don't give a shit about me or my Mum, no-one does." Reece began to walk away to his sleeping spot.

"Come on, son, she's trying to help," a familiar gentleman, with rotten teeth, suggested.

Reece brushed it off.

"Come on, Home," Reece ordered, walking to the place he had laid almost every night for as long as he could remember. The dog waited for a moment before following.

Reece exited, collected some packets of food, and a couple of tins of beer he had left, into a worn tote bag. He threw on his large overcoat and gloves before spotting the penknife he had used to kill the intruder. He collected it with the rest of his supplies and headed back to the fire.

George stood in front of him as he walked past.

"Where are you going, son?" he asked.

"Where do you think?" Reece answered. "To find my Mum."

"She's gone, son." George placed a loving hand on Reece's shoulder.

Reece knocked George's hand from him.

"I'm not your son."

George's head dropped. He spoke towards Reece's feet.

"We've always tried to do what's right. What your mother would have wanted."

After Reece didn't respond, George moved to one side to let him pass.

"Come on, boy," Reece called for Home to join him. "Walk."

"Be careful," Mary shouted from in front of the fire.

Reece left the sheltered area, filled with people that had treated him as part of their family. Home trailed slowly behind, he stopped before the exit and barked.

"Come on," Reece called.

Home hesitated. He barked again.

Mary collected the letter that she had protected for a large portion of her life: the message that she had never wanted to give to Reece. A letter than raised more questions than it solved.

Mary brushed soil off the letter, revealing the middle section that Reece skipped over previously.

The United World

'First, I want to tell you how much I love you. I am so proud to be able to call you my son. Your father and I love you more than anything in the world, and I hope that soon we will hold you in our arms again.'

Home ran back, rushing up to Mary with a whimper.
"What's the matter, boy?" Mary asked.
Reece was gone, alone into the cold night.

16

January 6th, 2040

D avid's eyes opened.
"He's coming to."
Shuffled movements and voices circled around him.
David found his vision was blurred. His head throbbed as bright light pounded and pummelled at the back of his brain. He tried to sit up and look around, but a shooting pain ran through his chest.
"Careful," a male voice urged.
Several pairs of hands helped him to a sitting position.
"Where am I?" David asked.
David's consciousness slowly returned.
He was sitting in a small room, underneath a bright, unprotected light above. Around him were several people in

tattered clothes, who, quite frankly looked like they were homeless.

"Listen, I, I, don't have any money. But I know people, I can get you whatever you want."

The man by his side knelt down to enter his line of vision. His smile seemed real enough, but then the amount of show business types that he'd met who also seemed genuine turned out to be quite the opposite.

"I'm not after your money, David," the man assured him.

"What, what do you want?"

Panic reared. David looked around him quickly to observe his surroundings. A sink, a chair, some more people, a boarded window, a door.

"We're not here to hurt you. If you're thinking of escaping, there is no need, you're free to leave. But first, I'd hope that you'd hear us out."

David looked at the man for the first time. He was older than him, maybe only by a decade or two. His scruffy beard and dishevelled appearance provided a mismatch for the wisdom that was apparent in his soft brown eyes.

Another onlooker passed the man a cup of water and a pill.

"We saw you pass out. Here." The man offered David a drink, which he accepted, and then a pill. David took it in his hand.

"What is it?"

"Nurofen, it's all we have."

David swallowed the pill and drained the water. He hadn't realised how thirsty he was.

"Thanks." David handed the cup back to an onlooker.

"We thought you'd had a heart attack or something. Lucky we got to you before that other fella."

Images of a young teen wielding a machete flashed through his mind.

"What happened?" David asked.

"One of them came for you."

"One of who?

"Them. The young ones that the government control," the man clarified.

David felt the urge to resist; to jump and flee, and to tell them that they were crazy. But then he remembered his audience. He remembered the people chasing him. He remembered the heinous scenes he saw on the street.

"How long have I been out for?"

"Since yesterday evening."

He rubbed his temples, which had begun to settle slightly. His breathing was laboured, but the pain in his chest felt more like a constant, yet dull, throb.

"What's – what's happening?" David finally responded.

"Let me show you. Are you alright to stand?"

David nodded.

"I think so."

The man helped David to his feet, and with his support, they made their way over to the boarded window. The window was covered with brown cardboard boxes and masking tape. Where the boxes met in the middle, there was a small section which was covered loosely.

The man pulled the edge of the box down in the corner slightly.

"Have a look." The man offered.

David leant in and peered through the small crack that had been presented between the boxes.

From a height he could see Manchester, he even recognised the street. They were just down a side street from the high street, in a building at least two stories from the ground.

"What am I looking for?" he asked.

"You'll see."

David looked to the right, which in the darkness appeared deserted. He shuffled around to get a better view through the gap and looked to the left.

Bright lights in the distance meant that it wasn't the dead of night just yet. He saw a delivery driver on an electric scooter cross over the tramline and turn down his street.

"It's been going on constantly. Only a matter of time, unfortunately," the man narrated. "Keep look-"

A loud bang caused David to jolt upright, losing sight of what was happening outside. A hand placed on his shoulder comforted him, and he looked back through the opening.

The delivery driver lay on the floor, dimly lit by nearby streetlamps. A girl, with her hair in two distinct ponytails, dressed in everyday attire, walked over to the driver. She held out something towards his head. The driver struggled beneath her, scampering to get away.

This time, the loud bang caused David's mouth to jolt open. He watched as the girl shot the delivery driver in the chest two more times until he stopped struggling.

The girl placed the gun back into her pink bag and walked back towards the high street.

"We've got to call the police!" David swung around to face the room. There were at least six or seven people in the small living room-come-kitchen.

"We can't. No phones. Not that they'd do any good. Police are no better, either."

David reached into his pocket where his old-fashioned flat-screen mobile device last was. All that he grasped were a few pieces of lint.

"Where's my phone?" he asked.

"Gone," the man confirmed.

"Why? Where is it?"

"They all have GPS tracking. That one would be registered to you, right?"

"Yes…"

"Then, wherever the phone is - you are. They can find you."

"What about lenses?"

"Even worse. We think that's how they're finding most people in hiding."

"How?"

"Satellites, people think. Tracking people who haven't been chipped."

"Come on."

The man scratched his head. He folded the cardboard covering down to shield them from the outside world once more.

"It's not really that hard to believe, though, is it?"

He led David over to the single makeshift bed, to which he perched on the edge. The man sat on the chair opposite.

The man turned to someone behind him.

"Get me the laptop."

The person nodded in return and exited the room. After a few moments, he returned with a chunky, heavy laptop.

"Bloody hell. That thing's prehistoric." David commented.

"Older models are the only ones that are safe to use. They're not chipped."

The man opened the laptop, booted it, and waited for ten seconds or so for it to load.

"This one has a VPN built-in so that it's untraceable."

The man tilted the screen so that David could see. He opened an incognito web browser window and loaded YouTube, then searched for 'The United Resistance'.

A channel appeared at the top of the search rankings with a million followers. The man clicked on it.

"Have you heard of The United Resistance?" he asked.

"Briefly. We spoke about it on my show."

"That's good. What did you say?"

David thought back to how his world began to fall apart.

"I questioned Miss-" David stopped himself. "Emily Cambersham about the acts of terror. She said that the acts are from those opposing the government."

"What you saw out of the window – did that look like an anti-government protest?"

David shook his head.

The man opened a new incognito browser window and entered a long web address he had memorised. It loaded with a username, password, and entry code box. He entered all three and the website loaded.

A chat forum loaded up, which listed thousands online down the right-hand side, and topics on the left. In the middle, a live chat updated frequently with discussion.

"This was set up by members of TUR - that's what we call them. Along the left, you'll see topics." the man moved his cursor to show the area of the screen he was referring to. "They've got a section for confirmed cases split by region. So, if we go to the North, then Manchester, in there we can report what just happened outside. Would you?"

David took the laptop. It was even bulkier than the one he had received for his eighteenth birthday.

"What do I type?"

"Start with the time. It happened a couple of minutes ago, say Twenty-one forty-five, and then write what you saw. Mention who the victim was and describe the person who did it."

David started writing.

'21.45 – delivery driver on a scooter shot in the street. Shot by a girl, mid to late teens, with ponytails and pink bag.'

"Is that alright?" David handed the laptop back over to the man.

"Perfect. We'll just send that, and it'll be modified by the admins and recorded."

"What else is on there?" David asked.

"Mostly information: what we know so far, who we know is in The United World, like Emily, Samuel, and some of their staff. We share photos of media reports as well."

"It's like a huge database." David admired.

"Technology, huh?" the man smiled. "Never thought I'd be sitting here on a laptop."

David leant back on the bed. His mansion seemed more than appealing right now, but for some reason, being surrounded by these people seemed to offer more support than his large home ever could.

"It's funny. We were all part of a resistance, long before it was given a name. But all it took was that video online, and suddenly everyone's coming together," the man considered. "Us lot, we've been together for years. We tend to move about, never stick to one place too long, but we've been here since it all kicked off a few days ago."

The men and women towards the edge of the room waved in David's direction. He held his hand up in reply.

"Tell me, what's your name?" David asked.

"Me?" the scruffy man replied. "My name's John, John Loche. Nice to meet ya."

David took the man's hard, workman-like hand in his own, and shook it.

"So, what do we do next?" David asked.

"We stay here, and we wait."

"Wait for what?"

"Don't worry. You'll soon see."

* * *

Out of the corner of David's field of vision, dim lights flickered through cracks in the cardboard across the window.

John walked up to the window, pulled back the viewing section, and looked out to the streets below.

"We're good," John ordered after a couple of moments.

John held open part of the cardboard as one of the resistance members walked over to the light switch. He flicked the lights on and off multiple times.

"Alright." John held his hand up, replacing the cardboard section across the window.

The person stopped, then left the light on.

David noticed his stomach growling for food, he had no time to think of that right now.

"What's going on?" he asked instead.

"Time to go," John responded.

"What? Where?"

"Out."

John and the crew began to head for the door.

"But it's not safe?" David noted.

"That flashing of light means the coast is clear."

"How is it clear?"

"They all seem to go to sleep at around the same time."

"Really?"

John nodded.

"Weird really. Apart from special occasions, the streets are empty by around one in the morning."

"Is it one o'clock?"

"About that, I'd guess."

"You coming?" another asked John.

John followed the others and walked towards the door.

A group of apparently homeless refugees being joined by an A-list celebrity; it would certainly make for an exciting dynamic for on-lookers. But somehow, he doubted the paparazzi were out tonight.

Blimey, he hated the media when they crossed the line, but were they safe? They were always out in the open, chasing stories. Was there even a media anymore?

David shook off the morbid thought and stood. He followed John and the resistance out of the small room, through a corridor, and out of the front door. A single person had remained behind to keep guard, he shouted from the door.

"Bring me back some crisps: chicken, or steak!"

The door closed tight behind them.

"Where are we going?" David whispered, following and staying as close to John as he could.

John continued walking through the hallway until they reached a door to the street. He turned around and spoke quietly to the newest member of the resistance.

"To get supplies. Listen, we should be fine. But you can stay behind if you like?"

"No, no, I want to see," David replied without a moment's hesitation. "Is it safe?"

"We're not certain, but if we're careful, stick to the side streets, and avoid others, we should be alright. Are you ready?"

As David took a deep breath to calm himself, he noticed that John appeared to be doing the same: he wasn't as calm as he was letting on. It didn't help his nerves.

David nodded. John pulled down on the handle and swung the door gently open. He allowed the other members to go first. David counted five others and John.

By the time he'd stepped out on the street, the others were all running in various directions, keeping low, and staying tucked in near houses on the paths best they could. David stepped out, and John joined him.

"Me and you, we're gonna check the dumpsters around there. They've been good to us so far."

John hunched down and started to jog across the road, towards a small alley across from the base. David followed suit - ducking down in his expensive formal wear, and polished black shoes that didn't provide the greatest of covers.

The night was quiet. It was the city of Manchester, and yet they could hear no loud music, little traffic, and thankfully, no screams or gunshots.

The long alleyway opened up and revealed two large dumpsters. One seemed to be for waste, the other recycling.

"Check the recycling, just in case, I'll go through this one." John pulled his fingerless gloves up further to make a point. "Got my gloves to help, don't I?"

The United World

It was quite a step down from presenting on national television, but it appeared that David was a survivor. It reminded him of the time he went on a celebrity television show. He had hated the idea of going to the jungle for four weeks to take part in survival trials, but his agent talked him into. It'd be good for his career… it'd help him get a bigger salary. His agent was, of course, right, but he wouldn't ever forget the experience of eating a raw fisheye or crawling through a floor filled with spiders and snakes, to collect a meal voucher.

David collected full, sea-through bags from the large dumpster. He tore them open and searched through one by one. This reminded him of some of the challenges he'd gone through on that show.

"Best things would be carrier bags, bottles, tubs, water, and food," John advised.

David found a plastic carrier bag almost immediately, shook off some food and placed it to the side. John took it and set some items he'd found inside.

Back to the challenge, then.

David looked through all of the bags in the dumpster, one by one, replacing them on one side as he did so – a process he'd worked out after the first two bags.

David had found some more plastic bags, a few clean large plastic bottles, and to his surprise some full packs of food that had been wrongly discarded.

After he'd finished the last bag, he looked over to John.

"Won't be much longer, just keep a lookout," he said.

David collected his findings together, pushing them down into the bags he had found, after which he stepped to the other side of John and looked out into the street. It was a fair distance, both ways, but there were access points that he could make out further behind him.

Stopping for a moment made him realise just how tired he was. Would he sleep in the room tonight? Would he get any sleep at all? Perhaps it might be safe to call his driver and head home.

"John?" David turned to face the man who had food and dirt covering his hands, as well as down his coat. He looked to be on the last bag of rubbish. "Where's your home?"

John stopped, threw the final bag back into the dumpster and packed his last food items into the bags.

"I don't have a home," he replied.

"But you must have one somewhere. What about before this?"

John shook his head.

"What about family?"

John picked up the bags from the floor.

"Pick it up, we're done," John responded.

John headed off in front of him, David found himself running to catch up.

They approached the door; John collected a key from his pocket, and, after looking both ways along the street, unlocked it. They entered with their supplies and John closed the door behind them.

David wanted to ask again, in case he hadn't heard him, but the man's expression had changed. If he learnt anything from his years of journalism training, it was when to ask more questions, and when to be quiet. To him, this definitely felt like the latter.

They walked in silence; back through the hallway towards the door they exited almost half an hour before. John rapped three times quickly, waited, rapped once, paused, and then three times again.

The door opened, and a resistance member greeted them, helping them with the bags.

The first thing John did was wash the dirt from his hands. He then took off his gloves, washed his hands with soap and water, and then placed his gloves on the windowsill to dry.

"Where should I put this?" David asked.

"Don't worry, Ric will sort it."

Ric gave David a nod and took the two plastic bags away that he had managed to fill with a variety of items. As well as the plastic bags and bottles, he had managed to find toothpaste, pain killers, and a few items of multipack food.

John sat back down on the chair. David hovered for a moment before taking his place opposite on the edge of the bed as before.

The two sat in awkward silence, the only sound coming from Ric who packed away various supplies in either the cupboards or fridge.

"Listen," John began. "I can't tell you what to do, but you're welcome to stay here if you like."

"Thank you," David responded, ending the conversation.

A single police siren broke through the silence. It faded away into the distance.

Ric left the room with some toiletries.

John placed his head in his hands, tiredness seemingly overcoming him, but before David could ask if he was alright, John began to speak.

"I lost them," he began. "They took them years ago." His hands began to shake.

"Who?" David probed gently.

"My wife... my kid."

John curled his hands into fists and tensed his upper body. He looked as if he was about to punch something.

"I couldn't save them."

"John, I'm sure-" David tried to console the stranger but was interrupted.

"No." John looked up, his eyes becoming red and watery. "I failed them." He took a deep breath and allowed his hands to fall back down slowly. "I broke my promise. I went back, and they were gone."

Ric re-entered the room, causing John to shuffle back to what would be considered a normal sitting position in his chair. He was still on high alert around them.

"I'll stay tonight," David confirmed. "Then perhaps after that, we could go to my place?"

If John was about to cry, David would never have known.

"That could work. How far is it from here?"

"About four or five miles," David confirmed.

John thought about the decision.

"But," David began. "It's got seven bedrooms, loads of bathrooms – and security cameras."

"Could be useful. Do you know which company provides them?"

David thought back, they were installed by a private firm, and the recordings were saved on a server in his basement.

"They're private."

"Not uploaded anywhere?"

David shook his head.

"Stored on a server."

John allowed himself a small smile, the first real smile David had seen since they met.

The United World

"Do you have a car?" John asked.

David nodded.

Ric joined the two of them on another chair, changing the subject.

"Good load tonight, boss. No chicken crisps though." He bemoaned. "Still, should keep us going for a couple of days. And you too, newbie."

He passed a pack of four cereal bars to John, who handed them out between the three of them.

David rushed to unwrap it and ate his in record time. He nodded in approval.

"We've got a plan." John began. "We'll talk when the others are back."

Ric jumped around on his seat, excitedly.

"Oh, boy, a plan! What are we doing?"

"When the others are back."

"Aw, man." Ric moaned.

"You might want to get some sleep. They could be a while." John commented.

"But I'm too excited," Ric added.

David kicked off his shoes, which provided a much-needed release of tension across the bridge of his foot. He leant back on the bed and pictured his large, king-sized bed and Egyptian cotton sheets.

17

January 6th, 2040

Reece had been walking for hours, no longer protected by the shelter in Camden Town.

Growing up on the streets, he knew London well, but he rarely ventured too far into the city - and it didn't help that it was dark. At least there weren't any drunks out, he thought to himself.

Usually, at this time of night around Camden or King's Cross, it would be filled with people spilling out of late-night drinking holes, but not tonight. Tonight, it was eerily quiet.

As he'd been raised to do for as long as he could remember, he stuck to the side streets. Then when he had to cross a major intersection, he made sure to keep to himself and focus on getting by without raising attention. Moving through alleyways and smaller streets also helped at this time of year to keep the freezing winds at bay.

It would be a more comfortable journey if Home had just listened and come with him. Perhaps he shouldn't have stormed off and left him behind – the thought continued to repeat in his mind. If he had to sleep on the streets tonight, Home would have helped keep him warm, that much he knew for sure.

He'd moved through King's Cross and around the edges of Leicester Square, through Soho, all the time moving towards Westminster.

Reece knew the direction well enough. He'd been around most of these popular tourist destinations before, most of the time begging with Mary. However, that was before the government ramped up the movement to stop street begging. People could now sign on for universal income, so there was no need for begging, well, that was the theory. Mary had told him the truth, that it was so the government could monitor people and make the world a better place for those who found begging offensive. Reece hadn't begged solo before, but if he had the opportunity, perhaps he'd have considered it.

A few people in the distance staggered out of a large brightly lit building. Reece moved closer, ensuring to remain in the shadows as best he could. It was a casino, and the men in front of him leant into each other as they walked. Luckily, there didn't seem to be anyone else around for their drunken singing to annoy.

Reece continued through the square, down past the fountain, and over another wide road, which he'd assumed would have been busier even at this time of night.

He'd reached the roundabout. This was as far as he'd made it before. Parliament was a straight walk down this main road, and that was where the headquarters for The United World sat - everyone seemingly knew this, even the homeless. He also knew that he needed to be careful.

Reece walked, constantly checking around him for people. He kept his head down and made sure that he remained as close to the walls as possible. However, he saw no one.

Just as he began to feel safe, a large, red double-decker bus approached. Reece allowed himself a moment to raise his eyes to meet it, but the digitally operated bus appeared empty as far as he could tell. He kept his head down and continued to walk.

Imposing buildings appeared to rise up on his right, many of them with extraordinary architecture to boast - large columns, and impressive brickwork, lit from underneath to accentuate the detail. A row of flags containing The United World branding hung overhead, as a man riding a large horse sat impressively in the middle of the road.

One thing that baffled Reece was the number of trees rising from the pavements all around; seemingly becoming more and more as he walked. It felt odd, like some sort of cover-up; a city in camouflage.

The row of black flags overhead displaying The United World continued. There must have been at least a hundred, probably more: he'd heard somewhere that there was one flag for each country in the world, but he wasn't sure if that was true. Reece looked at the logo. It was something he'd seen all his life, on the streets, on papers, on t-shirts, but looking up at a row of flags, all around, dominating, caused him to stop.

In the centre of each black flag were two hands coming together to shake hands. The hands had been edited to form the shape of a world: two hands, of different origins, coming together, to create a united world.

Reece lowered his eyes. He was where he needed to be. He turned down a street and walked underneath an arch. A plaque, displayed out of reach from the public, sat on the side of the fine stonework. It confirmed that he was in the right place - 'The United World'.

Another plaque pointed further ahead 'The Imperial War Museum. 225 metres.'

As the trees provided camouflage for the city, the beautifully stoned buildings provided the same for this large, black-fronted high-rise. Being careful with his approach, Reece knew that there would be some security present, even at this hour.

Out of the front of the colossal building were two monstrous guards in black. Two men weren't much, but they were enough to keep him at bay. Besides, perhaps there was a security system in place too.

Shit. Think, Reece. Think.

Reece stayed tucked in near the wall to avoid detection. He thought about his options. First of all, he thought, he could just go up and ask to speak to someone. If his mother was here, and they were as evil as he had been told, then that was not an option. The second choice was to stay alert and wait for an opportunity – and then what?

He observed the two guards standing as still as statues.

Come on, he thought. If they didn't move, he was completely out in the open.

Just as Reece started to rack his mind for a third choice the two guards turned and entered the building.

Reece dashed towards the front of the headquarters; on the ground floor, it looked like a reflective black glass. He reached the doors and peered through. No sign of the guards. Reece pulled the handle, but it was locked.

What would he do now? He hadn't really thought it through.

Reece left the front of the building, trying to keep his eyes down to the ground to avoid detection from any cameras that may be around. He moved around to the side. It was better around here, less chance of being monitored. He found another door and pushed. No good, that one was shut tight as well.

Could his family really be in there? It looked like a huge office block. When he stopped to think about it, lit by the mixture of starlight and LED lamps above, it seemed a little far-fetched. Still, he hadn't come this far to question himself. It was where his mother said she was heading, although years ago. If nothing else, maybe someone would remember her.

Reece pushed the door on the side of the building harder, but it held firm. He looked around, but there were no other entrances that he could see. There was, however, a single brick next to him on the floor.

Reece collected the brick in his hand. It seemed like the only way. He walked over to the glassed section by the side door and readied his swing. He pulled it back and began to drive it forward.

"There's no need for that." A man's voice cut through the night. "Come on, you can enter over here."

Reece followed the voice back around to the front of the building.

The man came into view as Reece approached. Straight away, he knew his identity.

Samuel Candrade was not someone Reece had ever met before, but he recognised him from, well, everywhere. It seemed a little strange that one of the most powerful, important and richest men in the world was standing out here, not even taken aback by a homeless person trying to break into his building.

"What do you want?" Reece asked, remaining over an arm's length away from Samuel.

"To show you something, come on in."

Reece dropped the brick. Samuel seemed so sure of himself, so unthreatened by him. He didn't seem to be a threat.

Samuel began walking, and Reece followed. The lights turned on as they entered. They walked past the two guards who turned and faced him. He felt their eyes burn into his flesh.

"Stand down," Samuel ordered. "Back to your posts."

The guards saluted and then exited back through the doors.

Reece followed Samuel through the front of the building, passed the bare, grand reception desk. After a short lag, the lights behind them turned off, one after another.

"Where is everyone?" Reece asked.

"Asleep, most likely," Samuel responded, still walking in front of Reece.

Even at this late hour, Samuel was dressed impeccably. One of the first things that Reece noticed was that his top collar button was still tied. Why would anyone do that? Reece wondered to himself. It was gone midnight, and no-one else seemed to be here.

They approached the end of the reception, and Samuel sat on one of the seats in the waiting area.

"Come, sit," he offered, calmly.

Reece sat across from him, keeping a table between them in case this man should try to grab him. He checked again for security but saw none.

"Tell me," Samuel began. "What brings you here at such a late hour?"

If the man was tired, he didn't let on.

Reece wondered what to say. How much could he guess about him? How much should he reveal?

"Come now boy, tell me the truth," Samuel asked, almost reading his mind.

"I came looking for my mother." Reece glanced in Samuel's direction to see if he could detect anything in his demeanour, but it remained stoic.

"Ah, I see. And why do you think your mother would be here, Mr…?"

"Loche," Reece replied. His last name felt foreign rolling from his tongue. As far as his life went, he was Reece - and Reece alone. "She wrote to me and told me she was here."

"Ah, did she now? We have many employees here, Mr Loche. As much as I'd like to, I'm afraid I can't remember every one of them. What was her first name, if I may be so kind as to ask?"

The edge of Samuel's lips rose up gently, into what looked like a welcoming smile.

The calming nature of this man annoyed Reece. He felt his mouth turning into a snarl. He focused his energy to remain calm. "Nora," Reece confirmed.

"Nora!" he paused for a moment. The pause was a little too long for Reece's liking. "Ah, Nora. My yes, she is a fine employee."

"She works here?" Reece asked, bewildered.

"Indeed, she does. In the laboratory downstairs."

"What, what-?" Reece began, unsure as to the direction of his line of questioning. There were too many questions to ask.

"She should be down there now, actually. If you'd like to go and see her?"

"Now? It's the middle of the night."

"A hard worker, your mother. She never stops." Samuel's smile widened as he displayed his glistening, white teeth. It reminded Reece of a grinning cartoon shark.

"Can I see her?" Reece asked, shifting uncomfortably, expecting something terrible to happen any moment.

"Follow me." Samuel rose from his chair, gestured for Reece to follow, and walked over towards the lifts. "You may have to stand a little closer when we're in the lift though, I'm afraid."

He was trying to be charming, but it just made Reece feel more on edge. He knew what he looked like and how he smelt. There was so little chance this man was there to help him, but yet, maybe his mother was here… and then he could see her again.

The lift approached quickly.

"After you," Samuel offered.

Reece hesitated before stepping in.

Samuel joined him, collected a plastic card from his wallet, tapped it against the lift's touch panel and then pressed the button for -2.

The lift door closed, and within moments they were travelling down - to where? Reece was unsure. He monitored Samuel, who stood tall, calm, and collected.

The lift came to a quick stop, and the door opened.

Samuel walked out into the corridor like he was on the way to yet another business meeting.

"What's down here?" Reece asked, as he stepped out of the lift, and rushed to keep up with his host.

"I told you," Samuel answered, not breaking his stride. "The laboratory."

Samuel removed his card once again and swiped a door, which opened, following his instructions.

"In here," Samuel instructed.

Reece allowed Samuel to enter first, following behind at a distance. The room opened up as he stepped through.

It was a giant, brightly lit room, filled with metal surfaces, scientific apparatus, strange-looking equipment, and computer stations.

"This is one of the main locations for testing."

Samuel began to walk around, somehow knowing that Reece was sure to follow. They walked around the right-hand side of the room.

"Over to your left." Samuel pointed at the testing stations. "Are areas where we check on vital signs of volunteers."

"What for?" Reece asked.

"To ensure that the implant is working correctly, that levels are being monitored and adapted correctly."

The words flew over Reece's head. As much as he'd like to ask further questions, he didn't understand what was happening.

"Over there." Samuel pointed to a room with multiple small metal surfaces. "Is where we perform new registrations. There are replicas of these units, albeit on a smaller scale, across the world."

"Why are you telling me this?" Reece asked.

"Come," Samuel instructed. "There's more to show you."

Samuel exited through a door at the end of the room. Reece followed hot on his heels, gaining distance slowly but surely, as he began to forget about survival – instead overcome with curiosity.

"Through here is the testing unit."

As he entered through the doorway, Reece noticed the clear fronted walls that showed people in cells before him.

"What… what's that?" Reece asked.

"Volunteers."

Each person had their own room, in an entirely see-through cell, without any form of privacy. All of them appeared to be asleep on small single beds in the corner of the rooms.

"Are they prisoners?" Reece questioned.

"They're free to go whenever they like."

"They look like… prison cells to me."

"Alright, if you don't believe me."

Samuel walked to a corner, entered a password on a computer and spoke a command.

"Basement two, release all units."

All of the room doors popped ajar, but the inhabitants remained sleeping.

"Hey, wake up!"

Reece ran towards the first room, leant through the opening.

"Wake up!"

The sleeping, middle-aged woman slowly came to.

"Who are you?" she asked, slightly agitated.

"I'm here to save you," he answered.

"Fuck off," she turned over to face the wall, away from Reece, and back towards slumber.

He exited the cell and looked at Samuel.

"See? Katie is proving to be a little difficult, but in time we'll get there. Care to try any of the others?"

Reece instinctively knew they would all be the same. He shook his head.

"Basement two. Lock all units."

The doors moved from a slightly ajar position to closed, and a locking sound echoed throughout.

"These people are the most recent batch of volunteers. There are some tests that we need to run, some scenarios that we need to engross them in, but I promise you that they are here willingly."

"What's next?" Reece asked, only really wanting to know about his mother.

Samuel smiled. He collected a different key card from his pocket than before - this one jet-black. They walked down to the end of the room. A locked door separated them from its contents.

"Do you want to see inside?"

Reece stopped himself from nodding instantly.

"What's in there?" he asked, instead.

"You wouldn't believe me if I told you. So…?"

Reece allowed himself to nod. All awareness of self-preservation had become a fleeting thought, as he became consumed by the chance of seeing his mother.

Samuel waved the black card along the side of the door. The light on the panel turned from red to green, and Samuel pulled it open. Inside, the room seemed darker than the invasive laboratory lighting.

Samuel held the door, waiting for Reece to pass. He chose this time to accept the invitation. He walked past Samuel, brushing his suit as he did so.

Reece stepped inside.

The room was darker, but now he was in here it seemed to just be a case of softer lighting. Reece could make out the lamps that lit this area in more of an open-plan living space.

In front of them was a sofa, over to one side a dining table, and past that a kitchen area.

"What is this?" Reece asked, walking through the empty apartment. He noticed a fish tank on the far wall, with several live fish swimming around. Next to it sat a picture of a baby in a small frame. The glass on the front of the frame was shattered.

The picture made him feel uneasy.

"Darling," a female voice entered from an adjoining bedroom. Reece closed his eyes at the sound of her voice. "What are you doing here so late?" she continued.

Reece already knew, even before he turned around that it was his mother that had just entered the room.

"Darling." The words sent daggers through his very being. He started to find it hard to breathe.

His mother would now be in her mid-forties, but she looked young, she looked healthy. She looked just like Reece imagined her to look – a beautiful woman, exuding warmth.

"Darling?" Nora walked over to Samuel and placed her arms around him. She placed a kiss on his cheek.

Samuel smiled in Reece's direction, locking his eyes on to his.

Reece couldn't help but let his mouth drop open slightly. "Who's your friend?" she asked.

Samuel broke the locked eyes with Reece. Instead, he focused on Nora. He took her hands in his and kissed her forehead.

"Would you get us both a drink?" he avoided the question.

"Of course. Tea?"

"That'd be great. Thank you."

Nora moved out of earshot, towards the kitchen space to make the refreshments.

Samuel walked across to Reece, brushing past him before sitting down on the sofa nearby. He patted the cushion next to him.

Reece walked over and sat in a chair next to the sofa.

"What the fuck?" Reece asked, his fingers digging into the edge of the chair cushion.

"Your mother and I are an item, as you can see."

"No. She would never leave me, not for this long."

"Your mother and I are very happy together." Samuel leant back, allowing the sofa to take his full weight. "Perhaps, if we get you some new clothes, give you a good wash, a nice haircut, maybe you could be part of our family."

Reece's hands ached from how tightly he gripped the chair.

"Your family?" Reece raised his voice but quickly caught himself. He continued with an aggressive whisper "She's my fucking Mum."

"You're just like your father." Samuel sighed.

"You don't know anything about my father." Reece snarled. "And you don't know my mother, either."

"Oh, that is just not true. I have known your mother for longer than you have, dear little Reece. Oh, what a problem you were growing up, what an absolute nightmare for her that was. You were such a troubled child."

"What the fuck are you on about?"

"You. You probably don't even remember." Samuel began to gesture with his hands. "But you acted out so much that your mother had to give you away. You were born evil, that's what she told me."

"She gave me up so that she could find my dad," Reece contradicted him.

"Oh, and who told you that?"

"It's in a letter."

"Letters are easy to forge, dear boy."

Reece sat in silence, overwhelmed by the situation.

"But then, a lot of things are easy to change, wouldn't you agree?" Samuel grinned.

Nora walked back over towards them, carrying a tray with two cups of tea and a small jug of milk.

She placed it down between the two of them. Her eyes caught Reece's for a moment. Was there a flicker of recognition?

"You didn't tell me who your friend was."

"Go ahead, why don't you introduce yourself." Samuel offered.

What would he say? Did she genuinely believe he was evil? That wasn't true, surely, but even if it was, Reece thought she might have believed it.

"I'm Roger," Reece replied. "I came in for a late-night tour." He thought of more lies. "I'm a journalist, writing a piece for the local newspaper."

"They still exist?" Nora asked.

"Of course they do, dear." Samuel allowed himself a rehearsed laugh.

They were selling him the idea of a picture-perfect family – or at least, they were trying. He was sure that was his mother, he felt it in his gut.

Samuel collected the porcelain cup, added milk and took a sip. Reece did the same. This is what he'd been missing all of his life: comfort, safety, and warmth.

"So, what do you think so far, Roger?" Nora asked.

Reece took his time to respond. His anger left him, but instead, he felt tears rise up and wet his eyes.

"It's great," Reece responded.

"Good." She studied him. "Have I met you before?"

Reece's heart skipped a beat.

The question hung in the air, no-one offering an answer.

"No, I'm probably just imagining it." She added. "Anyway, I had better get my beauty sleep."

Nora leant in and kissed Samuel on his head.

"Goodnight, Roger." She added as she exited.

The tears found Reece now, suddenly and completely.

"What is this?" he asked. "Is this real?"

"Oh, it's very real."

"Is she alright?" he asked.

"I take good care of her." Samuel smiled.

"Where's my father?"

"I couldn't tell you if I wanted to. The last time I was made aware of his location was up north, somewhere near Manchester."

"Manchester?"

Samuel nodded.

Or, perhaps his father was behind one of the doors that he was shown. Maybe there were dungeons further below the ground. Or, was he dead? His thoughts flooded his conscious, as the tears flooded his cheeks.

"Now, now. There's no need for that." Samuel began. "But tell me, now you've seen that your mother is fine and that your father isn't here, what will you do next?"

"I-" Reece focused on stopping his tears. "I don't know."

"Well, if you'd allow me to suggest the options, I believe there are two scenarios. One, walk out that door, go back to wherever you came from, and never return." It felt like a threat. "Or two, stay here with us."

"What?"

"It'd take some time, but we could tell her the truth. We could tell her everything: that we fixed you, and that you're all better now, resulting in you living here as one happy family."

"Why down here?"

"It's not safe out there, not for the moment - not for you, anyhow."

Reece's brain was overworked. He wanted to lie down; he was so tired from the discussion. He tried to suppress his yawn the best he could but failed.

"Actually," Samuel interjected excitedly. "I believe there is a better way."

Reece's eyelids grew heavy.

He tried to stand, but his legs wouldn't support his weight. Instead, he fell forward on to the table, sending his cup of tea halfway across the room, before rolling off on to the floor.

"Reece?" Samuel snapped his fingers towards Reece's motionless body. "Good."

Reece couldn't move. He tried to focus on Samuel's face above him but failed.

"You see, I've been expecting you to turn up here for quite some time. Now I would apologise for this, but my dear boy, my way is much more effective."

Darkness creeped into Reece's vision and the world around him disappeared.

18

June 2nd, 2023

As John approached the front of the house, he could see his boy - his baby turned toddler, jumping up and down with excitement at his arrival.

Nora and Reece waited for him outside. It was how they'd been living now for almost a year. Reece was getting older, and despite John hopping from spare room to spare room, and sofa to sofa, he had managed to save a good sum money.

John walked up to his family, ignored the movement in the curtains behind them, and grasped them in his arms.

"Daddy! Want to go up." Reece said, jumping towards him.

John picked up his son, and in one swift move, hoisted him above his head and down into a sitting position on his shoulders.

"Alright, hold on tight!"

John jogged around slowly; adjusting the height he walked at, bobbing up and down. Happy squeals let him know that he was doing a good job.

This was what he needed after a hard day's work. His kid melting away all of the stress, and although his lower back was hurting, a few drinks would sort that right out.

He ran around, occasionally checking that Reece wasn't too scared. Nora was quiet, a little too quiet for his liking. John grasped Reece and placed him safely back down on to the floor.

"Again, again!" he jumped up and down.

"I'm sorry buddy, why don't you show me how good you're getting at football?" John patted him on his head.

Reece nodded and toddled off to find the ball in the garden.

John walked up to Nora. She collapsed into his arms, crying.

Not again, surely. That bastard had promised it would never happen again.

John moved Nora's head away from his chest; he looked at her face and noticed the bruises masked with makeup.

"That fucking idiot. He's a dead man." John stormed towards the house, past his boy who was returning holding a plastic ball far too big for him, and over to the front door.

"No, John, no!" Nora shouted, but it was too late. His fist rapped at the door.

"Let me in, you piece of shit! I know you're in there."

"John, please."

Reece dropped the ball on to the ground.

"You get out here now, you fucking coward."

John slammed the door with the side of his fist.

"You're not getting rid of me this time, you hear me?"

Reece began to cry as his ball rolled away from him.

"John!" Nora pleaded, grasping at his arm, but even with all of her strength, she couldn't stop him from pummelling the door.

Reece fell down to his knees and cried.

Nora released her husband and ran over to her son.

"Alright, alright, it'll be alright." She picked him up and hugged him.

"Andy, you better let me in, because I'm not going anywhere. You want all of your neighbours to know what a piece of shit you really are?" John shouted, raising his voice for others in the neighbourhood to hear.

The curtain behind the living room window twitched.

John walked over to the window and banged on it with the back of his hand.

A crowd was beginning to form on the street; nosy neighbours looking in on something they likely deemed more dramatic than an episode of EastEnders.

John walked back over to the door and rapped again.

Sirens in the distance broke John out of his trance.

"Andrew called the cops?" he spoke to Nora before turning back to shout through the door. "The cops won't save you, Andy. You're going to get what's coming, one way or another. They're not going to stop it."

Nora placed Reece down on the floor, who clutched on tightly to her leg. She laid a hand on John's arm.

"Please, leave it. He's not worth it."

John broke the focus on the door that separated him from retribution; the arse-kicking Andy deserved.

John turned his attention to his wife and child.

"I know." John softened. "I just, I'm sorry."

His wife threw his arms around him as the approaching sirens loudened.

John removed an envelope of cash from his pocket.

"Put it with the rest." He handed it over to her. "After we've sorted this out, we can get out of here and never come back."

"I'm sorry." Nora threw her arms around her husband once more. Reece joined in and wrapped his arms around both of their legs.

"It's not your fault." He stroked her face, watching intently to make sure his words landed.

After he was sure the words had landed, John bent down to talk to his son - kneeling so he was almost at eye level.

"Daddy's got to go now, but I'll be back soon."

"No, Daddy. Play!" Reece begged.

"Sorry, champ."

Flickers of blue and red lit the front of the house. John noticed the curtain twitch again. Andrew knew that John's distrust for the police would make him flee.

"Shit." John stood back up and whispered to Nora.

"Go, John. Quickly."

The gate opened. Two police officers entered the gated path.

A moment to decide: should he run, head out around the back and jump a fence? Nora could help distract them long enough for him to escape. But what had he really done, what could they charge him with? Did he really want Reece to see him running like a criminal?

The United World

The last question stayed with him. He greeted the officers as they came down the path.

"Evening, officers." John began.

The officers approached.

"What seems to be the problem here?"

"Nothing, nothing."

The door opened behind the married couple. Andrew appeared, with his wife hidden behind him.

"These two were trying to break in," Andrew yelled.

He was looping Nora into this as well; didn't he even have a shred of dignity?

"That's not true, at all." John insisted.

"This is my parents' house," Nora began. "John is my husband, and we were just having a bit of a family quibble, that's all."

The police officers listened. It could have gone smoothly, but they noticed the bruising on Nora's face.

"Ma'am, are you alright?" One of the officers asked, stepping forward. "Are you alright, son?" he then asked Reece.

Reece hid behind his mother's legs.

"He beats her," Andrew shouted from the doorway. "And then he was threatening to come in here and beat me and my wife as well."

"You lying shit!" John yelled.

"Easy." The police officer interrupted. "Why don't we all take a ride down to the station and sort this mess out?"

He wanted to say it was Andrew, but if he did so here, he would surely kick Nora out. He'd have no ounce of guilt about putting a mother and child on to the street.

"I was angry at Andrew," John said. "I wanted a word with him, he'd taken some money."

"Liar!" he shouted.

"Anyway, I was banging on the door. I must have got a bit carried away."

"If you just come down to the station, we can get this sorted out."

John walked towards the officers.

"You only need me, officers. Please don't drag my wife and child into this."

Reece peered around his mother's legs.

The police officers looked at Nora, then the child, and nodded.

"Come with us, sir."

The police officer took John by the arm and led him down the path towards the car. Another stayed behind, likely to take down Andrew's bunch of lies as gospel.

John looked over his shoulder. Andrew had left the doorway and walked down to Nora's side. He took Reece by the arm and dragged him by his side.

He felt the rage bubble inside, but the presence of an officer was enough to keep him in check for now.

* * *

Nora sat on the sofa in tears.

"It'll be okay, darling," her mum comforted.

"They took him away," Nora sobbed.

Nora had put Reece to bed moments ago. He had never been a good sleeper, but tonight was especially trying. It had taken an hour and multiple attempts until he drifted off. Now, she could finally experience the situation – and the tears flowed.

"Why do you let him do this?" she whispered.

Her mother's face shifted, uncomfortably.

"Are you okay, Mum? I do worry about you."

"Don't be silly. Andrew takes good care of me."

"But look at what he did to my face." Tears had caused the makeup covering her bruises to run. "Look at what he did to me."

Her mother looked away.

"He wouldn't do that, he's a good man."

"Mum. Believe me. I'm your daughter."

Her mother continued to avoid eye contact.

"And he's my husband," she added.

"But he hit me."

"I'm sorry, dear. You just need to do as he says."

"Mum!"

"Enough, enough." Patricia began. "Let me get you some tea."

"I don't want any bloody tea!" Nora shouted.

Her mother stood up, walked out of the room and headed upstairs, leaving Nora to revel in her sadness.

Footsteps above meant only one thing. It wouldn't be long. She had nowhere to run.

The footsteps completed the staircase, arriving outside of the living room door.

Andrew's face peered in.

"Your no-good husband taken away by the police. I can't imagine how that feels." He stepped into the room.

"Go away," Nora sniffled, trying to stop the flow of her tears.

He walked over towards her, methodically, one slow step at a time.

"Your dead beat husband. He's pathetic," he spat.

"What do you want?"

"A bit of respect. I think I've earned that. All of these months, I've looked after you and that rotten child." Andrew stood tall in front of Nora.

"His name is Reece," Nora replied, rising to her feet.

The back of Andrew's hand met Nora's cheek, causing her to fall back to a sitting position. She held her hands up to her cheek.

"He's pathetic. Just like his father."

"He's not pathetic."

Andrew raised his fist again, causing Nora to cower. She used her arms to protect herself as best she could, meaning that Andrew couldn't hit her.

"Enough of that. Stay still. Stop crying," he ordered.

"No," Nora responded, kicking her feet out in Andrew's direction. As she flailed her foot connected with his midsection.

Andrew unbuckled his belt and pulled it through the loops in his trousers in one swift motion.

"You're going to pay for that, you ungrateful bitch."

"No, please. I'm sorry." Nora kicked her feet this time to scamper away from him on the couch.

Andrew folded his belt over in two.

"Please."

"Sit down."

Nora sat down as still as she could. Her hands were shaking.

"Please," she begged. "Don't."

"It's you or him," Andrew replied.

"No."

"How are you going to raise a child, when you have no respect for your elders?"

"Please, I do."

"Turn around."

"No, Andrew."

"Turn around," he insisted.

Nora shuffled around so that her back was facing Andrew.

"Pull your top up."

"Please, don't." she pleaded as she exposed her bare back.

Andrew walked away. She heard the door close behind her. However, her hope was dashed within seconds as she heard Andrew return.

"Don't scream too loud. You don't want to wake your precious boy."

Andrew raised the belt up behind her.

"This is for your own good."

Andrew brought down the fat, leather belt on to her exposed skin with a loud thwack.

Nora stopped herself from screaming.

"That's a good girl."

Andrew raised his belt and brought it down harder - this time it really connected. The punishment felt like she'd been shot with a gun. She tried her hardest to bite her lip but failed. She screamed.

"Shush now. Take it like a man."

Andrew brought down the belt again.

The third time hurt even more than the last, especially as he brought the belt down on the exact same area. Her scream loudened and then turned into a whimper.

She sat facing away from Andrew, shaking uncontrollably, exposed.

"Turn around."

Nora let her top fall down across her back, wincing from the pain as it did so. She turned around slowly, trying to control the amount she was shaking.

Andrew grabbed Nora by the chin. He clasped on so tight that she could feel his fingernails dig into the side of her face.

He spat at her as he talked.

"Don't you ever speak back to me, you hear me?!" Andrew shouted aggressively.

She could smell the whisky on his breath.

"Yes, sir."

Andrew held Nora's chin for a moment longer, before releasing it - seemingly satisfied with her answer. He allowed his belt to unravel, looped it back around his waist, and buckled it.

The rush of blood that had reddened his face had begun to fade. He turned his back on Nora, walked over to the door and opened it.

Nora prayed that he'd leave, that he'd go upstairs, or better still, go outside and get hit by a car. While he didn't go outside, she still found relief when she heard his footsteps retreating, followed by the slam of a door.

Nora rocked back and forth. The incredible and immediate pain had faded into a consistent throbbing. She moved a hand around to her back and retracted at the discomfort caused by her touch.

She couldn't take any more of this.

She reached for her mobile phone.

After the last beating, she'd charged her mobile and had been carrying it around with her. It felt like a loaded gun with the safety catch on. John had made her promise not to use it, but that was a long time ago, and she was left to deal with this man by herself.

For what felt like the first time in many years, Nora retrieved her small touch-screen mobile phone from her pocket and turned it on.

The phone lit up. Missed call after missed call - text after text. The numbers kept increasing. The benefits of having a pay-as-you- go sim card, she thought – she was still connected.

She loaded up the contacts, of which there were only a handful, and scrolled through until she stopped on Mary. She clicked the green dial symbol and placed it to her ear.

Nora thanked the heavens as the phone connected. Now she just needed Mary to pick up. It was pretty late, most likely past her bedtime. She wondered if she had found anyone since they last spoke; it was that long ago. She might even have kids of her own.

"Hello?" a tired female voice answered. Even after all of this time, Nora instantly recognised her accent that contained just a slight twang of cockney.

"Mary," Nora trailed off.

"Who is this?"

"Mary, it's Nora."

"Nora!" she shouted, causing Nora to move the headset away from her face. "What the hell, I haven't heard from you in years! How are you?"

Nora resisted the urge to unload, that wasn't what she needed right now... however tempting.

"Mary, I'm so sorry it's been ages. It's a long story."

"I've always got time for you." Mary interrupted.

Nora allowed herself the smallest of smiles before the discomfort of her fresh bruises pulled her crashing back to reality.

"I'll tell you everything, but not now. I... I need help. Sorry, I'm so sorry to call you, I didn't know..." Nora began to cry, her words falling into each other until they were incomprehensible.

"Oh no, are you okay? Try and tell me what's the matter."

"It's, it's, I'm with Andrew."

"Andrew?" Mary shouted. "You said you were never seeing him again."

"I know, I know, but..."

"No buts. You there now?"

"Yes," Nora replied after a moment's hesitation.

"Has he hit you?"

Nora made a noise to indicate a positive response.

"That fucking arsehole. If I get my hands on him."

"Not you too... I just need, I'm so sorry, I just need a place to stay."

"Of course, of course. I'll come right away."

"Are you sure? It's late."

"Roads will be clear, will only take me an hour. Just let me throw some clothes on."

"Thank you."

"Is it just you, or, I can't believe it's been so long – John, that's it, right? Is he still around?"

"John's around. But he's not here with me now. I'll have to leave him a note."

"Are you sure?"

"I can't stay in this house another second." Nora began to breakdown again.

"It's alright, pet, it's alright. I'll be there soon."

"Oh, but there is another."

"Another?"

Nora hesitated. She didn't want to reveal her son but saw no other choice.

"Reece. He's two and a half."

"Oh, right." There was a pause on the other end of the phone. "Why didn't you tell me?"

"It's a long story."

"Well, that's... that's amazing! Congratulations."

Mary had always wanted a child of her own. During the time they shared at college, she could not get Mary to stop talking about babies, toys, being a mother, yet one day out of nowhere, she suddenly did. It wasn't until weeks later that Nora discovered that Mary had been diagnosed with ovarian cancer and required an operation to have both of her ovaries removed. After that, she became distant, and when she had met John, their contact faded almost altogether. There was the occasional call or a text message to check-in, but that was all. When Nora found out that she was pregnant, she hadn't even told her for fear of upsetting her.

Since then, they had drifted.

A forgotten friendship.

"Is that alright?"

"Of course! What's he like?"

"He's-" Mary looked around the room. "He's amazing. I can't wait for you to meet him."

"Well, I'd better get a move on. Andrew still in the same place?"

"Same house. Same damn memories." Nora confirmed.

Same fucking Andrew, she thought.

"Is this still your number?"

"Yeah, it's been disconnected for a while."

"I was going to say. I've tried calling and texting. I was worried about you. I thought you'd died, or, I dunno, run off to Hawaii or something."

"I'll fill you in when I see you."

"Alright. See you soon."

"Thank you, so, so much. See you soon."

Nora disconnected the call.

She would collect her clothes, pack the spare cash that Andrew hadn't found, and get Reece ready. Another hour and she'd be out of this hellhole. But first, she needed to leave a note.

Nora walked around the front room and found a black pen and scrap of lined-paper. She started writing.

'My dearest John,

I'm so sorry I haven't been strong enough. I couldn't even wait for you. I just couldn't take it anymore. If I didn't leave, I don't know what I would have done.

I've called Mary, I'm sorry I had to. I'm going to stay with her in London for a few days until you're back. I pray you find this, but just in case, I'll leave a note for my mother to tell you.

See you soon, and love you always.

Nora xxx'

She added her mobile phone number and Mary's home address at the bottom of the letter and folded it in two. As much as she felt the urge to flee, she was torn. She was leaving behind her husband, the person whom she promised to always stand by. But she had to get out of here, she couldn't survive another day of this.

Besides, she calmed her thoughts, it wouldn't be long until she saw John again.

19

Jan 7th, 2040

Reece squirmed under his bedding, tossing from side to side.

Children were chasing him. Each one holding a different weapon. All of them slicing and hacking against his heels as he ran away. As he pushed himself to run faster, his legs instead moved slower, like running waist-deep in water. The children swarmed in. They cut at the back of his heels, then chopped at his legs. He fell to the floor as he screamed for help.

He shot up, gasping for breath, fighting off the sheets that covered him.

Where was he?

The room around him was dark, but he could make out the features as light filtered through the partially open doorway.

He slung his legs over the side of the bed. It was the most comfortable night's sleep he could remember - there were two pillows, a duvet, and clean blankets. He took a deep breath and breathed in the freshness of the fabric-conditioned sheets. They smelt like roses and freshly cut grass.

Despite what must have been a deep sleep, he felt groggy. His senses returned to him slowly.

He was fully clothed apart from his shoes. He must have slipped them off before lying down. Funny though; he didn't remember coming to bed.

He stood, uncertain at first: his legs had only just woken enough to stand. He moved them, one foot in front of another, wishing blood to pump through them and bring them to life. Gradually, more confidently with each step, he moved towards the crack in the doorway.

He wrapped his fingers around the edge of the door and pulled it open slowly. A lit corridor welcomed him.

Reece edged carefully out of the confines of the room and out into the narrow expanse.

To his right was a dead-end and, to his left, the corridor seemed to open out to another space. Leaning on the walls for support, he walked further out of the room.

Ahead, past a closed door to his side, the corridor opened out to the living area. There was a couch, a kitchen – it was where he had seen Samuel. It was where he had reunited with his mother.

He backed away from the opening. If Samuel was still there, then he sure as hell didn't want him to see him.

His legs felt better, stronger; capable now of carrying his weight. He removed his hand from the wall and noticed the closed door next to him. He had to see.

Reece clasped the metal door handle and carefully pulled it down. The door opened.

Light from outside spilt into the bedroom.

His mother lay asleep in bed. And thankfully, alone.

Was this her home, or her cage?

He longed to be next to her - to curl up in bed and wrap her arms around him. He wanted her to protect him from the world and keep him safe.

Reece took a few steps forward. The room was just light enough for him to explore.

The bed was a big single. It looked the same as his; the white covers clean and comfortable.

Next to the bed was a coffee table. On it perched a desk lamp and a half-drunk glass of water. Around from that was a large wooden wardrobe and an open door that presented an en-suite. Reece peered through and saw a large shower, bath, and sink area – all fully equipped with what someone might need for everyday use.

The only thing that struck him as odd was the lack of windows. Otherwise, it was a well-kept bedroom, like any other.

Wanting to know more about his mother, he tiptoed across to the wardrobe. He moved the door slightly to test the hinges, but after hearing no resistance, opened both doors completely.

The wardrobe accommodated few clothes. There seemed to be a couple of dresses, a few t-shirts, and a pair of jeans. It wasn't much. Then again, who was Reece to judge the number of clothes an average person would own?

Reece closed the wardrobe and walked over to the bed. He couldn't help himself. It was if his mother was calling for him in her sleep.

He perched lightly on the edge of the bed, making sure not to wake her. After he was convinced that he wasn't disrupting her sleep, he allowed the bed to take his full weight.

His mother was facing away from him. Her hair was mostly pulled back behind her head, allowing him to see her profile. It was as if he was looking into a photograph - staring into a distant memory that had suddenly fizzled into reality.

The desire to comfort her pulled at him. He allowed his hand to move towards her. Before he realised what he was doing, he stroked her hair and stared at her features.

He brushed her hair, using his fingers as a brush to move any free strands back behind her ear. Something seemed odd. There was a mark behind her ear. It was hard to see in the low light. Reece parted her hair and leaned in closer, revealing a small, raised scar.

"Reece?" his mother called, waking from a dream. "Reece?"

Reece shot up from the bed and backed away.

His mother rolled over; waking eyes taking in her environment.

"Oh, I'm sorry-. I was having a dream." Nora paused for a moment before continuing. "What are you doing here?"

Nora grabbed her covers and pulled them to her chest. She shuffled up the bed, against the wall, frightened.

"Were you, stroking my hair?" she accused.

"I'm sorry, I just-"

"Samuel! Samuel!" she shouted.

"Please."

"Samuel!"

Reece took a step closer, holding his hands out to try and demonstrate his lack of interest in putting his hands on her.

Her screaming worsened.

"Please," Reece bent down to look her in the eyes. "Don't you recognise me?"

"Get away!" she yelled. Nora kicked and twisted beneath the bed covers, to try and create distance.

"Mum…" the words slipped out from his mouth.

Nora stopped kicking.

"What did you say?" she whispered.

It was too soon. He hadn't prepared what he would say.

"You're my mother," he repeated.

Nora softened her appearance. A glimmer of recognition apparent.

"Reece?" Nora leant forward, inching closer to her son. "Is that really you?"

Reece found no words.

"My baby? It is you."

Nora reached out - her fingertips brushing his cheek before her hand enveloped one whole side of his face. She moved towards him for a hug that he had dreamed about so many times. He held his arms out to accept the loving warmth that only a mother can provide.

He leant in for an embrace he had dreamt about for so many days and nights. The only thing that distracted him were the approaching footsteps from behind. Before he could turn around, he felt a small, sharp pain in his neck.

Reece found himself falling to the ground. Reaching out for his mother, his eyes closed. Before darkness enveloped him entirely, he heard Samuel speak.

"It's time for you to join us."

* * *

David turned around from the bulky laptop, addressing the room.

"I've logged last night's activity and looked through some of the others. It seems like this isn't just happening in the UK, but from what I can see, across the world."

"Damn," John responded.

"I've created a new thread called 'what we know'. I've mentioned in there about timings, suggesting that it could be safe to move around at night."

A fellow member of the resistance passed John a sandwich, consisting of two pieces of white bread and some cheese.

"A few others have already replied. I've set myself as moderator, so they have to be approved before appearing. My thought was we could test suggestions carefully and create a list of items that would be useful for everyone."

"Way over my head but sounds like a good plan," John confirmed, before biting into his late dinner.

"Someone on here recently added that they've not seen any young people before four in the morning, so that could be our window. What I'd love to have is a graph of activity by time. Surely not everyone is asleep at the same time, but it gives us something to work with."

"What's that?" John asked, his interest suddenly piqued.

"That's Samuel Candrade." John scrolled back up to a photograph of the leader of The United Resistance.

"Is it recent?"

"Looks like it."

John squinted at the photograph.

"It can't be…"

"What is it?" David looked closer at the photo. It showed Samuel standing outside of the headquarters. Just behind him and to the side was a woman.

"Do you know her?" he asked.

John retreated into himself.

Members in the room continued to go about their daily business – split between preparing meals, playing cards, and fashioning weapons.

"Alright." David interrupted John's silent stare. "Tonight, we'll head over to my place. We can either walk – probably take a few hours - or we could try and get some form of transport. What do you think?"

John broke his concentration from the computer screen. He turned to David and replied quietly.

"It might be a bit risky to steal a car… Plus ain't no way we're all fitting in."

That was a good point.

"Alright, we'll go on foot."

"The walk will do these lot some good," John added, as he shook off whatever had spooked him earlier.

David had enjoyed stepping up to the plate and had almost instantly taken on the leadership role alongside John. They balanced each other well; John's brute strength and determination, with David's more calculated approach.

John finished his sandwich, downed some water and stood up. He walked around, checking on all of the other members.

"Are we all packed up?" he asked.

Affirmative nods filled the room.

"Good." John approached two guys who were playing a game of cards. "Who's winning?"

"Me," They both responded simultaneously.

"You guys packed?" John cracked a smile.

"Yes, sir."

"Alright then."

John sat back down next to David.

"Are you ready?" David asked.

John took a moment before answering.

"I hope so," he responded quietly, so only David could hear. "Can I can borrow a car?"

David nodded. "What for?" he asked.

"I've got a trip to make," John responded.

* * *

A few hours later, after the sun had long set, they were on their way.

In the black of night, it was much harder navigating than David had expected. Almost every trip he'd made in the past going in this direction was chauffeured. He'd be blissfully unaware, sitting in the back, either preparing for the show or practising some meditation exercises on the return leg. For that reason, it had taken them many hours.

He felt frustrated with himself at times. However, a positive word from John, or merely well-mannered silence and group perseverance, helped to keep his spirits high.

David was almost home, and they'd made it before the sun rose.

They had even found some food and drink along the way. It would come in handy – even though David's pantry was stocked full of tins and dry goods, the perishables such as bread and milk would soon spoil. When they arrived, that would be the first thing he'd sort.

It would be a change – moving from barely cooking for one, to being responsible for seven.

The multi-story mansion rose in the distance. They could build something here. There was space, for more of them even.

They approached the gates that protected the garden.

As silent as the night surrounding them, David entered a sequence of numbers into a key-code device. The large black gates opened with a click and presented the dark exterior of David's house.

David walked into the garden. He looked around, taking in the architectural beauty of his home, and noticed the others trailing slowly behind.

"Come on," he whispered. "It's safe. Everything's off the cloud."

David, John, and the other members of their group proceeded towards the front door. The gates closed automatically behind them.

David reached into his pocket but found no key. Damn, had he lost it last night?

John held out a set of door keys in front of him.

"Kept them for safekeeping," he smirked.

David took the key and placed it into the door and opened his home.

"Lights on," he ordered.

David ushered each member into the house. Holding the door open, he noticed all but a few wiping their feet on the doormat as they entered. Good manners were always appreciated.

John was the last to enter. He placed his hand on David's shoulder.

"The voice thing... there's no way *they* can hear us?"

The door behind them closed.

"Trust me. Cost thousands to install this system."

"You sure?"

"Positive."

John sighed.

"Don't worry, you'll all be safe here," David responded.

"Can I use your loo?" John asked.

"Of course. It's down the corridor to the right. Everyone else, make yourselves at home. Kitchen's down that way. Don't go eating everything!"

David pointed towards the kitchen, herding the resistance towards an area where food and water could provide much-needed sustenance. John exited to use the toilet.

David collected a few bags of provisions by the door and walked through to the kitchen.

Members were already retrieving items from their bags, placing food, drink, games and weapons on the sides.

"What kind of music do you like?" David asked as he observed the others.

Some shrugs answered him.

"Would you care for some Chopin?"

"Er, sure thing, boss."

He had gained their trust, and now he had the opportunity to educate them.

"Play Chopin playlist," David instructed.

Before long, music started.

"Volume low." He instructed.

The slow, melodic introduction eased its listeners: the volume now low enough for people to concentrate, but also for David to enjoy. He was home.

"Where do we put the food?"

"Pantry's over there, behind that door. Else you've got cupboards over there."

David decided it was easier if he showed people around.

"This is the fridge freezer. You can get fresh water from the front tap here. Anything that would spoil quickly, it'd be a good idea to put it in the freezer. Then all along, there are cupboards. Put whatever you like in them. And in here is the pantry."

David opened the pantry door. It was fully stocked with pasta, tins of soup and beans, flour, yeast, even toilet roll.

"Wow," a few people marvelled, as they approached.

"We need to be sensible and make it last, but help yourself." David offered. "My chef stocked it up for me."

"Your chef?" a member of the gang asked.

"Don't worry, only comes if I confirm. Fat chance of that happening now. I do have some plans to create a vegetable patch though; that way, we'll be able to become self-sufficient pretty quickly."

"Well, you've definitely got room for it." John entered the kitchen, marvelling at the space. "Never been one for classical music, though."

"No?"

"More of a classic rock guy."

"It'll grow on you."

"I'm not sure."

"Have you got any favourites?"

"AC/DC, Metallica maybe. The Unforgiven's a good one."

"Play Metallica, Unforgiven"

The slow, gentle guitar riff entered upon the sizeable open-plan kitchen space. After a few seconds, the main riff kicked in.

"That's more like it." John offered a small, nervous smile.

"There's a lot of similarities to classical music," David commented.

"Just wait for it."

John walked over to the counter to help with the unpacking and sorting of goods.

"This isn't bad," David thought out loud.

James Hetfield's lead vocals kick in as the lyrics start.

"Alright, maybe not for me." David quickly changed his opinion.

"It'll grow on you," John retorted, cheekily.

"After you've put that away, I'll show you to your rooms. Sorry, there are not enough beds…"

"We've come from a one-bedroom flat. I think they'll be alright." John responded.

"Don't worry, we can share," Ric said, pointing to his mate.

"A rug will do me fine," another added.

The last of the supplies were put away, and the gang circled around John and David for instructions.

John began.

"Well done. I'm sure you're all bloody knackered, so go get some rest, and we'll figure this all out in the morning."

The gang began to disperse.

"One more thing, David's in charge now. Lend him your strength, as you have me."

"Where you going?" Ric asked.

"Got to sort a few things. Can I count on you?"

"Yes, sir," Ric replied.

"But-" David began.

"You're going to be fine. You're more prepared than I ever was."

"What are you going to do?"

John picked up a sharp-edged weapon from the side. He turned and stared at David with determination in his eyes.

"I'm going to find my wife." He answered. "Now, where's the car?"

20

Jan 1st, 2025

Nora stared at her child without blinking. How was Reece already four years old? He'd grown so quickly. When she looked at him for long enough, she could even start to see his father's features coming through.

Nora wanted this moment to last. She knew that it could be the last time she watched her baby sleep for a while.

They'd had a lovely day. Mary had ordered a cake from the supermarket with four candles, of which they'd all eaten far too much. Reece played with his newest football, which was all Nora could afford as a present, that and some colouring books she had found from the local charity shop.

She should leave him to rest. She fought the urge to walk over and sit with him. Instead, she closed the door to the bedroom and left her child fast asleep on a small child-size camp bed.

Mary stood by her side and placed her arm around her shoulder.

"How's he doing?" she asked.

"Fine," Nora responded.

An unnatural silence lingered.

"I can't believe we didn't talk for so many years." Mary began.

"I know."

Mary playfully punched Nora's arm.

The ladies walked to the front room, out of earshot should Reece wake. Putting him to bed and watching trash television had become their evening routine.

Since Mary took them in, Nora's money had all but run out. She had hoped that John would find them, but still nothing. Now, however, she knew a potential reason why.

Luckily for the two of them, Mary had been kind enough to put them up free of charge. All that Mary wanted in return was for Nora to help out around the house, which of course she was more than happy to do.

But now her money was dwindling, and she still had to feed and clothe her child. More than that, she needed John back: she craved his warmth and pined for his massive arms to be wrapped around her at this moment.

Nora and Mary sat down on a two-seater sofa.

Mary picked up the television remote and pressed the power button.

"Whatcha in the mood for tonight?" Mary asked.

Nora didn't respond.

"Are you alright, pet?"

The United World

The television opened on BBC news. On the show, reports played of The United World, and the marvellous achievements so far, only five years into the regime.

They had minimised climate change across the globe. It had been a resounding success. Initiatives to provide greener working, mandated globally, had seen a mass uptake.

The reporter focused on some finer details into the year on year figures.

"I'm sorry," Nora finally responded. She didn't meet her friend's gaze.

Mary pressed the mute button, placed the controller down on the side and turned to Nora.

"What are you on about?"

"It's New Year's Day, and here you are, stuck with me." Nora began.

"Don't be silly. Having the two of you here is a blessing."

"You could be out there, meeting a fella."

"Never had much luck there, have I?" Mary responded.

"You've just not met the right one yet, that's all."

It was Mary's turn to stay quiet.

"Thank you for putting us up. It truly means the world-"

"Nora, I said no more thanking me." Mary interrupted. "Now, would you like a cuppa?"

"Thank-" Nora stopped herself. "I'll make it, but I was just wondering, not that we're religious, but I've got a question to ask."

Mary waited patiently.

Nora took a deep breath.

"Would you be Reece's Godmother?"

Mary's lips curled until her face beamed with the biggest smile Nora had seen in quite some time.

Mary leant in and hugged her friend. She grasped on, and only after more than a few seconds did she let go.

"Really?" Mary asked.

"One hundred percent."

"Ah, thank-"

"No thanking me either." Nora interrupted.

The two women burst into laughter. They pushed each other playfully like two school children that had just called each other names.

Nora's laughter eased first. She smiled. Yet, within a moment, her expression transformed from one of carefree to worry.

"Are you sure you're alright?" Mary asked.

It was time for the next part of the conversation, the part that Nora was not looking forward to.

"I..." she hesitated. "I got a text."

"Oh?"

"I'm not sure what to make of it."

"What does it say?"

Nora retrieved her old-fashioned mobile phone from her pocket that had somehow, to this date, lasted the test of time. She opened up the text message and handed it to Mary.

"It's from an unknown number. I'm not sure whether it's him or not, but Mary, I have to know."

Mary read the text out loud.

"Nora, I hope you get this someday. I'm sorry. I was stupid, I went to their HQ in London and was held captive. I have no way of finding you, and maybe that's for the best. Stay hidden. Keep Reece safe. I never stopped thinking about you... I hope that is at least something. Love John." She handed the phone back to Nora. "Jeez. Did you try ringing the number?"

"Disconnected. He must have remembered my number, rang it from a pay as you go, then destroyed it," Nora considered.

"When did you get it?"

"A few days ago."

"And you're only telling me now?" Mary asked.

"I didn't know what to think." Nora confided. "I tried the number. I wanted to focus on Reece's birthday. I didn't know…" her voice trailed off.

"Well, what are you going to do?"

Nora sighed.

The decision was one she had tossed around in her head over the last few nights. It was a decision she didn't want to make, but one she had been forced into.

"I want to find him," Nora answered.

"Of course, but he said to stay hidden…"

"If he's been taken, being held captive or something, I need to know." Nora interrupted.

"But what about Reece?"

"Mary." Nora took Mary's hands in hers. "What I'm about to ask is huge. I will understand if you say no." She took a breath, her words hard to find. "I can't take him with me. He's too young, and if it's dangerous, I can't put my baby at risk."

"So?" Mary elongated the word to encourage Nora to finish her thought.

"I've fought with this so much, but I have to do something. Would you look after him for me, just for a few days?"

Mary hesitated in her response.

"I'm not sure."

"I know I'm asking a lot. I just have to find him, I have to." Nora's eyes began to well up for the fourth or fifth time today.

"Oh darlin', please don't get upset. Whatever you need, you know I'm here for you."

"Are you sure?" Nora sniffled.

"Listen, he's my Godson now, am I right?"

Nora nodded.

"Then he's family." Mary rubbed Nora's hands with her thumbs. "You two are all the family I could ever ask for."

Nora found a laugh escape before she could contain it.

"I'm sorry, I just..." Nora exhaled. "It's real. I could see him again."

"I do hope you find him."

Mary squeezed Nora's hands. The pressure felt comforting. It made her feel more optimistic about her decision.

"Thank you."

"Where are you going?"

"He said he was at the headquarters, so I guess I'll start there."

"Be careful." Mary squirmed. "When are you going?"

"First thing tomorrow, before Reece wakes up."

"You're not going to say goodbye?"

Nora took her hands away from her friend's.

"I, I can't Mary. I can't do it."

"What do I tell him?"

"Just tell him that I've gone to find Daddy, and I'll be back as soon as I can. Tell him I love him, please. Tell him every day."

A look of contemplation washed over Mary's face before Nora continued.

"I don't have much, but I have around three hundred. I need a little bit for travel, but the rest is yours."

"Don't be silly." Mary rejected the offer.

"Please. At least take some for his food while I'm away."

"Just come back quickly, you hear me?" she smiled in a way that comforted her more than either of her parents ever could. "If you don't, I'll come and find ya."

"I bet you will." Nora returned the warm smile. She reached into her pocket and retrieved a folded photograph. "Please give this to Reece, just until I'm back."

Mary took the photograph and nodded. She opened it up and looked at the strip of pictures with John, Nora and Reece as a baby.

"How old is he here?"

"I don't even think he's a week old."

"Blimey."

"That was when John said we needed to leave, that people were after us."

"Do you believe him?"

"I- I don't know what to believe."

"Do you think he's, you know, alright?" Mary asked.

"Oh, John? Of course. He's s a bit paranoid, but he wouldn't make something like this up. There's no chance he'd have put up with Andrew for as long as he did if there wasn't something going on."

"So, the government are really out to get you?"

"I don't know."

The two of them sat in silence. Nora noticed Mary rubbing the bare part of her neck with her thumb and fingers.

"Thank you, Mary. You know, I love you so much."

"And I, you."

"You're the best friend I could ever ask for."

The two friends leant in for a hug that transformed from nerves and uncertainty to comforting smiles.

The two women ended their embrace and sat back into the sofa's natural grooves.

"I hope you find him."

"I have to, there's no other choice."

Mary unmuted the news. She started flicking through the channels before she found a game show that the two of them had grown accustomed to.

"There we go. Now, how about that cuppa?" Mary asked cheekily.

"On it." Nora rose from the couch and walked towards the kitchen.

She hoped she wouldn't be away from this for too long, and that this was all a misunderstanding. Still, deep down it didn't stop her from fearing the worst.

21

Jan 8th, 2040

Marc and Gary had grown accustomed to talking to a captivated audience on YouTube. Whenever Marc stopped to think about how it had come about, he couldn't believe that they'd already amassed a million subscribers. Yet, somehow, he didn't think a YouTube award for hitting that milestone would be arriving in the post anytime soon. There were far more important things at stake.

Gary set up the computer as before, preparing for their daily live stream. As a computer whiz, Gary had been sure to set up the VPN by default. They had also removed any personal information from the computer along with anything that could help to identify them from the camera shot.

They were simply two middle-aged men, bobbing up in the middle of an ocean – and that is how it needed to stay.

It had been just under a week since Marc was threatened. Then people on the streets started going crazy, and life, as he knew it, had changed forever. It was strange, though. Over the past few days, he felt like he was adapting to it like a fearful duck to tepid water – he was easing into it.

It was mostly the noises that echoed from outside that haunted him daily. They found him all day, every day: shouting, screaming, violence, and protesting. The result, however, was always the same - hundreds of lifeless bodies. The deceased were then cleared each morning by the same people who had put them there.

Marc and Gary had a small vantage point from one of the rooms upstairs. They had boarded all windows with various wood, cardboard and paper they had spare. For the edge of the downstairs window, they even used cereal boxes: which meant that the sight of a famous rooster now filled Marc with dread.

Like most of the people in their situation, they were in lockdown – and they had not left their homes.

Some of the chatter on the groups provided a small degree of comfort. They had read, and discussed on stream, that the streets were safe at night. He, for one, didn't want to test the theory until it was proven.

They had enough canned and frozen food to last for a while longer. The electricity was working, water flowing, and for now, they had no reason to leave. The main thing that concerned him was the diminishing supply of toilet roll. They were down to their final pack of four.

Feeling trapped inside had left him feeling caged. It was strange, as he had always been an indoors type. Marc was never really one for sports or outdoor exercise, but just the ability to go outside, and have a change of scenery was something he already missed.

Still, there were others worse off than them. There were so many others who had lost their lives, and, to make it worse, the mainstream media were covering events with such bias that it made Gary and his broadcasts even the more important.

As Gary entered the information for the live stream, Marc's mind wandered to the flavour of barbequed chicken. His mouth watered. He would kill for a few wings now, just four or six, crispy-skinned or regular. Beans on toast wasn't quite the same.

Even though their lives now focused around survival, he'd not spoken to Gary too much about their situation. They had simply adapted. Gary, in particular, had turned his focus on letting the people out there know the truth. There were also times when he'd had to stop Gary from revealing too much of the window upstairs, and potentially giving themselves away.

His priority was to go under the radar, and, if they found Gary, they found him.

The eye on the lens opened and the live stream began.

"Hello everyone," Gary opened, as Marc watched the live viewer ticker increase exponentially into the thousands. "Thank you for tuning in. We're here again to discuss the latest happenings here in the UK and across the world."

Gary looked down at his notes he had prepared for the broadcast.

"The news continues to ignore the deaths across the country. According to the government figures in the UK alone, there have been only a few hundred additional deaths over the past few days. I've seen hundreds outside of my window alone, so I know that is absolute horseshit."

Marc took a swig of his glass of water. He watched the live comments that scrolled too quickly to comprehend.

"Some viewers have set up a discord forum. I've added the link in the description. I'll remove it after the stream, so click on it now and sign up. It seems like people in there are sharing information about what they know about the brutal murders occurring across the world. They break it down by country, city, as well as having some tips for staying safe during a lockdown. You'll need to apply to join."

Gary rechecked his notes.

"Today is the 8th of January, twenty-forty. It has been four days since registrations closed for The United World. It has been four days of death."

Gary took a deep breath. Marc took the opportunity to keep the conversation going.

"Hey, everyone. On the forum, there's been some really interesting chat. I don't know if anyone on here has read them, but one of the things I've read is that it might be safer to go out at night. I'd say don't go out unless you really need to, but yeah, has anyone else heard that?" Marc trailed off.

With only a slight delay, the live comments filled with people agreeing with what he'd said, along with lots of people asking questions.

"Alright, it seems like a lot of you agree. If you can go to that channel and write what you know, it'd really help." Marc added.

"Cool," Gary interjected. "So today we're focusing again on what we actually know, what we think, and what's fake. Those are the three things we've been focusing on, and I think that's a good way to continue. If you disagree with something or have anything else to add, please let us know in the comments. We will try to go through them all afterwards."

Tens of thousands were now watching.

"What we know - the mainstream media are covering up the happenings around the world. That's a fact. You go on any large media site or channel, and it's not being reported correctly. There are a few smaller independent websites out there doing their best, but a lot of them have stopped being updated. So, what we know is mostly down to us. We know that in most cases, basic necessities such as water and electricity, continue to be provided. In terms of safety, we have boarded up our doors and windows, and so far, no one has tried to break in. A lot of others are reporting the same."

"So, if you can, stay inside and stay hidden," Marc added.

"On to the next point. We think the people who have been hired to kill us, whoever they are; however they're doing it, as we mentioned, seem to be less active at night. So, if you are desperate for food or medical equipment - that might be your best chance."

"We don't know for sure, though." Marc contributed.

"There's some more interesting information from the forum. Apparently, any person under the age of twenty is a threat. Family, friends, it doesn't matter. If you know someone under the age of twenty, you have to distance yourselves."

"Now, we don't know for sure it's all young people, and we've seen some older people too."

"Yeah, that's true. But, from what we've read – and what we've seen – there's definitely a pattern. Just be careful. If you absolutely have to talk to anyone, keep your social circle to the smallest number possible. That way, you'll minimise the risk."

Gary took a sip of his water before continuing.

"And we know what's fake. If you look on any of the news sites, they're all claiming the same thing. Violent protests from those not registered: people from our side killing others because of disagreements, because of beliefs. I mean, we have what, almost one hundred thousand people watching now - I would bet that almost all of you would agree with me that is complete bollocks."

The comments section screamed once more with approval.

Marc decided he had something of merit to add.

"You know, we're just two normal guys, trying to help people out there. It's amazing seeing the number of people here listening to us."

"Together, we can beat this," Gary said. "There's a silent killer out there, and like a disease, we can't tell who is infected, but if we stay safe, and stay in contact online, then we can all get through this."

"Have we got our guest, mate?" Marc asked his friend.

"Oh yeah."

Gary clicked away on the keyboard as the viewing figures continued to rise. Another window appeared alongside theirs, simulating a video conference.

David Stern appeared in a non-descript, small white room. He waved once to the camera.

Even now, being this close to a celebrity gave Marc a fluttering feeling in his stomach. He found his mouth turn dry. Luckily, Gary was the one to introduce him.

"We've got David Stern on the line. David, thanks for joining us."

"Of course, thanks for having me," David replied.

"So it was, what, a few days ago when you had your last show. Can you tell us what happened?" Gary played host to the television host.

"Sure. I was in the middle of the show, just like normal. There was a, I don't know how to describe it - a weird feeling in the air. I was just going about the show, and then after the conversation with Miss-" David looked visibly annoyed as he corrected himself, "Emily Cambersham, the entire audience, filled with young people, all stood up at the same time. They looked at me, emotionless, and then they started to charge. I turned and ran. Luckily, I made it out of the building."

Marc leant towards the camera to make sure his question was heard.

"Do you know why?" he croaked.

"I have some ideas."

"Would you share them with us?" Marc asked again.

"Alright. Well, don't take my word for it. I'll try to be as factual as I can, but, all of those that have been registered have been chipped. As far as I have been told, it's a form of GPS tracking so that people are correctly accounted for should they commit a crime, all of that. A better world. However, from what I've read from various people online, including a whistleblower from the government, the chip does a lot more than that."

"Do you know what?" Gary asked.

"I stayed up all last night reading report after report. I can't verify all of them, but this one guy captured my attention. I searched his name, and his employment appeared in a historical page. Again, I don't know if this is completely correct, but he claimed that the chips were used to alter chemicals in the brain. That way, the government could reduce levels of aggression in those who needed it."

"What about increasing it?" Marc mused.

Someone knocked in the background of David's stream. He turned around and addressed him.

"Yeah, just check in the cupboards. I'll be out in a bit."

"Who was that?" Marc asked.

"A friend," David replied.

Keeping his cards close to his chest was a tact that Marc understood all too well.

"Surely there have to be bodies, organisations that would stop this from happening?" Gary implored.

"I don't know. But look out your window, does that look normal to you?"

They didn't need to look. It did not.

"How about you guys," David continued. "Have you learnt anything of value?"

Marc and Gary took a moment before replying – dead air no longer an issue in what was turning quickly into a dystopian nightmare.

"I don't think so," Gary responded first.

"What stops them attacking each other?" Marc asked.

"It's got to be to do with the GPS of the chip? Some sort of recognition." David answered.

"So potentially if you got your hands on a chip…" Marc trailed off.

"It could work. Maybe there's a scientist watching who could look into it?"

"So, what you're saying," Gary began. "Is that if you could get hold of a working microchip, and carry it around with you, it just might cloak you from detection?"

"Who knows? That's one idea. Another option could be to create a chip that replicates the one that The United World have created, or perhaps some device that blocks detection altogether."

"Like a frequency jammer?" Gary asked.

"Something like that."

"Well, David, thank you for coming on and talking to us. I know you've got a lot to sort out."

"My pleasure. Anytime you chaps need me, just give me a message. Stay safe, everyone."

David signed off, leaving a stutter in the stream.

"Shall we play the footage?" Marc asked Gary.

"Good idea." Gary turned his attention back to the audience. "We've received lots of videos from people. If you have anything you want to send in for us to share and discuss, please send it through on the forum. Sign up anonymously, use a VPN, and that way, we can all do our best to remain undetected."

"This video is pretty horrible." Marc changed the subject back to the matter in hand. "I wouldn't watch it if you are a bit squeamish."

"It's important," Gary argued. "Watch it if you can. Hold on, I'll just load it up."

Gary exited the live video playback on the computer and opened a video from his desktop. He right-clicked and chose cast, and clicked play.

The live stream changed to show a shaky hand-held video of a man and woman walking hand-in-hand in the middle of a countryside lane. The person recording them was walking a good twenty or thirty meters behind – recording the trees, bushes and potential wildlife around.

"This was shared yesterday afternoon, apparently from the Hertfordshire area." Gary narrated over the top of the video.

In the distance, a small person wearing black tights and a pink top walked up towards them. As the person came into focus a little more, it appeared to be a young girl.

The recording was tracking the views of the person walking behind the couple as he looked around.

A scream pulled his focus to the couple ahead.

The girl was standing over a body.

The girl was stabbing the other as he flailed his arms in her direction.

The man recording stopped in his tracks.

"What the fuck?" he said under his breath, just audible enough to hear.

The second victim fell to the floor.

The girl looked up. She started to walk and close the gap.

"Mister," she said, only slightly raising her voice. "Mister, can you help me?"

He fumbled backwards, placing his feet behind him, but all the while keeping his focus ahead.

"What are you?" he shouted back.

"Mister, please, they were trying to hurt me."

The girl closed in towards him until she was only a handful of metres away.

He noticed the knife, that dripped with blood, held behind her.

"I've lost my Mummy and Daddy," she said all too innocently.

"Get away from me!" the man yelled, to no effect.

The girl approached. She held the knife out in front of her.

The man turned, losing visuals on the girl, and ran in the opposite direction. He huffed and panted; his breathing grew heavy and tired quickly, yet he continued to run as the woodland surrounding him whirred by.

"Get away! I haven't done anything wrong!"

From the audio, it was clear that he was beginning to sob.

He slowed his retreat slightly so that he could look behind him. The girl was standing in the same position that he had seen her last time. She wasn't even following him.

The man didn't wait for much longer before returning to his retreat; this time he did so with a steady jog. He narrated what he had seen as he did so.

"It's Saturday," he struggled to breathe and talk at the same time. "It's.. the sixth… seventh of Jan…u…ary, I think." He turned back but saw no one chasing him. He allowed himself a moment to catch his breath. "I've just witnessed two people being murdered by a, well, a small girl with a knife. I don't know…" He trailed off. He began to walk in the same direction he was heading. "I was just out for a walk, to stretch my legs. Oh, my God. What the hell?"

The footage shook as he began to run again.

Gary closed the video. He and Marc returned to full screen on stream.

"There's so many showing the same thing. A young person killing someone in cold blood, showing no remorse." Gary said.

"It's horrible," Marc observed.

"The more we know our enemy, the more we learn, and the more we understand. The more we can combat it. Keep sharing the videos, no matter how hard it is, it's important."

Marc hoped that would be the last violent video he'd have to watch, but knew that there would be many, many more.

Gary lined up the next one.

* * *

The large screen on the wall displayed Marc and Gary on their live stream.

Emily sat in her office, watching the two of them closely. She clicked a button on her ear.

"Phone Samuel," she instructed.

The phone rang and then rang some more. It didn't usually take Samuel this long to answer. Two more rings and she'd have to try again later.

On the final ring, Samuel picked up.

"Hello?" he sounded out of breath.

"Are you alright?" Emily asked.

"Yes, yes. Do you have an update?"

"Very well. Yes, the streamers are giving away a lot of information about our operation. Some of it is guesswork, but some of it could be harmful to us."

"How are they finding out information?"

"Well," Emily ran the tips of her fingers against where a necklace might have been. "Mr Stern made an appearance."

"Mr Stern?" Samuel asked. His tone indicated that he wasn't as surprised as she had assumed he would be.

"Yes. He divulged information about me, and about the microchip."

"Surely they're just guessing. Putting two and two together?"

Emily breathed deeply before she had to deliver the unfortunate news. However, it was something that could not be passed over with pleasantries.

"There's a whistleblower, sir."

"A what?" Samuel's voice rose.

"A whistleblower, someone who's informed-"

"I know what a whistleblower is, Miss Cambersham." His voice smoothed over the individual moment of frustration. "Please go on."

"They said it's a government official. They have released information on the microchip in context to the balancing of chemicals."

"Anything else?"

"No. That and eye-witness accounts… videos of murders."

"That doesn't matter."

Emily could tell, even with his near pitch-perfect response, that he had been taken slightly aback.

"No?" She asked.

"In the grand scheme of things, it's just a minuscule blip. Besides, we know who they are and where they live."

"There is a forum as well, a discord server."

"We're well aware."

"But why?" Emily began.

"Why haven't we stopped them?" he asked.

"Yes." Emily cleared her throat.

Emily could tell that Samuel was sipping his scotch; savouring the taste – and the power.

"Would you not agree that it's better to fight an enemy you can see than to fight one blind?"

Emily supposed that made sense. She agreed.

"It's always better to know thine enemy, Miss Cambersham. I imagine you would know enough about that matter."

He was referring, of course, to the man who had raped her - the man who had raped many others. She knew every little detail about that despicable excuse of a human being. She probably knew him better than anyone else in this world, and just thinking about him filled her with contempt.

"I understand," she responded. "But why not block their stream?"

"Until we have succeeded, there will always be resistance. We should know all we can about them, to be able to monitor their communications and to gauge their influence."

She waited as he took another sip.

"And then, when the time comes, we'll simply destroy them."

The call disconnected. Samuel was obviously in no mood for small talk.

Emily turned the volume back up on the stream and continued to watch as the two innocent men rallied hundreds of thousands to their cause.

22

Jan 8th, 2040

John knew the streets of London when he saw them.
What John didn't know, however, was just how impactful the dead bodies that littered the streets from the night before would prove to be. The lifeless that lay before him on his journey increased as he moved centrally through the capital. It was the worst he'd seen, so far.

If he stopped and checked on them, if he showed just an ounce of empathy he could be discovered, and then he'd never see his family again. He couldn't allow that to happen.

John drove through the city at a snail's pace. He thought back to his distaste for the city when things were normal: the streets were always over-packed, there were tourists everywhere, and crime was rife. But looking back, he realised that perhaps it wasn't as bad as he had imagined; he had settled down in one of the rougher areas, after all. What was happening now, however, was something else entirely.

It had been a long time since he'd driven any distance of note. Still, after a few issues, such as remembering where the indicators were, not to mention the occasional accidental squirting of windscreen fluid, he had taken back to it well. Besides, it wasn't as hard as in his youth. There wasn't a clutch to worry about, automatic parking was standard, and there were nowhere near as many arseholes on the road.

His main issues were with avoiding the bodies that littered the road and the rising sun.

The clock on the car's dashboard read 05.50.

The lifeless streets he had previously driven past, started to slowly become busier. If someone was to notice him, if people were to come for him now, he'd have nowhere to go.

He was almost at The United World headquarters, but perhaps it would be best to park up and continue on foot. It was an option between driving in full force or moving in the shadows. Against a worldwide government, he assumed the latter would be the better choice.

John turned off down a side road, located an empty spot away from a bus lane, slowed the car, and clicked the park button.

All of this area used to be a low emission zone – for a few years motorised vehicles had been banned from Zone 1, but since mandating electric vehicles, the inability to drive through had been lifted.

After the automatic sensors had assisted with a perfect park, John collected the machete from the passenger seat. He turned his hood up to avoid detection from cameras and opened the door.

The United World

John stepped out on to a newspaper, blowing through the streets. The newspaper headline read 'A United Success'. Below the headline was a picture of Samuel and Emily shaking hands. He wiped his shoe on the paper and exited the car.

The sun hadn't risen yet, which would still give him some cover, but he'd need to move quickly.

Sticking to the sides of buildings, with both his face and weapon concealed, he stalked through the side streets of Westminster towards his goal.

If what he'd seen was any indication, people in The United World would be awake now, they'd be getting ready for the day, exercising, eating well, and some would be outside: those were people he needed to avoid.

Step by step, inch by inch, he closed in on the headquarters of the most powerful organisation in the history of the world - and quite possibly, the woman he still loved after all of these years.

* * *

Reece opened his eyes.

There was something peculiar about his dream.

As he became more aware of his surroundings, he attempted to grasp hold of a memory but, as he tried to focus, it merely slipped through his consciousness, like water rushing through a colander.

The memory was gone.

He rubbed the top of his forehead and sat up in bed.

Reece was usually tired and lethargic when he awoke, but not today. He felt ready to take on the world.

Reece swung his legs from beneath the soft, white covers, and his bare feet found the cold floor below.

To the right, he noticed a pile of clothes. He stood and walked over towards them. There was a pair of black trousers, a black shirt, fresh socks and even a new pair of black shoes. He leant in and smelt the fabric conditioner. The scent of the clothes reminded him of a fresh meadow.

Reece placed his clothes and shoes under his arm. Somehow, he knew what to do next – the stench that followed him was all the instruction he required. He walked across the room, pushed open a door, and walked into the adjacent en-suite.

He placed the fresh clothes on the toilet seat and turned the shower taps on. Instantly he was greeted with a strong stream of boiling hot water.

Reece placed his hand under the scalding water. He watched his skin turn red under the current. It was too hot. He removed his hand, slowly, and adjusted the temperature.

Steam filled the small bathroom as Reece slipped off his boxer shorts and stepped into the cubicle.

The water and steam lashed at his naked body.

There was a soap dispenser attached to the wall, which Reece pumped a few times, filling his hand with enough gel to cover his torso.

A brown river flowed from his body.

Reece scrubbed at his skin, removing all of the dirt and dead skin that had found itself a home.

He pumped the soap dispenser again and pulled his fingers through his hair. The knots and clumps of dried dirt required a lot of cleaning. However, with a lot of scrubbing and a few more applications of soap, the water ran clean.

Reece finished washing, turned the taps off and stepped out of the shower. He found a white towel and dried himself.

Cleanliness was suddenly very important, and after the shower he felt rejuvenated. Taking a deep breath, he noticed the lack of body odour to which he had become accustomed.

The clothes that he put on fitted almost perfectly. After putting on the last garment, he slipped on the shoes and tied the laces. He hadn't been taught the proper way, so he simply tied a knot and then tucked the laces into the shoe beside his foot.

Looking in the mirror, he felt like he looked acceptable from the head down. His floppy, brown hair fitted the desired image, but his unkempt facial hair needed to go.

Luckily, there was a shaving kit by the sink – a pair of small scissors, a shaver, and a bar of soap. Reece began with the scissors.

Tuft after tuft, his facial hair fell away from his face into the bowl below. He felt his appearance evolve with each snip. After a while, his facial hair was trimmed enough to attempt a shave.

He picked up the soap, lathered his face, and then picked up the sharp shaver. He noticed the reddened skin on the back of his hand from the hot water, but it didn't bother him.

The sharp metal ran against his face, relieving the stubble.

Reece turned the tap on so that the hair ran down the plughole as he continued to update his appearance – a nick or two, here or there, did nothing to put him off finishing the job.

He had never been shown how to shave before. He did his best, with what intuition he had.

Washing off the soap, splashing his face with warm water, he felt the sting of the cuts, but instead of sharp piercing pains, they were small and dulled.

He looked at himself in the mirror. Apart from several red dots on his neck, and a few nicks on his jawline, he'd done a good job for his first shave.

Here he was, clean, shaved, dressed smartly – possibly all for the first time.

Reece had been reborn.

He cleaned the hairs from the sink, tidied the bathroom, and exited back into the bedroom.

He felt a need to tidy behind him as he went. He made the bed, which provided comfort, and then walked towards the door, which led to the corridor. With a push, it opened silently.

Walking down the fully lit corridor, with no hesitation, he approached the open kitchen dining area.

His mother was boiling the kettle.

"Morning," he introduced his presence.

"Reece!" Nora walked over and wrapped her arms around his shoulders. "Good morning. Would you like a tea?"

"Yes, please," he responded, politely.

"Have a seat, and I'll bring it over."

His mother planted a kiss on his cheek, unwrapped her arms from him, and flicked the kettle on.

Reece walked across to the sofa. As he did so, he saw a picture frame on the side. The glass was smashed, but inside, the picture looked good as new. It was a photograph of Reece, Nora, and Samuel. A happy family.

Reece shook off the strange feeling of déjà vu from the image and headed towards the sofa. He sat down, but instead of leaning back against the cushions, he sat up straight – concentrating on posture over comfort.

The rising whistle of the kettle quickly grew before it descended.

"Would you like sugar?" his mother asked from across the room.

"No, thank you," Reece responded.

His mother brought over two cups of tea. She placed one in front of him on the coffee table, and one to the side of him.

"How are you today?" Reece asked.

"Me? Oh, I'm fine." His mother smiled before walking back to the kitchen space. "How are you, darling?"

He didn't even have a chance to contemplate the notion before the words left his lips.

"I'm good, thank you."

Reece picked up the cup that had been placed before him and lifted it to his lips. He felt the hot air tickle the exposed skin on his face. He blew the drink a few times before taking a sip and placing it back down to the table.

A heavy door opened. It slammed shut moments later.

Samuel walked in, dressed in a smart grey suit.

He walked over to Nora and planted a kiss on her cheek.

"Good morning," he said.

"Morning." Nora smiled back. "Your tea is on the table."

Samuel nodded and walked over to the sofa beside Reece.

"How are you feeling?" he began tentatively.

"Good. How are you?" Reece responded.

Samuel took a few moments to respond, he seemed to be studying Reece.

"I'm fine."

Samuel collected the cup of tea from the table, took a sip, and leant back into the cushioned support.

"How are you settling in?" he asked.

"Great," Reece replied.

"I see you found the shaver I left for you."

Reece nodded.

Samuel stood up, leant forward and looked closer at Reece's face.

"Hmm. You have done a good job. And I am very fond of your attire."

Reece felt no emotion towards what he was wearing - it was merely clothing.

"Very good." Samuel sat back down, sipped his tea, and turned to Nora.

"Would you whip us up some breakfast, dear?"

"Of course," Nora responded. "Are scrambled eggs alright?"

"That'll be fine." Samuel turned to Reece. "Go help your mother out, boy."

Reece had no reason not to do as he was told.

He wasn't experienced with cracking eggs, so he was in charge of the bread. He toasted two pieces of bread, waited for them to pop out, and then placed them on a plate.

"The marge is in the fridge," Nora informed him.

Reece retrieved the olive oil spread from the fridge, scooped a large dollop on one end of a knife, and spread it across the two pieces evenly.

Nora poured eggs on top of the toast. She gave Reece a knife and a clean fork.

"Take it to your father," she said.

Reece took the breakfast and cutlery over to Samuel. He placed it in front of him.

Without a mention of gratitude, he started to eat.

"Salt, where's the salt?" Samuel spat.

"Oh, I'm sorry dear." Nora panicked, fetching the saltshaker from the cupboard. She hurried and placed it down on the table.

Samuel ground some small flakes of salt that landed delicately atop the eggs, after which, he wolfed the meal down.

He was with family now: he didn't have to maintain his perfect exterior.

Reece stood by the couch, unsure as to what to do next.

"Sit, boy," Samuel instructed.

Reece did as he was told. He sat, took another sip of his cooling tea, and waited for Samuel to finish eating. It took only a handful of seconds.

Samuel threw the knife and fork on the empty plate, sat back, and sighed.

Something irked Reece just a little. There was something in the way Samuel threw down the cutlery. Something wasn't quite right. Why was he demanding salt so aggressively?

Reece looked up. He realised that Samuel had been observing his thoughts.

"Feeling alright?" Samuel asked.

Reece took a moment to respond. It was a moment too long.

"I said, are you feeling alright?" he asked again, louder, leaning forward as he did so.

"I think so," Reece responded.

"What are you thinking right now?"

"I, I don't know. I'm a bit confused."

"I see."

Samuel retrieved a mobile device from his pocket. He pressed his thumbprint against the reverse, and the previously black screen came to life.

He clicked a few buttons.

"What's that?" Reece asked.

"This is the next phase. Tell me, how do you feel now?"

Samuel slid his finger along the device.

"I don't-" Reece began to talk, but his sentence remained unfinished. Instead, he felt a wave wash over him. He felt a soothing sensation splash inside of his mind, taking away with it any negative thoughts or feelings.

"Better?" Samuel asked.

"Better," Reece responded. "Shall I help mother?" he asked.

"That's a great idea."

Samuel placed the device back in his pocket as Reece collected the dishes and took them to the kitchen.

"Here you go," Reece handed the plates over to his mother.

"Thank you, darling. Why don't you ask if your father would like another drink?"

He would. He would walk over to his father. *His father?* He would ask his father if he wanted a drink. *He would ask Samuel if he wanted a drink.* Who was this man?

The wave crashed against the thoughts and dragged them into an ocean of forgotten memories.

"Father. Would you like a drink?"

"That would be lovely, son," Samuel responded.

Samuel's phone rang, causing him to stand and move over to the side of the room. Reece could hear him, and despite knowing not to listen in, couldn't help but to take in the information.

"He's here? *Now?*" Samuel sighed as he pressed a finger to his temple. "Very well. Please see that he's looked after. I'll be there shortly."

23

Jan 8th, 2040

Despite her best efforts, Emily found no sleep last night. She was unsure as to what had come over her. When she was young, she could be described as an anarchist or, at least, a leader. She would lead rallies and protests, force change, and always get a good night's sleep. Yet now, while she was the face of The United World, she felt hollow; a completely different person from her driven younger self. The thought would not leave her.

Was that why she had come to Samuel's office before work? Was she hoping that he'd be sitting in his seat, feet up on the desk, looking as composed as ever? Perhaps he'd have helped her see that she's just feeling anxious, that this is just a difficult time in the bigger picture. It needn't matter, because that was not the case.

Emily walked past an empty reception desk, happy that his overly eager receptionist wasn't in just yet. She continued walking naturally and pushed open the glass door.

Her heart pounded rapidly. Perhaps it was the strain of a restless night, or maybe it was because she knew she was doing something untoward.

Emily stepped into Samuel's office. His large desk filled the room in an imposing manner. The sight stirred the memory of Samuel's hands running over her – his alcoholic breath mixing with hers. The door clicked shut behind her.

Emily moved around to the back of the desk, ignoring the magnificent view out across the capital. Besides, she didn't want to see any more dead bodies if she could help it.

She placed her derrière in the most expensive leather chair one would ever hope to sit in. However, now was not the time to notice the brilliant lumbar support, the padded memory foam cushion, or the silky-smooth touch. Emily leant forward and opened the first of the drawers; she'd start with the bottom and work her way up.

In the first sat multiple documents. Plans, agreements, and proposals – they were all things she'd seen before. Why he'd have something physical when everything was digital, she'd never know. Next to them, of course, was a bottle of scotch on its side, and two crystal tumblers. She placed the documents back as she found them.

The next drawer down contained a notebook, a single pen, and the television remote. She felt a pang of pride for her peer: Samuel was extremely organised.

Flicking through the notebook, the majority of the pages were blank. A few pages contained some phone numbers, some web addresses, some items of food. It seemed to be perfectly legitimate.

The third drawer was empty.

There was a small slither above it, which looked like it contained something, but would not pull open. It was locked, but there was no hole for a key.

Emily felt around inside the top drawer. She felt the bottom, the sides, and then knelt on the floor as she traced her fingers across the roof. She felt a small notch and flicked it to one side. The hidden top drawer sprung open.

Emily took her seat back on the leather chair and, with a deep breath, she prepared to open the drawer. It was only large enough to contain a single folder, a tablet, or necessary documentation. Emily wasn't sure which she hoped it was.

The drawer slid open, presenting a small, black, mobile electronic device, similar to that of a mobile phone. Beside it was a black key card, with no detail.

She collected the electronic device and held down a button on the side. The screen, which covered the entire front, turned on with a message - 'Enter Pin'.

Typical. There were six digitals to enter and only numbers to choose. She would have to make an educated guess.

She tried his birthday. Incorrect.

She tried her birthday; it was worth a shot, after all. However, when the guess proved to be wrong, she actually felt somewhat relieved.

Emily thought about possible dates, but only one more came to mind - the date that The United World first formed. The first of January 2020. Surely, he wouldn't use such an obvious date as that? The face of The United World turned hacker entered the digits 010120, and to her surprise, the device unlocked.

The screen contained a list of names in alphabetical order – family name first, followed by the given. Her heart skipped a beat when she saw the fourth down the list... Miss Cambersham, Emily.

Not knowing what the device pertained to, but searching for clarity, she clicked on her name.

The screen switched instantly to multiple horizontal sliders, all of which seemed to be at different levels. Emily studied the text beside the sliding scales, which each displayed names of various chemicals – some of which she recognised, and others which she did not. Emily struggled to fathom what she held in her hand.

One scale, in particular, caught her eye. It was the second line down, which appeared to be around three-quarters of the way full, titled dopamine and followed by other chemicals. Dopamine, however, was the only word she knew of its effects. In a nutshell, it was a hormone that occurred naturally within the brain that induced a happy feeling. There was more to it than that, but that was the gist of it.

She clicked on the scale and dragged it to the left so that it emptied completely.

Emily fell from the chair, crashing to the floor. She clutched at her head, as the pain rose to a blinding, uncontrollable level. It felt like a thousand knives were stabbing her behind the eyes at once.

She sat, writhing in agony before eventually, the pain became too much, and she passed out.

* * *

Emily opened her eyes.

She hadn't had a migraine this bad in, well, she couldn't even remember when. She thought that she had simply grown out of them, but here she was, in her boss's office, sprawled out on the floor with one of the worst she'd experienced.

Jeez, she was sprawled out on Samuel's floor.

Emily got to her feet, pushing herself up into the chair. She sat back and took a deep breath.

She squinted through the dimming but constant pain and picked up the mobile device. She re-entered the pin, clicked on her name, and saw that the dopamine levels were now depleted. The pain she felt in her head had dimmed from a thousand knives to just one or two - but the stabbing remained. She considered raising it slightly but thought against it.

Despite finding pain, she also found a sense of clarity.

Her single-minded and focused thoughts began to fall away, like a distant feather slowly making its way to the floor. She began to think of her mother, her disgrace of a father, and her friends from a lifetime ago. She hadn't seen anyone from her previous life for so long.

Tears welled up.

No, she thought to herself, this is no time to succumb to feeling sorry for herself: she couldn't simply sit here until Samuel came and found her. What would she say to him? How would he react? She'd seen some of the people downstairs that he'd locked away. She'd seen the people that he'd taken kicking and screaming.

And Emily had allowed it.

Emily considered destroying the device, but for the time being, thought it wise to turn it off and place it in her pocket. She collected the black key card, pushed the drawer back into position, and stood up as quickly as her tired legs would allow.

She needed some painkillers, and as soon as she'd returned everything exactly as she'd found it, she'd have to collect some.

Emily positioned the chair back at the desk, in the position that she remembered seeing it. She dusted the armrests and checked it from across the room. Perfect. She opened the door and exited the room.

"Oh, mornin' Miss Camberhsam." A female voice approached from the other side of the hall. "What are you doing here so early? Emily recognised the high-pitched nosiness of the receptionist instantly.

"Good morning." Emily attempted to collect herself as best as possible. She turned and looked at Amanda, who was approaching the desk. Trying her best to seem professional, she responded.

"I was just looking for Samuel."

Amanda sat down, placed her bag on the floor, and began applying her lipstick. It was a hot pink colour.

"But you know he's not scheduled to be in his office until nine."

"Of course. Silly me."

Amanda paused her application.

"Are you alright, Miss Cambersham?"

"Me? Oh yes, just a bit of a headache."

Emily felt the beady eyes of interrogation upon her. That, and the throbbing in her head caused her to wince.

"Strange. You do look a bit under the weather."

"Yes, perhaps I should head home," she suggested.

"Yeah, maybe."

Emily began to move away but was stopped in her tracks after only a single step.

"I'll just let Samuel know you were here."

Amanda put down her lipstick; only half applied, picked up the phone, pressed a single button and waited for an answer.

Panic ran through Emily's veins. The feeling was alien to her. She couldn't remember the last time she felt this vulnerable, this scared, and most importantly, this threatened.

"Mr Candrade?" Amanda began.

As thoughts from her past threatened to rise to her conscious, she stepped towards Amanda and pressed down the button to end the call.

"Hey!" Amanda interjected.

"That won't be necessary," Emily instructed.

Emily took the phone from the receptionist and placed it back down.

Amanda shot a fierce look in Emily's direction.

"Where is Samuel now?" she asked.

"I don't work for you," Amanda replied.

"No, but you know who I am." Emily calmed herself; playing the role she had been playing all these years.

"But something's not right. Hey, why were you in his office?"

"I was looking for Samuel," Emily replied calmly.

"Well then, let me give 'im a call."

"No."

Amanda reached for the telephone, but Emily grabbed her wrist before she could do so. In response, Amanda rose to her feet and tried to overpower Emily. This was the last thing she needed as her head pounded, causing her vision to darken.

Emily and Amanda grappled, moving away from the desk. Emily felt something rise within her, a primal urge to push this young, attractive girl down to the ground. Luckily for Emily, Samuel liked his receptionists petite.

Biting through the pain, she removed her right hand from the grapple and pulled on Amanda's hair. She shrieked and buckled to a kneeling position.

Without thinking, Emily dragged the receptionist by the hair towards a door. As she did so, she struggled to catch her breath.

The annoying receptionist who often shot her a snarky glance, or a fake smile, was now on her arse being dragged by her hair towards an open closet.

Amanda kicked and screamed. Luckily there didn't seem to be anyone else in yet. It must still be early. Emily had to hand it to her, she was committed to serving Samuel, but she also wondered why she was so loyal. Perhaps it was the money.

"Get in there."

Emily dragged Amanda to her feet and pushed her into a small broom closet - which she assumed must have been used previously by some overnight cleaners.

"No, no!" Amanda screamed as she fell backwards over an empty mop bucket.

Before there was an opportunity, Emily slammed the door closed and with all of her weight, forced herself back to prevent an escape. She felt the door buckle as Amanda pulled at the handle and pushed with all of her might.

"Help, help!" Amanda's muffled screams echoed through the hallway. "Help!"

Emily needed to do something, anything. She looked over at the desk, was there a key to lock the door? No, even if there was, she'd escape. Time was ticking by, and it wouldn't be too long until someone came within earshot.

"Help!" Amanda cried.

Emily thought about Amanda's blind loyalty. Something clicked. She felt around in her pockets and removed the electronic mobile device.

It was a long shot, but she was on it, so perhaps Amanda was.

Emily entered the pin, scrolled down the list – realising she wasn't aware of Amanda's last name. Scrolling, scrolling, stop. There was an Amanda.

She clicked on the name.

"Please," Emily prayed out loud - covered only by Amanda's cries for help.

The dopamine level was almost full, similar to hers when she first saw the device. It was worth a shot. She slid the slider all the way down to zero.

The crying stopped.

A thud echoed from the other side of the door as Amanda's body hit the floor.

Emily eased her weight from the door gradually. She opened the closet and saw Amanda lying there, pink lipstick still only half-applied. Emily closed the door, sprinted to the reception desk, and found a ring of keys in the top drawer.

Emily tried a few of them unsuccessfully, but on the fourth attempt, the closet locked. She slid down the door, exhausted. Her migraine threatened to overwhelm her conscious, but the adrenaline levels were keeping it at bay for now.

Rising to her feet, she walked over to the reception. She hid the keys in the bottom drawer. That would keep Amanda at bay for a while at least. Besides, when she came to, perhaps she'd see things a little differently.

Emily straightened her clothes, pulled her fringe away from her face, and walked over to the elevators.

Next, she needed to know what secrets the black key card was hiding.

24

Jan 8th, 2040

The tight fabric restraints pulled at John's wrists. He stood upright, tied to the wall in a small, glass-fronted cell. He was able to move and kick his feet, but nothing more.

The desire to call for help had long left him. He had tried for what seemed like hours, and all it had done was leave him with a sore throat, an increasing thirst, and an intensifying rage.

He took a few deep breaths as he tried to remember what Nora told him - focus on his breathing. Breathe in, breathe out, breathe in, breathe out. He did so, and even though it only helped a little, a little was enough for the moment.

How had it been so long since he last saw his wife? How had he left it so long? Time continued to spiral at a rapid pace, and with each passing day, his belief that his wife and child were better off without him grew stronger. He had been selfish. He had been afraid. Then, before he knew where the time had gone, years had passed.

John had no recollection of how he came to wake up in this cell, or who had imprisoned him. The last thing he remembered was reaching The United World headquarters and investigating a rear entrance.

It didn't matter, anyhow. This was what he felt like he deserved. He was living meal to meal, and surviving day to day, He'd pushed it one step too far, and it had finally caught up with him. It was only a matter of time. It was quite ironic looking back - John believed that the government was tracking his every move years ago, but when comparing it to today – especially the destructive happenings of the last week – it was like night and day.

His mind skipped. Anger rose, followed quickly by a dull acceptance. Loving memories came only seconds before a wave of self-loathing set in. He was trapped, and the punishment came as much from within.

John was so caught up in his inner turmoil that he didn't notice a figure walking up to the glass door and pushing it open.

"Ah, Mr Loche," a male voice interrupted.

John snapped from his daze. He pulled his head from his chest and looked forward. Whatever drugs were in his system must not have fully worn off, because his sight was a little hazy. He could, however, make out three figures in front of him.

The man in the middle approached him and spoke.

"Hello, Mr Loche? Are you with us?"

John tried to focus on the smartly dressed man in grey in front of him.

"Who are you?"

John squinted harder but struggled to make out his features.

"Surely, you must remember me?"

John tried to place his voice, it was one he recognised, but the fog in his mind prevented him from making the connection.

"Well, if you don't remember who I am, perhaps you'll recognise my family?"

Thoughts echoed within the chamber.

"No? Well, let me refresh your memory in that case. Darling, why don't you say hello to our guest?"

"Hello," Nora said, shyly.

He would recognise that sweet voice anywhere. The way she said hello reminded him of how she'd answer the phone to a stranger.

"Nora!" he gasped.

"Nice to meet you."

"Nora!" he fought the restraints keeping him in place, contracting his large arms, with all the strength he could muster. "Nora, it's me! It's John!"

"John?" Nora asked.

"An old friend," Samuel added.

Nora made a sound of acknowledgement, like she would when she'd solved an answer on a crossword in the paper.

"What the fuck have you done?" John shouted. He noticed saliva trickle down his chin. "I'm your husband."

"Now, John. They don't know-"

"Dad?" Reece asked, standing in place.

"No, son, he's trying to confuse you." The blurry figure turned to the boy, only a little shorter than him.

"Reece?" John's heart fluttered. "Reece, is that you?"

"Dad?" Reece asked again, ignoring the pleas of Samuel, but remaining monotonous with his question.

"Yes, son, it's your dad."

"What are you-"

The blurry figure of his son hit the floor.

"Reece!" John shouted.

"Calm down Mr Loche," John instructed. "He's simply taking a bit of a nap. I think he needs a little more time in the lab... a few more alterations are required."

"Nora!"

The figure that began to come into focus was the object of his affection, there was no doubt. Even before the blurriness left, he could picture her face – down to every single detail.

"Nora, help me!" he shouted again.

"Now, now, if you don't settle down, you'll have to take a nap yourself... and where's the fun in that?"

"You son of a bitch," John retorted. "When I get out of here-"

Samuel's laugh cut John's threat short.

"Nora?" John questioned one more time, to no avail.

"Is he okay, dear?" Nora asked, but not directed towards him, but to Samuel.

"Quiet," Samuel ordered, to which Nora immediately obeyed. "Go and find someone to find Miss Cambersham. Instruct her to take our boy to the lab for his shots."

"Like holiday jabs?" she asked, without expression.

"Exactly. Now be a good wife and do as you're told."

"Yes, darling. Where are we going on holiday?"

"I don't know," Samuel answered shortly.

"We're going back to Cornwall," John interjected. "We're going to rent that little campervan again like we did before we had Reece. We'll walk along the beach, spend the evenings with a bottle of wine, watching the waves crash against the shore."

"That'd be nice," Nora answered.

"I love you," John whispered.

"I love you too." Nora trailed off, as the figure of his wife exited the room.

"Interesting," Samuel considered.

The figure walked closer. His face came fully into focus. It was a face John recognised, of course, from news articles, and media coverage – he was only surpassed by Emily Cambersham in terms of public recognition. Perhaps she would be here soon also. He was aware of how much power these two individuals would have – for all intents and purposes, they were untouchable.

"I thought she would have forgotten everything, but perhaps I didn't go deep enough."

"What did you do?" John asked.

"All I did was give her the life she deserves. I gave her a fresh start, a loving family, a steady home."

"You bastard."

Samuel began to laugh, but before he had the chance to fully open his mouth, John forced all of the spit in his mouth explosively into his face.

The laugh became a scowl.

Samuel reached into his pocket, retrieved a handkerchief, and brushed the saliva from his face.

"You're a baboon, no wonder your wife left you," Samuel spat in return.

"I'll-" John began to raise his voice.

"If you do that again I'll kill the boy."

John's words fell away from his tongue. He lowered his head in the direction of his felled son.

"Now, let me say that I don't want to, but I wouldn't recommend forcing my hand." Samuel looked directly into John's eyes. "You know how we found him? The poor boy was just looking around outside for a way in, oblivious to the hundreds of security cameras. Well, like father like son, I guess."

"What did you do to him?"

"The boy? I merely gave him a little boost... and a tune-up." Samuel began. "Originally, he wasn't a part of my vision, but to give Nora something so dear to her heart... you know, I still wasn't sure what to do when he arrived, but when she recognised him, I knew I had to take him in... I'm a bit of a softie, you see?"

John's neck hurt from holding his head upright for so long, his ears hurt even more.

"What do you want?" he asked.

"I want what we all want. A united world, one where people can feel safe to walk the streets at night, a world without unnecessary murders and assaults, a world without crime, a world without poverty, without racism."

"And this is how you're going to do that?"

"I will do whatever needs to be done. It is all for the greater good."

"You and your people are killing millions - millions! Is that for the greater good?"

A blurred shadow in the distance caught John's eye for a second.

"Everyone had a choice. Comply and live with us or the alternative. Those that did not are now facing the ramifications of their decision."

"You don't even feel guilty, do you?"

"Why would I feel guilty? It was a free choice."

"A choice between death and mind control! Look at my son on the ground. Look what you've done to him. Doesn't that make you feel guilty, for fuck's sake? There is no choice!"

Samuel took a step forward until he was face to face with the man whom he held captive. John felt his eyes burn into the back of his head with intensity.

"I saved them."

John placed his feet together and stood up tall. He rose above Samuel by a few inches.

"You saved yourself," John returned the intense gaze. He noticed a female figure enter the cell and considered that this might be his final opportunity to talk. He would be heard. "You're a weasel. You're an excuse of a human being."

"I am your leader. I am your God. I can control whoever I want. Maybe I can even control you."

Samuel's forehead suddenly scrunched, and his eyes rolled back into his head. He collapsed to the floor.

"You can't control me anymore." Emily Cambersham stood inches away from John, holding the needle that had pierced Samuel's neck.

"What?" John began to ask, but before he finished, Emily was already untying his restraints.

"Please trust me. We have to get out of here."

John nodded. His left arm fell to his side, followed shortly after by his right. The moment that the restraints left his wrists, he jumped across the floor and crouched down by his son.

Reece and Nora were the only positive things he dreamt about; the distant possibility of seeing them again had kept him in this world. John cradled Reece's head in his arms. He thought back to the day he picked him up as a baby for the first time in the hospital. For the first time in many hardened years, tears found him.

"Is he going to be okay?" John asked.

Emily searched Samuel's pockets.

"Did he inject him?"

"Yes."

"He should be fine; it's probably the same as what I used."

John struggled to find his breath. He wanted to punch Samuel's face into the ground, to smash and smash until nothing was left. He rose to his feet.

Emily held up a hand to him. She removed a black mobile device from Samuel's pocket, stood up, and stamped her high heel down on to the screen. The first stamp deflected off of the device, but the second cracked the screen. The third, fourth, and fifth dismantled it completely.

"Will you help me restrain him?" Emily asked.

His fist unclenched. What he really wanted was to kill him. But this was at least some form of retribution.

John nodded, and in one clean motion, scooped the middle-aged man to his feet. He held Samuel in a bear grip as Emily fastened each of his wrists to the wall.

"Let him go."

John released the body, and after a few unnatural jarring movements, Samuel came to a rest in the same shackles that John found himself in moments before.

Emily retrieved a lipstick from her pocket, she unscrewed the cap and wrote a message to him on the floor.

'YOU ARE NOT OUR GOD.'

The pink lipstick ran out.

"That will have to do." Emily turned to John and gestured towards Reece. "Can you carry him?"

John knelt down, picked up his son gently, and trying his best to bend from the knees, he picked up his scrawny, yet heavy and unconscious son.

Emily removed a device from her pocket, similar to the one that she had just destroyed.

"What's that?"

"I don't really know, but it seems to affect people somehow. Your son's name is Reece? Reece Loche?"

John nodded and watched as Emily scrolled through the device until she found Loche, Reece.

"What are you doing?"

"I'm lowering some of his chemical levels. I'm not sure what they all do, but I lowered mine, and here I am."

Emily was the public face of The United World, and now she was betraying the only person more powerful than her. It didn't make sense, but if anything, she had rescued him. He'd give her the benefit of the doubt for now.

"Be careful."

He watched Emily reduce one level to the left, and then another halfway.

"I need to research some of the effects, but I believe this first one is linked to his mood and behaviour."

"Is there one on there that links to memory?"

"I'm not sure," Emily responded truthfully.

If there was, he could get Nora back.

"What now?" John asked.

"We get out of here." Emily began to move towards the door.

"Wait. It's not safe out there."

"It will be for us. You didn't register, did you?"

John shook his head.

"That makes it complicated. I could see if I could fit you with a microchip. The lab technician should believe that you're a delayed registree."

"No fucking way."

He'd spent the last eighteen years living on edge for fear of the government. There was no chance in hell he'd let anyone put a microchip in him.

"Perhaps just installing it in your hand would be enough to avoid detection?"

"What if I carry it?" John asked, unwilling to move from his stance on the matter.

"If we just go to the lab, it will only take a second, and a very minor incision."

"No fucking microchip," John responded firmly.

Emily took a moment before responding.

"Very well, we can sow it into the seam of your shirt, or perhaps your boot. We'll need to test whether it works, though."

"Okay. I can carry it for now, though. Where to?"

"We need to go to the lab. However, if they see you, they'll know something is amiss. I should go by myself and meet you afterwards."

"I need to find my wife."

"Where is she?"

"She went to find you. Didn't you see her?"

"No." Emily thought for a moment before removing a black card from her pocket. "But I know where she might be."

After leaving the cell, John arrived a few minutes later at a heavy-looking security door, his biceps were burning from not only holding his son for so long, but also for being held in restraints. But he was Reece's father, and he would not put him down until he was safe. He pulled him up a little closer to his chest to relieve some of the pressure on his arms.

Emily wafted the black card against the keypad, and the door clicked open.

John pushed it open with his large boot, and Emily proceeded first.

"I'm sorry darling, I couldn't find anyone to help, so I came back here to make a start on the ironing. I hope you don't mind."

The sound of a glass smashing on the ground echoed through the space that John and Emily walked into.

John walked over to the sofa and placed Reece gently down. He positioned him so that he was sitting.

"Reece?" Nora power walked over towards him. "Did his injections do this to him?"

"Yes," Emily replied. "They had an adverse effect."

"Oh no. Will he be alright?"

"Your son will be fine."

"Oh, good." Nora turned to face the shattered glass. "Oh, I am so sorry, please take a seat, I don't want you to stand on any of the glass."

Nora scurried away out of sight.

"She doesn't know who I am."

John walked around, taking in the place where his wife seemed to be living. It was modern but lacked all personality and familiarity - apart from this one picture.

John walked over to the photo of Nora, Reece and Samuel.

He turned it around, slid the back section off, pulled the image out and ripped Samuel's face from the photo. He folded it and placed it in his pocket, placing the photo frame face down on the table.

Nora came back into the room, holding a brush and pan. She quickly cleaned the broken glass without a fuss.

John examined her every move. She worked efficiently, and without any comment. That wasn't the Nora he knew; hell, if she had to clean a sink full of dishes, he'd hear about it for hours.

"Nora?" John asked.

Nora finished sweeping the last fragment up and then looked up in John's direction.

"Yes?"

"Don't you recognise me?"

"Of course I do," Nora replied.

A glimmer of hope radiated through John's being.

"You were in the cell with Samuel."

The glimmer vanished.

"I'm so sorry, I've not even offered you a drink, you must be thirsty. Would you like a tea? Coffee? Miss Cambersham?"

Emily shook her head. John stood still.

"Why don't you fetch Reece some water for when he wakes up?" Emily suggested.

"That's a great idea," Nora walked over towards the kitchen.

Emily walked to John's side.

"I don't understand why she can't remember, but perhaps there's a solution on here?"

Emily removed the mobile device once more and began to inspect it.

"Here you are, darling." Nora walked over to Reece's side and placed a glass of water on the table in front of him.

Emily loaded up Nora's profile on the device. She noticed the dopamine levels were raised to their highest.

"Would you sit down next to Reece for a moment?"

Nora did as she was asked.

Emily flicked the switch all the way to the left. Nora began twitching and flailing on the sofa. John ran over to her side.

"That seems to be the normal reaction," Emily stated, a little too business-like for John's liking.

John held Nora in his aching arms. He noticed the twitching calming as she began to fade into unconsciousness. When she stopped completely, John held her in his arms and squeezed her tightly to him. He laid her back gently in the chair, seated next to his son.

"Will she be okay?" he asked.

"She should be," Emily responded. "If you stay here, I'll be back shortly with the chip."

"But what if she wakes up?"

"I'm sure you can handle her."

Emily walked towards the large door, tapped the black card on the panel, exited and closed the door behind her.

"But what if she doesn't remember me?"

John sat on the couch opposite his unconscious family and prayed that this was the reunion he had hoped for.

25

Jan 8th, 2040

David Stern prepared to address the world. The YouTube channel that Marc and Gary had built was the best platform for his message. The two Londoners had agreed to give him complete access. Not only did they need to spread the load in terms of responsibility should anything happen to them, but the face of the resistance needed to be someone that the public could get behind. David Stern was a respected talk show host, who was used to being in the public eye, so they thought if anyone was the right fit, it was him.

Whilst Marc was proud of building the resistance online with his best friend, he knew that he was no spokesperson. If the public was to come together and revolt against the government, worldwide, the spokesperson needed to be someone with a voice, someone who could rally the troops.

It turned out that David was in the right place at the right time. He had joined the chat previously, and the messages that Marc looked through, even then, showed that people believed he was the brains behind the whole operation. And while it bruised their egos, there were more important things to consider.

So, instead of leading the stream this afternoon, they had released the reins. Today they were mere viewers, along with tens of thousands of others who flocked to the stream.

Marc and Gary still had access to the analytics and moderation part of the stream, so, as the countdown to the live stream began, they watched the messages flood in. As always, there were too many to read in real-time, but Marc would look over some of them later. It had become not only a hobby of his but an obsession.

"Thirty seconds. Want another drink?" Marc asked.

"Got any beers?" Gary asked.

Marc laughed. It had been a few days since they'd had any alcohol left in the house. They hadn't dared to venture outside since their lockdown began.

"Think we've got some squash left?"

"No bourbon?"

"'Fraid not."

"I'm alright then."

The basic countdown timer, that Gary had created in a few minutes on a video editing software, approached the final few seconds.

"Alright then. Let's see what was so important." Gary said, as the countdown hit zero.

The United World

David Stern sat in the same room as his previous video chat on the stream. He looked tired, but there was a steely determination resonating from the way he spoke.

"Hello everyone. I hope you don't mind me taking over the stream today," David began. "Today is an important day. Today is the first day where we plan a retaliation. It's been over a week since the government first threatened us, and since then they have killed millions. It's not a conspiracy theory, it's not bollocks, it's the truth. I imagine most of you have seen it with your own eyes, but we know that the government is behind the deaths of innocent people across the world. I, for one, will not stand for it, and I hope every one of you watching will join me in rising up. We need to take back our neighbourhoods, take back our towns and cities, and eventually take back the world."

Bloody hell, Marc thought, this guy didn't half know how to deliver a monologue. He sat in awe, glued to the screen.

"I have created a base for myself and several others. I implore you to do the same. Make sure that the people are those whom you can trust, and whatever you do, are not registered and part of The United World. I believe the first step in taking on the government is to create centralised bases, safe spaces in each location for people of the resistance to call a temporary home."

David took a breath before continuing.

"Now, to start with, the bases need to be small. If there's too many in one single space, it will be seen as an easy target. However, if you can create small bases of ten to twenty, then there is hope."

Marc looked at Gary, who was leaning back in his chair.

"We've done alright, just the two of us," Gary mused.

"Might not be a bad idea though," Marc countered.

"I hope you don't mind me taking the reins. I'd just like to say thank you to the two founders of this channel, who have given me access today. Without the two of you, this platform wouldn't exist."

The ego-stroking felt nice, especially coming from a celebrity – even during these difficult times.

"The forums linked will be our home for discussion. All reports, sightings, information, strategies, and the like, is to be posted there. On there, I'm told there's a team of moderators, whose job it is to certify the information. Once certified, it will be made available to the public. Please check the forum daily - and use a VPN at all times."

David took a moment to sip a glass of water beside him, which came into and returned out of shot.

"So, the first item of today's meeting is to form small bases with trusted individuals. Secondly, as far as we're aware, the registered members of The United World are far less active at night. Any movements outside of your properties should be restricted to those times. The exact information can be found on the forum as to the safest times, but it may be a case of needing to adapt our sleeping schedules for the time being. And third, I just want to say keep your heads up high. No-one wanted to be in this situation, but like it or not, this is where we find ourselves; we are not only in a battle of life and death, but also in one to preserve hope and freedom. If we give in, life as we know it will surely be eradicated, and replaced by, well quite frankly, we'd be replaced by slaves. Because that's what those people out there are, they're slaves to the government, doing as they are told."

"He's not wrong," Gary spoke over the talk show host to Marc. "They are slaves."

"Well, I suppose if they don't have a choice?" Marc posed.

"That's a slave. Someone who's forced to obey without question."

"So, the registration. It was registering to become a slave?'"

Gary scrunched his shoulders.

"I guess so."

"Shit."

"Bet you're glad you didn't go now."

Gary and Marc turned their focus back to the speech being made by the new face of the resistance.

"Tonight, long after dark, I ask you to go out on the streets, but be careful - stick to the shadows, and engage with people who look in a similar position to you, from a safe distance. Form those connections, share supplies, and make sure to tell others about this news. Tonight will be the first step in forming a defence against the terrible acts of those who are supposed to protect us."

"Shall we go out tonight?" Marc asked.

"I dunno," Gary responded.

"We've been so safe and secure; it'd be good to have a little look?"

"I suppose you're right, and see if we can find some supplies at the same time."

"Could do." Marc sat back and listened to the ongoing speech.

"What you can expect on here from today are daily updates - with updates and next steps. The most important thing at the moment is the gathering of information and the validation of data. With that, we can start to recognise patterns, and from that, weaknesses. Once that happens, we shall have an opportunity to correct this. It won't be easy - in fact when we free ourselves from the shackles that have been placed around our necks, that day will go down as the most important in history. That is the magnitude of the situation. This is what we need to do, and this channel is going to be how we communicate moving forward, I hope-"

The screen turned black.

Marc and Gary looked at each other, dumbfounded.

"Refresh it," Marc suggested.

Gary refreshed the stream, but instead of being greeted by David, instead received a message:

'This video has been removed due to hateful speech that violates our terms and conditions.'

"Shit." Gary gasped. "Shit, shit, shit."

"What's happened?" Marc asked.

"It's down," Gary responded. He hit the keyboard in frustration. "Oh, no."

Gary clicked on the top right corner to go to the account profile. It opened their profile page for the resistance.

'Your account has been suspended for violating YouTube's terms and conditions. Please contact a member of the team for more information.'

"Damnit!" Gary leant back in his chair, crunching his hair in his hands.

"What do we do?" Marc asked.

"I dunno. I guess they found us." Gary leant forward on his knees.

"Check the forum," Marc suggested.

Gary entered the web address for the forum manually and clicked enter. To both of their relief, it was still online.

"Look, there's a new topic."

A topic at the top of the updates forum posted one second ago read 'YouTube channel removed. Stay tuned for updates.'

"Fuck," Gary sighed.

"Damn. I guess it was good while it lasted." Marc mused. "Quite a rush being a bit famous."

"We didn't even get any of the benefits."

"Whatcha mean?"

"Like, no girls throwing themselves over us, no free holidays in the Bahamas, that kinda thing. You know, like all the influencers get."

"Oh yeah." Marc thought for a second. "Well, if this is the new, you know, normal, we couldn't do any of that anyway."

The two friends sat in silence as realisation sank in. This could be their future for an extended time. And now, there was no internet platform to offer safety.

For the first time since lockdown, Marc felt alone.

"I guess, later on, we just go out and try and meet people?" Gary suggested.

"At least they'll recognise us."

"That's true. Hey?" Gary turned to Marc.

"What?"

"Maybe there'll be some chicks out there."

Marc felt a laugh rise up, but not enough so that it escaped. Instead, he smiled softly.

"Maybe, mate. Maybe."

Marc patted the shoulder of his friend, who sat rubbing his eyes in distress.

"It'll be alright. Should we email David?"

Gary focused back on the screen.

"Good idea."

"Alright then."

With Marc's help, Gary wrote an email to David explaining the situation. They suggested that the forum was now the home of the resistance, and for him to be the face of the fight against the government. Tonight, they, like many others, would all go outside and try to make alliances with those nearby – and then tomorrow they would report back.

After all, tomorrow was another day.

* * *

Despite sitting on a comfortable sofa next to his family, John was on edge. He'd been sitting, waiting now for what felt like well over an hour. What could be taking Emily so long? At least his wife and son were sitting next to him, and in here, at least for the time being, they were safe.

John closed his eyes and allowed the memories to find him.

He thought back to the day that he was arrested by the police. John remembered his skin crawling as the officer repeated the information that they had on him and his family: it triggered his anxiety. If anything, he realised now that he overreacted – maybe he even needed to see a shrink. He knew it was his fault, and not returning to his family was the worst mistake he had ever made. It was a mistake that he'd have to live with for the rest of his life.

Reece groaned.

John turned and saw his son moving slowly like he was waking from a long nap.

Whilst being out of his life, Reece had grown into an impressive man. He recognised parts of himself, especially in the jawline and areas of his face. The main difference was the scrawniness of Reece in comparison to his bulkier physique.

Reece opened his eyes.

"Dad?" he said groggily.

"Reece. Are you okay?"

John didn't want to scare his son away; he also knew that he had little right to do much else than sit still – despite wanting to move across and wrap his arms around his son.

"Dad? Is that you?" Reece's eyes seemed to be focusing on his surroundings. "Where am I?"

Reece started to shift frantically in his seat.

"Where am I?" he asked, louder.

"It's alright, son. You're safe now."

Reece examined his surroundings. It seemed as if he was just as paranoid as John.

"Where are we?"

"We're at The United World."

"What?" Reece rose to his feet, his legs almost buckling beneath him. "We need to get out of here."

"It's alright." John stood beside him.

"Mum?" Reece looked at his unconscious mother. "MUM!?" he shouted, edging past John.

Reece placed his hands on his mother's shoulders and shook her. Her head wobbled back and forth without any support from her neck muscles, before sliding forward to rest of her chest.

"She's sleeping. She should be awake soon."

John wanted to put a supportive hand on Reece's shoulder. Instead, he stood behind him and waited for his son to turn to face him.

After a few moments, Reece turned and examined John's face.

"Dad?" Reece asked again.

John allowed himself a small smile.

"Son."

John could guess what Reece was thinking. He noticed uncertainty appear in his eyes - he recognised it instantly from glances of himself in reflections that he'd seen many times before.

"It's alright. I'm here." John said.

"Are you sure we're safe?" Reece asked.

"I think so. As safe as we can be." John answered as truthfully as he could.

John moved his arms out a little to invite the beginning of a hug. Instead, Reece moved and sat back on the sofa. He rubbed his temples as John chose to join him sitting down.

"What happened? I don't remember." Reece asked.

"All I know is that I came here looking for you and your mother, and when I got here, I was ambushed. They held me as a prisoner, and the worst thing..." John wondered how truthful to be; however, he saw no reason to lie to his son. He deserved that at least. "The worst thing, was this man, Sam?"

"Samuel?" Reece suggested.

"Yeah, Samuel. The piece of shit had you and your mother by his side. Only, your Mom didn't recognise me. She'd completely forgotten who I was. I almost gave up, but you..."

"What?" Reece leant forward, closing the gap between father and son.

"You recognised me, Reece. You saw me."

Reece leant back against the cushioned support and held his head in his hands.

"I don't remember that."

"And then, Samuel injected you with something, and you passed out."

Reece sat silently. After a while, he turned to his father.

"How did we get here?"

"Someone saved me."

"Who?"

As if on cue, the door opened. Emily walked in.

"I've got your chip; sorry it took so long."

"You!" Reece jumped to his feet and ran over in Emily's direction. "I'll kill you."

"No. Reece!"

John jumped to his feet, but he was no match for the rapidness of youth. He ran after his son, who reached Emily first, grabbing her by her blouse.

"Why did you do this?" He shouted at her. "Dad, I got her!"

John caught up to them. He leant on his knees to catch his breath.

"Son, she's here to help us."

"What?" John noticed Reece's hands trembling.

John placed a hand on his son's arm, instinctively.

"Please. It's true."

Reece's clenched jaw softened slightly.

"I'm sorry, Reece," Emily said. "I cannot change the things I have done, but I can help to make things better."

"Why?" Reece held on to her.

"I could tell you every reason. I was drugged, for one. I was also manipulated and lied to for another. Yet I feel that even so, I was partly responsible for all of this. I can only apologise. I had no clue of the scale that Samuel was creating."

"She was the one that freed me."

"She was?"

"She was the one that saved my life... and yours."

Reece uncurled his fingers. Emily's blouse slipped through his fingers.

"I'm ever so sorry," Emily said.

"Did you get the chip?" John asked.

"Yes, it was more difficult than expected, however. Each chip has to be registered to an individual. As I didn't want to invade your privacy, I had to find a recently deceased individual, remove them from the deceased list, and register that information to your chip."

John processed the information.

"I also had to match it with some DNA in the morgue."

"What do you mean?"

"Some things are better left unsaid."

John nodded.

Emily walked around a stationary Reece. She handed John the brand-new microchip. She walked to the sofa across from Nora and sat down.

John looked at the small microchip in the palm of his hand. It was smaller than the one he remembered from Reece's birth, but it still generated the same amount of dread. He placed it in his pocket for now, knowing full well that as soon as possible he'd get rid of it.

"Come on, son." John placed a hand on his son's shoulder. Reece turned slowly and joined John on the same sofa as Nora.

"I also managed to alter the registration information of Nora and Reece. That way, if anyone looks for them directly, they'll be impossible to find."

"What about you?"

Emily shook her head.

"Why not?"

"I have unfinished business here. I was the one who introduced the Public Protection Bill - perhaps I can halt it."

"So, we'll be safe? Outside?" John asked.

"I believe so," Emily answered. "But I would still suggest remaining away from any means of surveillance and ensure that you're hard to identify."

Nora began to stir.

Reece noticed before anyone else.

"Mum!"

The person John recognised as his wife shot up from her seating position and defensively jumped to her feet. She held her hands in front of her.

"Where's my Samuel?"

"He's gone." John held his hand in front of him to indicate that they meant no threat.

"What have you done with him?"

"Mum?" Reece asked, rising to his feet at the same time as his dad. Reece approached his mother.

"You. Did you do something to him? It was all fine until you came back."

"What?" Reece asked, shocked.

"She doesn't know what she's saying. Don't listen to her." Emily said from a distance.

"Miss Cambersham. Where is Samuel?" Nora approached her.

"Listen, dear." Emily reached out and put an arm around her shoulder. "I hate to be the one to tell you this, but Samuel is gone."

"What?"

"He's left you."

"No, he would never."

"He didn't deserve you."

Nora remained still.

"I wonder if you can handle the truth?"

"Samuel always told me the truth."

"Not so, my dear. Come, sit down."

Emily led Nora to the sofa and sat her down opposite herself, John and Reece.

"This is your son. His name is Reece."

Nora remained still. Her eyes traced their faces.

"This is your husband, John."

"John?" Nora asked. "No. No. My husband is Samuel. Samuel!" she became agitated.

"Remember Cornwall," John said. "Remember walking hand in hand. We got soaked because we walked too far, and then it chucked it down with rain."

Nora's eyes processed the information.

"I don't know."

Whilst she didn't vocalise the truth, John could see her posture relaxing.

"I am your husband. I know that I've been gone for too long, and, well… I'm just so, so damn sorry." John looked at Reece. "Both of you, I let you down."

"But, what about Samuel?" she asked.

"He's kept you here," Emily answered. "I don't know how long. You've been his personal project, if you will."

John felt the anger rise inside of him. He fought it down - after all, this was all his fault.

"Please come with us," Reece begged. "We can get out of here and be a family."

"I don't know," Nora replied.

Emily walked over to Nora.

"Listen to me. Samuel is gone, he's had to go away. He wants you to be happy. He would want you to go with your son and keep him safe."

A tear fell from Nora's eye. She nodded.

Emily helped her to her feet.

"But you are not my husband." Nora pointed in John's direction.

He deserved that. Even if it came from a place of untruth. Even if it hurt more than any weapon could. He earned every moment.

"But he will always be your son... our son," John replied.

Nora shook her head. She walked over to Reece.

"Mum!" he said, muffled by her arms wrapping around him.

At least Reece and Nora had found each other, at least they were safe.

"You'll come with us?" Reece asked.

"Okay," Nora tentatively replied.

Emily opened the door.

"I can only apologise for my actions up to this point. I hope that, one day, I can make it up to you."

"Where do we go?" John asked.

"I know somewhere," Reece replied. "One thing first, though." He pulled at his collar. "Let me get my old clothes back on first. I can't stand this thing." He pulled at the collar of his shirt.

John smiled in his direction. He was his father's son.

26

Jan 8th, 2040

Reece and his family walked through the streets of London. They couldn't run towards the screams of those in need, and it tore him apart – there were just too many people they thought were registered, and far too few of them.

They'd witnessed, in their eyelines, men and women, old and young, being brutally murdered as they walked. They kept their distance but could not avoid the lifeless bodies that impeded their path. Reece shuddered at the mere thought of this happening worldwide.

Reece turned a corner and crossed over a roundabout. No cars appeared to be on the streets, except for the occasional driverless bus containing a handful of people going about their day as normal.

"Did Samuel do anything to you?" John asked Nora after a long period of silence.

"He only cared for me," came the reply.

His father left the questioning there.

Reece's heart filled with the smallest amount of joy when the desolate warehouse came into sight.

"This way," he instructed.

Nora followed closely behind, while John followed last. Reece noticed that he was keeping an eye on their surroundings.

As they walked, Reece and John covered their faces as best they could. The two of them hunched their shoulders and pulled their tops up towards their faces, trying to at least cover their mouth and nose somewhat. Nora wasn't quite so concerned. However, she was worried about the cold air.

"Is this where we're going?" she asked.

"Come on."

Reece walked across the open car park.

A dog barked in the distance.

"Home!" Reece shouted and ran towards the shelter in front.

Home bound towards him like a leaping gazelle.

"Home!"

The two met in the middle of the car park.

Home leapt from the floor into the midsection of Reece, knocking the air from his lungs, and his feet from under him. He toppled backwards.

Reece tried to catch his breath - from the air that had left his lungs, and the tongue that lashed at his face.

"Get off!" Reece wriggled underneath the paws of his loyal companion. "Get off!" he laughed.

Reece tussled Home's face and managed to sit up. Home nuzzled in underneath his armpit but continued to try to lick him.

"Are you alright?" Nora asked, leaning down to check on her son.

"Who's that?" John asked as he approached.

"This is Home, my dog." Reece laughed again as Home's tongue managed to find his neck. He then tried to lick Nora, who bounced back upright.

"Home, huh?" John asked, peering out towards the warehouse in front of them.

"He won't bite," Reece assured. "Not unless you deserve it."

John walked closer and held his hand out for Home to sniff it, before tussling the fur on his neck.

"How long has he been with you?" John asked.

"He's always been here, longer than me."

"And where exactly are we?"

Reece rose to his feet, petted Home on the head, and started walking towards the boarded entrance of the warehouse where he had laid his head for as long as he could remember. His family followed close by.

"This is where I live."

He couldn't see his father's face, but he knew that hearing that must have hurt him.

"It's okay, it's better inside."

Reece walked to the plank that protected the inside of the shelter from the elements. He pulled it apart, and before he could do anything, Home jumped through.

Nora and John proceeded through the gap, with Reece following last. He replaced the plank, and the three of them were greeted by near darkness.

"Follow me," Reece said as he and Home bounded inwards, away from the only source of a nearby light source.

He could hear Nora and John muttering to each other behind him. The fact that they were even talking to each other filled him with hope.

Before his parents had time to argue, a distant flicker lit the path ahead. They approached the roaring fire and the community of the homeless.

"Reece!" Mary shouted as she saw him walk through the opening. "Did you find them?"

Mary wrapped her arms around him.

"Did you... shave?" she asked, as she took another look at him. "And you smell really good!"

As she let him go, Reece simply gestured behind him. Nora and John walked in.

"Hello," John said formally. Nora remained silent.

"Nora?" Mary asked. "Nora, is that you?"

"Ma- Mary?" she asked tentatively.

"Oh, my God. It is you!"

Mary released her grasp around Reece and ran towards Nora, meeting her with an enormous hug.

"I've missed you."

"Mary?" Nora asked again.

John stood, waiting patiently. Reece walked up beside him, as did Home. Together they studied Nora as she talked to her former friend.

"How are you, my dear? Oh, how I've missed you."

"I- I haven't seen you for years," Nora thought aloud.

"So many years. I'm sorry he ended up here, but I've kept him safe."

"Who?"

"Your boy. Reece."

The United World

Reece fidgeted, unsure as to where to look as Mary gestured towards him. He saw John and Home staring at each other.

"Why was Reece here?" Nora asked.

"You told me to keep him safe."

"I did?" she asked.

"Don't you remember?"

Nora shook her head.

Mary's face dropped.

"It's okay, dear. You left Reece with me, remember, when you went to find John."

Nora looked towards John and then back to Mary.

"Don't you remember?"

Nora shook her head.

"You left Reece with me when he was, I can't remember how old now?"

"Four," Nora said.

"That's right. So, you remember?"

Nora shook her head, wincing.

"I remember his birthday," Nora said. "I remember him chasing his ball."

"Good."

Nora held her head.

"I remember, leaving." She gritted her teeth. "I did. I left him. Didn't I?"

Nora grasped her head. Reece watched as she stumbled over her next word, and her eyes rolled backwards.

"Nora!" John jumped over to her side, quicker than Reece could react. He caught her as her knees buckled.

"I've got her," John said, lying her down on the sodden ground below their feet. "Can someone get me a pillow and water? Reece?"

Home whined in Nora's direction.

Reece nodded. He ran towards where his bed was set up a few nights before. Exactly as he left it. He scurried through a plastic bag of his left-behind stash - a few cans of beer, crisps, chocolate biscuits, chewing gum, ah a bottle of Ribena. That would do. He grabbed the drink and his single pillow from his bed.

"Here you go." Reece ran, pillow first, back over to his family. He placed the pillow underneath his mother's head, without a care for how muddy and damp it'd get and handed the purple bottle to John.

"Has this happened before?" Mary asked.

John shook his head.

"It might be the chip," he suggested.

"What?" Mary asked.

"She's got a microchip in there" John pointed to the side of her head. "One that the government put in. I think it's blocking her memories, or got rid of them, or it's doing something."

Reece had no reason to disagree.

"She passed out before, so did Reece, and they were fine when they woke up. Maybe we shouldn't get her to try to remember anything else for the moment." John said.

Reece placed a hand on his shoulder. John knew that meant that she wouldn't remember anything about him, or their past together.

John shrugged the hand away and scooped up Nora in one swift motion.

"Where's your bed?" John asked. "I, er, do you have a bed?"

"Yeah, follow me." Reece picked up the pillow from the ground and the bottle of Ribena that John had left behind.

Reece led them to his only plot of personal space he'd ever known. He quickly felt uneasy about the beer cans on show and the empty food packets that were sitting around the bed. He quickly kicked those to the side as John and Mary followed him. Home had his own intentions, as he walked over and sat by the fire.

Reece placed the pillow back on the bed and collected the cover. John laid Nora down in a more comfortable setting, and Reece set the cover across her for warmth – although the fire was offering support as well.

John looked at Nora for a moment as Reece waited to hear his thoughts.

"Let's let her rest."

Reece nodded.

"We can sit with Home," Reece suggested. "By the fire."

"Alright," John replied.

Before they left, Reece reached into his bag and collected two beers.

"Hey, er Dad… you want one?" Reece smiled.

"No thanks, son." John smiled back.

Reece put one of the beers back but then thought better of having one for himself. He left them both behind.

Reece gave his mother a kiss on the cheek, before leaving her to rest and joining Home by the fire.

"So, this is where you stay?" John asked Reece as they sat.

Reece felt the heat dance across his face.

"Yeah, I've been here with Mary as long as I can remember. Isn't that right?"

"Sure is," Mary replied.

"Why- how did you end up here?" John asked.

"It's a long story," Mary said. "Nora told us you warned her about the government. Then when she left to find you, and we didn't hear from her, we started getting these weird messages. I thought it was just a coincidence, but then I noticed these black cars on the street. Well, one day I was on the phone talking to a friend about it, and I kept hearing clicking and breathing on the other line. I started going paranoid, I tell ya. I knew I wasn't crazy, though." She stopped for a moment. "I wish I could have given him a better home."

John stared into the fire. The sound of wood cracking and popping filled the silence.

"You did better than me," he replied.

Home nuzzled into John's hand, flicking it upwards.

"He wants you to stroke him," Reece commented.

John lifted his hand and patted Home.

"He likes you," Mary commented. "Knows you're family."

Home circled around John's feet before lying down across both of them. John patted his chest before sitting back.

At that moment, there were so many questions that Reece wanted to ask. And there were even more thoughts that he wanted to scream. It was just too much.

Instead, he said nothing.

A few people gathered around the fire, taking in its warmth before Reece noticed something.

"Is it me, or are there less people here?"

Mary took a moment to respond.

"A lot have gone."

"Left?" Reece asked. "Where'd they go?"

Mary shrugged her shoulders.

"Could be dead," John answered. "Sorry to say."

The silence grew once more.

Reece unscrewed the Ribena bottle, took a sip and passed it to Mary, who, after taking a sip, handed it to John.

Reece heard footsteps approaching from behind. They all turned around.

George walked towards them, holding his arm up to his chest.

"Are you alright?" Mary rose to her feet and greeted him. She grabbed his arm and looked at it. "What are we going to do with you?"

"What happened?" Reece asked as he stood.

"Got a couple of them, only small, but they were proper comin' for me good." George began. He winced as Mary inspected his injury. "I couldn't do it, I couldn't get 'em first. But when they started comin' for me, I had to protect myself."

The flickers of the fire revealed George's bloodstained clothing, one item at a time.

"Come on. Let me see to ya. Again!" Mary said, leading George off. "Doesn't look too bad, few small cuts. Oh, and you see who's back?"

"Hey, buddy," George said to Reece. "Nice to see ya."

"And you."

"Who's that?" He asked as he was being led off.

"This is my Dad."

George offered a wave in John's direction as Mary escorted him away.

The father and son passed the time in silence. Two generations under a single roof.

Over time, the strength of the fire faded, as did Reece's desire to turn to shout and scream at his father for leaving him, and even more so for not protecting his mother. It would take many more evenings by the fire to forgive, but for now, he only needed to forget.

"Hi," Nora said tentatively, as she sat down in between John and Reece.

"Mum!" Reece hugged his mother as she sat next to him.

"How's the head?" John asked.

"It's a bit painful... but it's okay."

John's smile quickly faded.

Reece released his mother from his tight grasp.

"Are you sure you're okay? He asked.

Nora looked at Reece. She brought her hand up to his cheek. The warmth of her hands made his heart skip a beat.

"I'm getting there." She smiled.

Home barked, jealous of the attention.

"Come here, boy." Reece tapped his lap, causing Home to jump up at him and lick the air around his face.

He saw his parents laughing as he tried to push Home away from his face.

The terrors that were to find them. The journeys they needed to face. It was all background noise, and, for now, Reece could not care less. He was with his family.

And that was all he'd ever wanted.

* * *

The restraints that had held Samuel hung, empty.

The message on the floor had been ferociously scraped away, as by the claws of a wild beast.

Outside of the room, footsteps could be heard walking through the corridors.

The United World

The sound of shoes stomping on concrete stopped. Moments later, the elevator arrived with a short and pleasant alert. The doors opened and then closed shut.

On the twentieth floor, the elevator doors opened.

Samuel walked out, limping slightly, and rubbing at his wrists. His once polished shoes were scuffed, and the fronts covered with pink lipstick.

"Amanda!" He shouted. "Amanda!" he cried louder.

A noise came from the closet next to the reception desk.

"Amanda?" he said towards the closed door.

He tried the handle, but it was locked. He let out a frustrated scream and kicked the door, but they were made from sturdy material.

He walked over to the reception area and checked the top of the desk. It was immaculately clean, and there was no key. He tried the top drawer, throwing its contents out on to the ground, then the middle drawer, and finally the bottom. He found it.

Samuel grabbed the key, slammed the drawer shut, and paced over to the closet.

Frustrated by the inability to open the door, he slammed it with the palm of his hand. The scurrying noises from the other side stopped. He focused and unlocked the door on the next attempt.

Samuel pulled the door open but found himself greeted by something he didn't expect – his receptionist running at him, full force, with the pointed end of a broom handle.

The broom hit him in his chest, causing him to double over and fall to his knees.

"Oh, Samuel," Amanda said, only now realising who rescued her from the closet. "I thought it was that other bitch."

"Bitch?" Samuel wheezed.

"Emily. I've been locked in there for hours. I could have died, you know?"

"Emily?" he wheezed again, as he concentrated on catching his breath.

"And you. What the fuck did you do to me?" She dropped the broom and walked over so that she was standing over him. "Did you drug me or something?"

"What?"

"You fucking drugged me. You're sick, you know that?"

His lungs began to fill with air once more. He placed his hands on his knees and stood slowly.

"It's all your fault." She started to scream at him.

Samuel turned from her and walked towards his office. He felt a hand around his arm stop and twist him around.

"What the fuck did you do to me?" Amanda shouted at him. She raised her index finger and pointed it at his face, aggressively. "You fucking shitbag. You're no better than any of them out there."

"Listen, calm down." Samuel placed an arm on Amanda's waist, a place he had touched on multiple occasions before, so much so that it had become commonplace.

She tore his hand away from her waist.

"Don't you touch me!" she screamed.

Amanda shoved Samuel in the chest with two hands, forcing him to take a couple of steps backwards.

Samuel found himself laughing.

"What the fuck are you laughing at?"

"You."

"Fuck you."

"You're pathetic, just like all of them."

Amanda's face turned from a milky pale to a blistering bright red. She jumped in Samuel's direction. However, Samuel was quick for his age. He sidestepped, and Amanda fell face-first on to the floor with a crack.

Amanda stood, turned, and faced Samuel. Her jaw was beginning to swell, and her lip was bleeding.

Samuel laughed harder.

"Fook you," she yelled, "I'm going to th' police."

Amanda stormed off towards the elevator. He could stop her. He could show her how pathetic she really was. He could revel in her humanity.

The elevator door chimed, and with a final insult, she was gone.

Never mind.

He had more important issues to contend with.

Samuel straightened his tie and walked into his office.

He was immediately afraid that something had been taken, despite the perfect appearance. He bolted to his table, opened the top drawer, clicked the secret lever and opened the concealed hiding space. Please let his device be there. Damn it, it was gone.

He forced his clenched fists down on the rich mahogany table. Someone had turned on him, but who? He thought back to the command to bring Miss Cambersham to him. Surely it couldn't be her?

Samuel slammed the table again and leant forward to rest the side of his face against the cold, expensive tabletop.

He breathed.

He couldn't control his playthings anymore. He had selected them all for his own personal beta program: their data was his alone, and none of them were even on the system. However, he found the onrushing despair quickly leave him. He could create a new device, and he could begin a new test. They were mere ants to him, anyhow; they meant nothing.

Besides, he had the best scientists in the world at his fingertips. Who knew what was possible, given enough time and resources?

Samuel sighed, lifted his head and swivelled in his chair. He looked down on the people below.

"Don't worry, my people. It will all be fixed soon."

There was still a cleansing occurring. The world was becoming purer by the minute. And, for Samuel, this was just the beginning.

- END OF BOOK 1 -

Now they've found each other, will Reece, John and Nora find a way to stop Samuel, and The United World, once and for all?

Find out in Off the Grid, book 2 of The United World.

ACKNOWLEDGMENTS

Writing a book is scary. Not only because of the length of time it takes to create the plot and get words down, but because it's putting a piece of yourself out into the world. Like in many aspects of life, what makes it that much easier is having incredible people around you to help.

I'd like to thank a few people, without whom the book would not be anywhere near what it is today.

First of all, a gigantic thank you to my fiancée, **Sarah Carter,** for another great cover design. Not only that, but for the constant support and belief, and putting up with me when I've had my head stuck in the laptop.

Thank you to my advanced reader team – **Lucy Morris, Claire Piper and Tina Cavalier**. Your feedback has been invaluable. Hearing your thoughts as I wrote really helped to shape and strengthen the story.

Thank you to **Alison Carter** for, once again, giving the book a final read and pointing out a few (hundred) grammar mistakes - even one that was in this sentence.

Mum, **Dad**, and **all of my family and friends** (you know who you are), thank you - I couldn't do it without you.

And finally, **<u>thanks to you</u>**, the reader. Having you read these words means more than you could ever know, and I hope that you enjoy the rest of the series.

Craig Priestley is a fiction author based in London, UK. He graduated from the University of Greenwich in 2008 with a Bachelor of Arts degree in Media Writing. After graduating, he worked in television production and advertising as an award-winning producer – but the love for creative writing remained.

He released his first novel, Watchers, in January 2020, which is available here: www.amazon.com/dp/B083ZDMVY8

SOCIAL MEDIA:
Facebook.com/AuthorPriestley
Instagram @AuthorPriestley
Twitter @AuthorPriestley